STORM

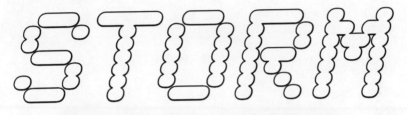

DAVE PEARSON

ISBN # 9781453829554
Published by Stand Up America, USA
Bigfork, Montana

Printed in the United States of America

ACKNOWLEDGEMENTS

STORM has been an amazing journey that has taken a decade from initial concept to putting "pen to paper" to final print.

First, I'd like to extend a special thank you to author, editor, and journalist Lt. Col. W. Thomas Smith, Jr., who patiently worked with me as a new author. You are a great writer, teacher, mentor, and friend. I'm certain you grew tired of saying "show, don't tell" and "unnecessary" over the past two years. Thank you for making me a better writer.

Thanks to CDR Mark Divine, who was given a very rough draft early on. You provided me with expertise and inspiration, and ultimately made this dream a reality.

To my friends, new and old, who came to strengthen this work without expecting anything in return, I have immense gratitude. Thanks to Scot Hutchinson for your enthusiasm for the story and feedback early on. Thanks to LCDR Matthew E. Harris for your valuable insight as a Navy officer and avid reader. I appreciate your attention to detail. Thanks to Parker Hays for your helpful criticism and for enhancing the moral dilemmas faced by the characters. Thanks to Marilyn Benner for your incredible ability to make dialogue flow, and for spending many hours on edits. Thanks to Omayra Marrero and Liza Rosenman for finding last-minute errors and for adding fresh vantage points.

Thanks also to CDR Pete Berardi, MAJ Kevin Dobzyniak, Jeff Faragher, Meredith Heffner, and countless others who supported this novel and contributed the intangibles to make it better.

This work would not have been possible without the talented and patient team at Stand Up America Publishing. Thanks to publisher MG Paul Vallely, cover designer Heidi Roedel, editor Kathleen Hawkins and layout designer Victoria Kane.

Finally, I'd like to thank my family. Thanks to my parents David and Angelica, my grandfather Wallace and brother Ben, for their undying support of all my outlandish adventures. To my seven-month-old son Walker, thanks for sitting in my lap "helping" me with the final edits. I can't wait until you're old enough to read it. Thanks to my in-laws, Lauri, Justin, and "baby" Justin, for offering encouragement and timely feedback. Last, but by no means least, thanks to my wife Erika, who was forced to listen to the numerous storyline changes, character development ideas, and plot twists. I love you.

If I forgot to mention your name, it was unintentional. Please accept a sincere thank you.

SEAL FIT is the training program created by Navy SEAL CDR Mark Divine, the technical adviser to STORM. SEAL FIT combines training of the mind, body and spirit in the Warrior-Athlete tradition. Integrating CrossFit and endurance, mental toughness and durability training, SEAL FIT is designed to meet the specific needs of all serious athletes who must work at or near peak capacity for long periods of time. Join the ranks of those who have found SEAL FIT to be extremely demanding, effective and rewarding. If you are ready to step it up, their program is a good starting point.

Visit www.SEALFIT.com
to learn more about this extraordinary program!

TABLE OF CONTENTS

PROLOGUE THE HACK

NEW BERN, NORTH CAROLINA
JULY 20

THE EARLY MORNING STORM descended on the coastal town of New Bern, North Carolina, as fifteen-year-old hacker Dutch lay awake in bed. The hard rain cracked against his window. A whistling wind occasionally buffeted the window's frame. It was nearly three in the morning.

Dutch crawled out of bed and tiptoed across the dark room to his small wooden desk. Cognizant of his parents' bedroom across the hall, he quietly eased onto his wobbly aluminum folding chair, spacing apart the sharp creaking sounds it created.

Once seated, he pulled his Commodore 64 desktop computer closer to the desk's edge. He felt along its side, finding the switch and turning it on. Seconds later the screen's glow lit the room. The disk drive began to read the 5-¼-inch disk with a quiet scratch, but at this hour, it seemed to echo throughout the entire house.

As Dutch waited for the computer to boot, he glanced down to the wall at his right, taking note of the two phone jacks that enabled access to different phone lines in his bedroom. One line was used for voice calls. The other line, given as a birthday gift, was linked to the 2400-baud modem of his computer. His parents felt if they encouraged his enthusiasm for computers it would keep him busy and out of trouble.

Dutch smiled at the thought.

The disk drive light flickered and finally dimmed; the computer had finished booting. He changed disks, pecked several commands, and initiated loading of his terminal software.

Dutch turned and glanced at the digital wall clock as he waited for the software to load. It was exactly 3 a.m. Using his voice line, he dialed into the long-distance carrier. At the tone, he entered a long-distance code, waited for a second tone, and dialed the phone number he wanted: a *loop*. Loops were two phone numbers, usually consecutive, that were used by phone companies for testing. For hackers, loops acted as a two-way chat-line. Experienced hackers usually avoided dialing their own home phone numbers. It would be like submitting fingerprints to the FBI's doorstep; therefore, they used loops. The 1,000-hertz tone buzzed for several seconds, then went quiet, confirming the connection to the low-end part of the loop. Nobody was on the other end...yet.

On the other side of town, another teenager walked along the bank of a tiny ditch that ran behind a dozen homes. Lightning streaked across the sky, illuminating the oak trees as he passed each backyard. Only seconds separated each burst of thunder. Thirty-miles-per-hour gusts blew the rain sideways in great sheets.

Spyder was determined to keep his promise to Dutch. Of course, Spyder was not his real name but an alias, as was Dutch. The hometown friends were hackers working yet another night as they did most nights during summer school.

Spyder's black raincoat whipped in the wind as he tried to keep its hood over his face, but the rain continued to sting his eyes. Even though the black bag strapped across his chest was waterproof, he feared the equipment inside was getting wet. Spyder finally reached his destination—the *can*—a green-colored ground unit that housed the neighborhood's telephone lines. He pulled the black bag over his head and lowered it to the ground, then dropped to one knee and quickly unzipped the bag, trying to shelter its contents from the rain.

With a tiny, dim flashlight gripped between his teeth to guide his eyes through the darkness, Spyder unscrewed the latch door of the can. Once it was open, he saw a meshwork of wires, cables, and dangling splices. Working through the tangled connections, he found one of the splices, but it slipped between his fingers. Damn rain. He tried again. Repeatedly, the splices slipped from his wet fingers. Rain beat into his eyes. He blinked. Finally, he held onto a splice and successfully connected his red phone. Within seconds, he heard a dial tone. Spyder then entered a series of digits into the red phone's keypad and connected into the high end of the loop. A low-frequency click sounded.

"About time," Dutch whispered.

"My Mom woke up when I was almost out the window," Spyder replied. "I had to wait until she went back to bed before I could try to sneak out again."

"Well, let's get to it," Dutch said.

"Yeah, this storm has me a little nervous," Spyder replied.

"Don't get so jumpy that you let the rain screw up the connection."

"Screw you, Dutch!" Spyder snapped. "It's bad out here. And why am I always the one who has to run around in the middle of the night while you sit there at home doing the fun part?"

"Because you're the only one with a car, remember?"

"When your ass gets a car, I'm the one that's gonna be staying home," Spyder replied, as a crooked lightning streak flashed in the distance. Seconds later, deafening thunder shook the ground.

"Damn, did you hear that?" Dutch exclaimed, keeping his voice low.

"Hear it? Dude, I felt it!" Spyder whispered angrily. "I'm outta here if that keeps up. The target is asinine anyway."

"Don't start, man. We all agreed SSI is hot," Dutch replied. Sentinel Software Industries had caught Dutch's attention at the start of the summer when he read the headlines of his father's newspaper sitting on the living room coffee table: *Sentinel Software Industries Wins Bid for Government Security System*. Dutch's heart had raced as he read the article. SSI claimed to be the next generation in database and security software. It was perfect. And for months now, every other night like clockwork, they had secretly been trying to hack into SSI.

"We're picking up our pace. Tonight we're going for *root* access," Dutch declared.

"It's about time we did something different," Spyder complained as he repeatedly blinked the rain from his eyes. "We haven't gotten anywhere in two months."

"Will you stop whining and get the others online?" Dutch asked.

There were three others, all teenagers. Together, they comprised an underground hacking crew who called themselves STORM. Dutch and Spyder knew nothing personal about them. No real names. No home phone numbers. No hometowns. No personal information was ever exchanged. STORM's strength stemmed from this anonymity. Communication was achieved by secret e-mails via bulletin board systems (precursor systems to Internet websites), voice messages via stolen voice mailboxes, files stored on university networks, and phone calls via loops and *bridges* (hacker lingo for conference lines). These tactics not only protected them from law enforcement; they protected them from each other. If one of them was ever busted, they could offer up no information.

Spyder and Dutch had broken this rule of anonymity long before STORM existed. Unbeknownst to the others, they were friends before they were hackers, first meeting in elementary school. While Dutch prided himself as a *hacker*, the others had their niches, too. Spyder was the *phreaker* in the group. *Phreaking*, a portmanteau of the words "phone" and "freak," was the act of manipulating telephone networks, mostly in order to gain free phone calls.

"Hang on," Spyder said.

First up was Sting Ray. They called him Ray for short.

Spyder dialed a series of digits into his keypad until he reached the loop, where he waited. The low-frequency click sounded as Ray was connected. "Ray, ya there?" Spyder asked.

"What took you so long?" Ray demanded tersely. "I was about

to hang up." Ray was the *phisher* in the group. Stemming from the words phreaking and fishing, *phishing* was the act of obtaining secure information under false pretenses, such as acting like an employee. Ray was the only one who could pull it off. His raspy voice with a New England accent made him sound much older than the others.

At first, little was known about the SSI target, yet Ray quickly put the pieces in place. Starting with the published corporate phone numbers, he eventually unveiled all lines linked to the company. Acting as an employee, Ray then phoned company telephone operators and conned them into releasing additional private phone numbers. Using a *war dialer* program, Ray systematically searched the 9,999 phone numbers of each SSI area code and prefix for a computer carrier. After many nights, STORM finally discovered the computer access line they sought.

"Hang on again," Spyder said.

Next up was Skye. Thirty seconds later, she was connected.

Skye was the only girl in the group. She was the *analyst*, and as such, had a knack for detail. She had already mapped out the system and knew how to exploit it.

SSI was running Unix, a computer operating system first released in 1969. Unix had many programs that operated within its system, and and those programs held weaknesses. They could be executed without user ID authentication. Using Unix's File Transfer Protocol, STORM had gained access to the */etc/passwd* file, which contained all registered user IDs. Nine out of ten systems held vulnerability in the linked password. New user IDs were tied to a standard password that was configured by the system operator, or SYSOP.

Skye had raced through thousands of user ID-password combinations. Nothing. STORM's next break had come with the discovery that the passwords were stored in a separate */etc/shadow* file. Unfortunately, the file was encrypted. SSI was not like other systems.

"Y'all won't believe what I found," Skye exclaimed, her thick drawl giving away her southern roots.

"Whatcha find?" Dutch queried, anxious to get her latest update.

"Is everybody else on the line yet?" she asked.

"No, gimme a second," Spyder replied.

Skreemer was next. He was STORM's leader. Skreemer liked coordinating hacks and worked solely from pay phones. He was also the *cracker* of the group. *Cracking* was the act of getting around software copy protection. As soon as new video games were released, Skreemer had them cracked. When his entry click resounded through the conference line, they all said, at nearly the same time, "Skreemer?"

"What's new?" Skreemer shot back, his voice filled with enthusiasm.

"I found one!" Skye exclaimed. Daily for the past month, she had diligently searched through thousands of e-mails stored off-line, hunting for default IDs, passwords, anything that would give them access. Twenty-four hours earlier, Skye had finally stumbled across an e-mail from the system administrator to a user named "Joe Norman." It had been dated one week back. Buried within the text of the e-mail, and far more hidden than a needle in a haystack, had been a default user ID and its corresponding password.

"User ID is *jnorman*. Password is *pwd25*," Skye declared.

"No shit!" Skreemer blurted out.

"It's showtime!" Spyder added.

Dutch shot straight up in his chair. Using his computer line, he rapidly dialed into a second loop. Spyder simultaneously dialed into the same second loop and joined him. Like making a three-way call, Spyder connected Dutch's computer to the SSI mainframe and enabled the hack.

Although using the extensive number of connections deteriorated their quality, it provided a call not traceable to STORM. Traces would only lead to the unfortunate owners of different residential phone lines near the telephone *can*.

The speaker of Dutch's modem trumpeted the familiar sounds of logging on: whistling jumping from a low, deep frequency to progressively higher frequencies until they were connected. On his computer monitor, the cursor jumped down a few spaces, then paused, then continued to jump down to the bottom of the monitor. The lone word *login*: suddenly appeared against the black screen.

Dutch immediately typed in the user ID: *jnorman* and password: *pwd25*.

A box popped up. "Login incorrect," Dutch read aloud.

"Make sure it's not case sensitive," Skreemer said. "Let's try out all our options."

Dutch proceeded to try user ID: *JNORMAN* with the same password.

Nothing.

Fearing that the system had been configured to limit logon attempts to three, they hung up in hopes of preventing the target system from recording too many failed attempts.

"Did you hear that clicking?" Spyder asked nervously.

"What clicking?" Ray asked.

"I didn't hear any clicking," Skreemer chimed in.

"No click. I need a new line, Spyder," Dutch remarked.

Once logged on again under a new phone line, Dutch attempted two more iterations. The conference line was dead silent, awaiting word from Dutch about what he saw on his computer screen.

"Damn!" Dutch hissed, as *login incorrect* flashed on the screen once again.

"The e-mail's too old," Skye said. "They must have changed the password already."

"I got an idea," Dutch said.

Several loud clicks blasted through the line as lightning cracked across the sky. The line went dead.

"Hello?" Dutch whispered several times. Silence permeated the conference line.

Both lines went dead. Dutch tried several times to get back a dial tone, but there was none to be found. Disappointed, he gazed across the room at his bookshelf, which neatly held several Unix operating system manuals. For the past week, he had been studying a possibility to gain access via *sendmail*, a mail transfer agent used by Unix. A way that would get him root access.

A minute passed as he tried the phone again. The humming of a dial tone sounded. Dutch quickly dialed back into the loop. Fortunately, Spyder was at the other end.

"Think it was the storm?" Dutch asked.

"Hell yeah!" Spyder replied. "I felt my fingertips goin' numb. Lightning damn near barbequed me. Listen, I'm outta here. We can try again tomorrow when this storm's gone."

"Wait, I have an idea that I've gotta try," Dutch said.

"No way," Spyder replied.

"Buffer overflow attack using *sendmail* to execute the */bin/sh* file to gain root access."

"Dude, can't this wait until tomorrow?"

"Spyder, one try."

"The storm's gettin' really bad out here," Spyder replied nervously, as a crackling bolt of lightning ripped across the sky.

"Gimme one chance," Dutch begged.

"One," Spyder replied, finally giving in.

Spyder's hands trembled as he grasped the wet line wiring and nervously tried to make the connection. His shifting eyes blinked at the flashing night sky. Once connected, he reluctantly dialed the phone number and reconnected Dutch to the SSI mainframe. *Login:* with a flashing cursor again appeared on Dutch's monitor.

Several commands later, Dutch connected to the *sendmail* program and sent his pre-programmed data to the *VRFY* command.

"Did you hear that clicking?" Spyder asked.

"Damn, you're paranoid tonight!"

"Dude! Listen. Let's call it a night and try this thing another time. I'm gonna get my ass shocked out here."

Booms of thunder—one right after another—shook the ground beneath him.

"Don't hang up on me," Dutch insisted. "We're close; I can feel it."

PROLOGUE

Once more Spyder went against his better judgment and waited. The passing minutes felt like an eternity. A huge bolt of lightning sparked in the darkness as the voice line cut in and out.

"You have one minute," Spyder warned with finality. "I'm timing you." He began to count the seconds on his digital watch.

With eyes fixed on the screen, Dutch awaited word from the flashing cursor.

Finally, the cursor brought life back to the blank screen, as *Access to Compound Five Database Granted* glowed on the monitor. The screen quickly filled with menus. Dutch glanced across the titles reading *Exercise Parameters, Security Systems-Perimeter/Core, Power Grid/Back-up.*

"We're in!" Dutch announced excitedly, keeping his voice low.

Not hearing Dutch over the fierce storm, Spyder started to pack up his equipment. Dutch began erasing the log files that contained records of his presence on SSI's network. He then proceeded to set up a backdoor, a fictitious user ID with password for future access to the system. Dutch glanced at his watch: 3:32 a.m. With a click of his finger he performed his final act and uploaded a harmless computer virus. It would create a diversion. "Thirty seconds and we'll be done, Spyder," he whispered.

"There's some lights, Dutch," Spyder mumbled. "I gotta go."

"Don't hang up. Twenty more seconds."

"I see fucking lights."

"It's probably just a neighbor. There's no way they can find us."

"They just did," Spyder said, as he tore out the phone line.

The telephone connections with Dutch immediately went dead as a string of random characters lay plastered across his computer screen.

A brief pause preceded the scramble back onto his computer. Dutch typed furiously, logging onto a university computer network. He then quickly pecked out an e-mail to Skreemer. It read: "Something's wrong. Spyder may be busted, but we got in. I know you barely check this system, but I felt this one was the safest. I set up the following backdoor. User ID is FIVE; password is FIVE. Total ROOT access. Programmed so it doesn't write to the log file when you log in. Don't know how long this backdoor will stay open. SSI is big time. Don't use this one as a file-sharing network for the team. It's huge. I really don't know what it is, but it's bigger than any of us imagined. I'm going to lay low to see how this all plays out. I'll e-mail again here in a couple of weeks. Damn, Skreemer, if this is my last communication with you, it was one hell of a run."

After he hit "send," Dutch logged off and yanked the line from the back of his modem. Immediately, he pressed eject, removed the 5-¼-inch disk from the floppy drive, and placed it on the desk. Leaping up from his chair, he reached under his dresser drawer and pulled out a dusty steel U-shaped magnet.

Dutch clutched the magnet tightly and stared outside his window at the vicious storm. His hand began to tremble as he imagined Spyder running from the police. For three years, their lives had been defined by worldly adventures and exhilarating hacks, places of a depth few truly knew. In an instant, it could all be gone.

Dutch glanced back at the disk, a repository of hacker tools, programs, and codes. He slowly pulled the disk to the magnet, passing the disk beneath it several times, permanently erasing its contents. Instinct told him this was their last hack.

*   *   *

Once a blur, the lights coalesced onto Spyder. He frantically shoved the equipment into his bag, slung it over his shoulder, and dashed into the large ditch behind the house. As he emerged on the opposite side, the mud slipped under his boot, sending him crashing to the ground. Covered in black silt, he glanced back only to see the darkness become light. He sprinted across the open grassy field, heading toward his car parked half a mile away on a quiet dirt road.

Finally, Spyder saw his blue 1986 Corsica. He crawled through a second ditch and fumbled with his keys as he bolted across the wet road that now looked more like a small river. Spyder glanced back to see the pursuing lights illuminating the wet, grassy field. Jumping into his vehicle, he switched on the ignition. Leaving the lights off, he began to drive. Car lights appeared from both ends of the desolate, deeply rutted dirt road. Spyder was sixteen, scared and alone. He felt abandoned and knew his fate.

CHAPTER 1 THE FIVE

TWENTY YEARS LATER

"War brings out two distinct aspects of human behavior—the very best a man can be and the very worst."
— LCDR Michael J. Walsh (USN – Ret.), former Navy SEAL

NAVAL AMPHIBIOUS BASE
CORONADO, CALIFORNIA
MAY 20

A PURPLE MOON illuminated the crashing waves along the strand of Coronado, California. It was close to midnight...quiet, cool, and starry. Five shadows began to move along the moonlit beach. They were five U.S. Navy SEALs, members of the super-secret DEVGRU. Formerly known as SEAL Team Six, the counter-terrorist unit was disbanded and replaced by DEVGRU, known throughout the world only within a few top-level military circuits as the most elite CT unit in the U.S. armed forces.

The SEALs were testing the Objective Force Warrior, the U.S. Defense Department's successor to the Land Warrior, a multi-billion-dollar project plagued by funding gaps and technological glitches that was subsequently cancelled. The OFW was the solution, designed to make the soldier a complete weapon system by fusing together myriad battlefield technologies and digitally linking the operator to an intrasquad Local Area Network. From flip-down heads-up displays, to weapon-mounted thermal sighting and night vision, to GPS-navigated digital mapping and real time intelligence, the operator had tactical situational awareness and thus was more durable, efficient, and lethal.

Extensive training was necessary to adapt to the new equipment. Although the team was well attuned to some of the technologies, many features were new. The researchers and engineers pushed the technological envelope of fighting in the digital age. Rigorous testing allowed the SEALs ample opportunity to express their opinions and concerns. There could be no better source for criticism.

In the pursuit to simulate real combat conditions, this specific exercise forced the SEALs into sleep-deprivation for three days. Using the Augmented Cognition-enabled software, the computer recognized delayed neuro-cognitive functioning of the sleep-deprived operators, and adjusted the inflow of tactical combat data and communications.

The bright moon and clear skies had forced the SEAL team to come ashore two miles from their destination—a thirty-foot watchtower.

The dark wooden tower stood alone like a giant sentinel overlooking the sand dune embankment. The five moved swiftly across the soft sand, easing their pace as they closed in on its lurking presence. Based on previous intelligence, two soldiers watched the beach from the tower's tiny deck on top, while two more guarded its base. The mission was to covertly infiltrate the tower and retrieve a black box presumably containing detailed enemy strategic plans. They would be using simunition weapons, which would allow them to shoot paint rounds out of a real weapon.

On the other side, Kathryn "Kat" Lange accompanied the guards on top of the tower. Her eyes canvassed the ground for SEALs.

After finishing top of her class with a Masters in Mechanical Engineering from Massachusetts Institute of Technology, Kat had opted out of pursuing a PhD, and instead joined Edge Defense Industries. Though only thirty-two, she'd easily climbed the ranks of EDI, mainly due to her contributions to the technological advancements in the OFW. Three years ago, EDI's CEO had advanced her to head the top-secret project known as *Compound Five,* or C5. Since then, hundred hour workweeks were the norm, and sleep was a thing of the past. She had never imagined working for EDI on top-secret military projects, much less sitting in the top of a Navy SEAL watchtower, observing the project in real time.

Earlier in the day, Kat had been briefed on the training exercise. Omitted from the brief were details of the special group of SEALs she was about to observe. The classified CT unit known as DEVGRU was far beyond simply competent SEAL operators.

Of this particular fourteen-man DEVGRU platoon, five were selected to be part of the future C5 exercise one month away. They were known as the YUMA team, chiefed by patrol leader Sean Graves. Moving twenty feet ahead of Graves was point man Ron Spiers. His primary duty was to prevent his team from walking into an ambush. Further back was the M60 machine gunner, Terrance Rock, who was nearly double the size of any other team member. Rico Cordova was the radioman and known to most as the master of clandestine operations. His existence was covert, his movements silent, his presence nearly invisible, and he prided himself on this. Not to mention his ability to communicate with the umbrella command element whenever and wherever he needed.

Matt Campbell was the last one in the group, some thirty feet behind Cordova. He was the Special Operations Technician medic. He had completed the Navy Hospital Corpsman school and gone on to BUD/S (Basic Underwater Demolition/SEAL) training, then to the U.S. Army "Goat Lab" or 18 Delta medic course, an eleven-month course on field medicine. Beyond that was on-the-job training with various SEAL platoons.

"Kat, stay down!" whispered the tower guard several feet from her. "They'll make their move soon." Kat glanced toward the ocean and searched for signs. Every time she thought she saw movement on the dark coast, she realized it was her mind deceiving her. She squatted down, gazed at the tiny black box resting on the watchtower's wooden deck, and wondered how the SEALs would be able to snatch the box.

"It hardly seems fair," Kat whispered to the sailor beside her, while peering through a small crack in the tower's wooden beam. "We can see everything from up here." The tower guard momentarily smiled, glancing at the other guard next to him, well aware that an OFW-equipped DEVGRU would be attacking any minute. He put his finger to his lips, instructing Kat to remain silent.

Kat turned her attention back to the sea and listened to the rolling surf. The tower was protected by hidden guards and was inaccessible except by a flimsy wooden ladder. Trip wires and mines surrounded it.

It seemed an impossible task for the attacking SEAL team.

*   *   *

"YUMA. Plan Alpha Two is a go," crackled a voice over the SEALs' headsets.

"Good copy," Graves replied.

Point man Spiers slowed the team and cautiously traversed the sandy beach. As in any training exercise, intelligence had to be taken with a grain of salt. Intel was essential, yet the rule was to trust no one but yourself and your team. Spiers flipped down the visor of the helmet, eyeing the heads-up display equivalent to two seventeen-inch computer monitors. He glanced at the satellite image, verifying his position on GPS. Searching the dark with his M4-mounted night optics, he slowly proceeded forward, dropping flat to the ground and slithering through the damp sand. As he saw one of the guards on the ground, he instinctively dropped a virtual chemlight on the target, instantly notifying the team of the enemy's location. No need for voice communication anymore.

Spiers' eyes shot across the landscape. The second guard was missing. It was a trap. He was reluctant to push forward without sighting the crucial watchman. He switched his helmet over to infrared.

Nothing.

Campbell stayed behind, remaining hidden near the ocean, as the trailing end of the surf washed over his black boots. Cordova received the digital signal to move into position. He then moved across the mine-laden beach, positioning himself almost beneath the first guard. He was so close. It was as though the guard was looking right at him, but somehow Cordova could not be seen. Now was the perfect time to eliminate the enemy, yet there was no word yet on the second guard.

Graves instructed Rock to begin traversing the minefield. Graves himself was already midway across. From a small bunker, a tiny flicker of motion betrayed the second guard. He was buried among the sand with what appeared to be a sniper rifle.

Spiers quickly signaled to Graves and Rock to cease movement until he was in better position to make his kill. He pulled his small sidearm from its holster and crawled to the edge of the bunker. Then he signaled Cordova.

Three seconds later, two silenced shots fired from Cordova's weapon pounded the guard in the chest, instantly bringing him to the ground. Spiers hit his target in the back with a single shot, but not before the guard got one shot off. Once that shot hit the eardrums of the tower guards, the sound of gunfire filled the beach air, while three red flares illuminated the night sky.

The sand danced as the automatic weapons brought the beach to life. Rock was the most exposed. He opened fire with his M60, blanketing simunition bullets onto the tower, as though he could see directly through the tower at the guard that had taken aim. For the moment, there was no return fire.

Campbell pushed forward, firing at the opposition. Though a medic, he was also a "shooter." Viewing the scene through the helmet-mounted computer and sensor display, he saw his own location and also those of his enemies, directing his fire to these locations as reported by the other operator sub-systems.

Kat watched as Cordova worked almost magically up the tower, firing shots off at every free second. She had a hard time convincing herself that this was a drill. The gunfire echoed with realism. Everything moved so fast. She tried not to blink. She watched as the tower guard next to her pulled his sidearm, aiming at the door that separated him from the attacking SEALs.

From the ground, Rock peppered the tower with bullets, forcing the tower guard to lie flat, as Cordova forced his way into the entrance. He appeared to come from the ceiling as he fired two shots, neither one missing his targets. Cordova charged in, stopping for a moment and staring at the unexpected presence of Kat. He captured her image with the helmet camera and scanned through the enemy mug shots. No match.

Flipping up his helmet visor, Cordova stood in front of her, staring with the whites of his eyes piercing beyond his blackened face. He reached down and retrieved the black box. "YUMA, we have the target," he stated, stepping backwards with his sidearm still aimed at Kat. He disappeared down the stairs and jumped nearly ten feet onto the ground. Kat crawled to the door's edge on the tower, looking down only to see the darkness he had already disappeared into.

It seemed impossible. She knew it was an exercise, another level of testing the OFW, giving the SEALs another chance to get used to it. But the team on the ground, as well as in the tower, had known they were coming. It was a trap. Never mind that.

Kat turned to the two guards in the tower with her. They only shook their heads.

CHAPTER 2 CONTACT

NEW BERN, NORTH CAROLINA
MAY 21

THE LATE FRIDAY NIGHT CROWD poured into the tiny eclectic diner, quickly filling up the remaining open booths. The regulars had already claimed their row of a dozen stools lining a counter facing the kitchen, as the disheveled customers hovered over their coffees purchased with loose change.

One man at the counter was distinctly different. Dressed in a three-piece pinstriped suit, he shunned any conversation and made no eye contact. He merely stared at the few sips of coffee that remained in his cup.

"Hey buddy, sure's a nice lookin' suit you's got on," the man seated beside him said with a hoarse Louisiana drawl.

The man only nodded.

"You's from around here?" the southerner asked. Again, no reply.

The slim, meticulously dressed man adjusted his thin, silver-wired Versace glasses and scanned the restaurant, his eyes determined and focused. He threw back a last gulp of coffee, then tossed a twenty-dollar bill down that easily covered the cost of his late-night eggs and hash browns. Slowly he stood up, stretching over six feet tall, and, without a word, walked away.

As he reached a wall of pay phones in the back of the restaurant, a gray-haired woman in her sixties was using the single functional phone. The second phone held an "out of order" cardboard note pinned between the receiver and cradle. With a quick glance at his Tag Heuer wristwatch, he inched closer to the woman, towering over her.

"Excuse you," she said irritably.

Holding out another twenty-dollar bill, he handed it to the woman as he reached out for the phone.

"I'll call you later," she said, snatching the twenty. She handed him the phone and walked away. With practiced precision, the man dialed a series of numbers, finally hearing the click he desired.

"Have you found him yet?" the voice at the other end asked.

"I found him," the man at the pay phone replied.

"You sure it's him?"

"I have no doubt."

"Do you still think we need him?"

"Absolutely."

"We should contact him, then."

"Consider it done."

*   *   *

The rain bounced from the tow-truck windshield as the wipers cut through sheets of water. John Newark could barely see five feet in front of him as he searched for the gray Chevy car illegally parked in front of the fire hydrant. Last call was rapidly approaching as several bar-hoppers exited the local bar in varying stages of inebriation, scurrying sloppily through the rain. It was towing calls like this that made him nervous, as he hoped to avoid any confrontation with an intoxicated car owner.

"Come on, who needs a fire hydrant during a torrential downpour anyway," he thought.

But that was not up to him. He got the call. He made the run.

Locating the '89 Chevy, John quickly backed up the tow truck.

The beeps echoed throughout the street. Reluctant to battle the rain, he slowly stepped out. Rain found its way around his black raincoat, drenching his clothes.

Within minutes, the car's frame was linked to the overlift and was ready to roll.

"Hey! Wait a minute!" a voice came screaming across the street as two men stumbled towards him. Almost back inside the tow truck, John stopped and turned around.

"You're not towing my damn car!" the short, stout man yelled, as he got closer with his winded breathing and slurred speech. Unfortunately, a second man, lanky and at least half a foot taller than John's five-foot-seven-inch frame, approached as well.

Before John could say a word, the tall figure worked his way behind him in small steps.

"Easy, guys," John said, thinking about lowering the car so he could get out of the rain and avoid the altercation. "I don't want any trouble."

"What's your fuckin' problem?" the shorter man yelled, moving in front of John. The stout man threw his body behind a slow drunken punch. John stepped back and leaned to the right, as the strike missed. He quickly leapt forward with fist clenched and jacked the short man in his jaw, sending him hard to the concrete.

The tall man charged from the side, his fist pounding into the back of John's head as he dropped him to the ground. With John momentarily stunned, the lanky man kicked again and again at John's ribcage.

With the next kick headed for his face, John latched onto the man's foot and ankle, twisted his leg, and sent the man tumbling to the ground. Without getting up, John crawled beside the tall man, latched onto his thinning, rain-soaked hair and slammed his skull into the ground with two short bursts. He jumped up and dashed for his open truck door, where the keys dangled from the ignition. Quickly starting the engine, he peeled off, the tiny car jerking behind. "Why do I do this shit?" he muttered to himself. Adrenaline coursed through his veins like a pain medication, numbing his bruised ribcage and skull.

John was flustered as he searched the truck for his cell phone, feeling along the seat while continuing to drive faster. His tow truck had all the necessary amenities. The cigarette lighter powered the small portable radio that blasted the rattling sounds of an unknown rock band. The old CB radio rested on the mid-panel as a backup. On the passenger floor mat lay ten empty Pepsi cans and well over a dozen partially eaten bags of assorted chips. His glove compartment carried a stun gun—not much good that did now.

Searching beneath his seat with his right hand, he grasped a discarded, crinkled photo and lifted it up to his eyes. It was a picture of his ex-fiancé. Since the split, he worked extra shifts, most of them overnight, in a vain attempt to keep himself busy and the thought of her distant. He quickly tossed the photo back onto the floor mat.

Five minutes passed before his rage subsided enough to even consider reporting the incident to the police. He finally noticed the clattering cell phone in the far left corner of his dashboard. As he reached for it, the phone unexpectedly rang.

"I'm done for the night," John answered.

"Hello, Dutch." The sharp, calm voice pierced through the receiver.

No words came to John's lips. He unknowingly slowed to twenty-five miles-per-hour, not having heard his alias Dutch for twenty years.

"It took a little longer than a couple of weeks," the man continued.

Dutch glanced at the caller ID: unknown.

"Skreemer?" Dutch asked.

"This line isn't secure. Go to the pay phone at the L&D Convenient Mart on Oaks Road. Five minutes." The line went dead.

Dutch drove another half mile before yanking the steering wheel and making a harsh U-turn; the towed Chevy jerked and skidded behind. The store was less than three minutes away. He finally pulled beside the pay phone and nervously scanned the parking lot, noting only one parked car.

The pay phone was ringing. He picked it up without saying a word.

"Don't use any handles. This line isn't secure. We can't talk for long."

"Who is this?" Dutch asked.

"You know who this is," the man said, choosing his words cautiously.

"Twenty years ago, you went to a place. I can't say the name because this line is not secure. Fortunately, you sent me an e-mail that let me visit that place many times. Did you ever want to know what that place was?"

"Is this some kind of joke?" Dutch said, skeptically.

"No joke," the man said. Beyond the words, Dutch honed in on the voice, analyzing the inflection, tonality, and pronunciation, attempting to verify Skreemer as the caller. "The place you uncovered is a testing ground for DARPA, the Defense Advanced Research Projects Agency, a facility testing the next generation warfare technology. We're talking weapons, combat technologies, tracking and communication systems, robotics—you name it. Top counter-terrorist units from Britain, Canada, New Zealand, and France, even U.S. Navy SEALs, will be participating in an exercise at this facility in one month. Do you want to know more?"

Dutch pulled the phone away from his ear. The dripping rain ran off his raincoat hood and over his face. He closed his eyes for several seconds. The old hacker slang raced through his mind: extenders, diverters, PBXs, sweeps, black boxing, phreaking, cracking, pins, codez, and warez. STORM and his old friend Spyder flashed through his thoughts, as the rambunctious sound of partygoers reached his ears from a honking passing car, snapping him out of his transient daze.

Upon opening his eyes, he caught a glimpse of his reflection in his truck's side-view mirror. His face was bruised. One eye was nearly swollen shut. His gaze shifted behind him to the car that he had just towed.

The voice resembled an older Skreemer. But what if it wasn't him? And why, after all these years, would Skreemer contact him? Dutch had enough problems to deal with.

Without a response, he gently set the phone down on its cradle and got back into his truck.

CHAPTER 3 LOST MEMORY

NEW BERN, NORTH CAROLINA
MAY 21

ARRIVING at *Marks' Towing & Auto Repair,* Dutch pulled up to the chain-link fence topped with spiraled barbed wire. As he stepped out of the truck his boots slid into the slick mud. It was eerily quiet, except for the slow trickle of rain that pattered on the hood of his raincoat. Unlocking the padlocked gate, he pushed and released it, hoping it would swing freely. The thick sludge stopped its momentum. Tensely, he shoved it fully open, then hurried back to his truck.

After pulling the truck through the entrance, he locked the gate behind him. He then backed the truck into the far corner of the unpaved parking lot. While unloading the small Chevy, his eyes shifted between the surrounding darkness and the car. He saw imagined shadows and heard sounds that on any other night would have gone unnoticed.

With the towed car unloaded, Dutch headed to the shop's front door. Nervously fumbling with the keys, he managed to get it open. Once inside, he hurried to the office computer desk and eased into the rolling office chair, pulling the metallic-beaded chain of the desk lamp. A dim glow lit the room. With an older, bulky computer monitor and keyboard on the desktop, he reached down beneath the desk and slid his fingertips along the computer casing until he connected with the power button. The computer's soft humming broke the silence.

Booting completed, Dutch clicked on the Internet software and began the search.

First up, *DARPA*. The Defense Advanced Research Projects Agency's website flashed on the screen. Dutch clicked on the drop-down menu *Offices*.

A new screen revealed DARPA's technical offices: *Defense Sciences, Microsystems Technology, Tactical Technology, Strategic Technology, and Information Processing Techniques*.

Dutch jumped from menu to menu, searching for the various DARPA programs. His eyes glanced across the descriptions: *Dynamic Optical Tags, Defense Against Cyber Attacks on Mobile Ad Hoc Network Systems, Tactical Mobile Robotics, Navy Photonics, NeoVision, Peak Soldier Performance, Surviving Blood Loss, Training Superiority Program, Jigsaw, Eyeball, Crosshairs*. For twenty minutes Dutch hunted. There was no mention of Compound Five.

He then searched the Internet for Sentinel Software Incorporated, the corporation he had hacked twenty years ago. A list of websites appeared, including the corporate website, multiple editorials, and several news and investment reports. The ninth option down caught his eye: *SSI loses bid on major defense contract*.

A thunderous boom came from outside the building. Dutch quickly turned off the lamp and computer and sat in the darkness for several seconds. He moved to the window and searched the dark parking lot. Had the owner of the towed Chevy found him?

With keys in hand, Dutch left the building and sprinted to his silver Ford Escort. As he drove off, he glanced through his rearview mirror.

Nobody was there.

*   *   *

Driving home along New Bern's quiet, dark streets, Dutch felt his paranoia intensifying, an unfounded suspicion since he knew he had done nothing wrong or illegal. What bothered him was that he had been found. His secret identity had been uncovered. But he was not Dutch anymore, no longer a hacker.

The inescapable questions crept repeatedly into his mind. Was STORM still together? Why had he been contacted? Was that even Skreemer?

Dutch interrupted his whirlwind of thoughts and focused on his recollection of Skreemer. Skreemer was a friend without a face, a personality created only from a voice. Their first interaction had been on a hacker's *bridge*, a conference call service borrowed from businesses during the overnight hours. Bridges were useful for making new contacts in the realm of hacking. Most hackers carelessly trusted the other callers on the line. In reality, it was impossible to tell who was to be trusted—who was FBI or hacker. Supposedly, there were clues. Some hackers tattooed terms like lamer or elite to others, indicating various levels of hacking knowledge. They would ask for never-before used codes (*virgin codez*) or the latest cracked software (*warez*) as a sort of test. Others thought an older voice meant trouble.

Dutch and Skreemer had paid no attention to this. These clues could easily be decoys. And for that reason, they only talked via loops and bridges. This made it possible to talk to each other without ever exchanging home phone numbers. Skreemer took it a step further and always operated from a pay phone.

Immediately, Dutch and Skreemer had worked fluidly together, and they soon became close friends—as close as two people could get without meeting face-to-face or knowing each other's true identity, or even knowing real first names.

Several months after meeting, they established the underground hacking group: STORM. Underground—a distinction that meant their pursuit would remain unknown even to the hacking community. Most hacking groups searched for recognition by plastering their aliases and group names onto software they cracked or computer networks they hacked. Skreemer and Dutch wanted STORM to remain a ghost, recognized only for its incredible hacks, not for its name.

Over the year that followed, STORM added members, eventually including Spyder, Ray, and Skye. With this group of five, STORM took on impressive targets. Their intent was never malicious. Their reasoning could only be likened to that of mountain climbers attempting Mount Everest. They wanted to show that it could be done. It was the challenge that was enticing.

*   *   *

Dutch finally reached his apartment. He was exhausted but could not sleep. For hours, he stared at the ceiling fan, wide awake.

Getting out of bed, Dutch walked over to his bedroom closet. He reached up and felt around on the shelf above his head, his hand finally grasping the worn file folder. A layer of dust had accumulated on the graying folder; Dutch wiped and smacked the file, watching the dust float into the air. He dropped it onto the bed, then sat down. Slowly he unwrapped the loose string and wrapper. Delicately, he opened the folder he had not looked at in over five years.

"Felony seen in boy's use of computer," the first newspaper headline read. He flipped to the next, "Teen charged in computer scheme." Clipping after clipping, he sifted through the headlines. There were no names in the papers, only mention of a teenager: his old friend Ryan, alias Spyder.

Back then, hacking was Ryan's escape from the emotionally and physically abusive world in which he lived. He was caught more than once sneaking out of his house, only to meet with the repercussions of a stern fist from an alcoholic stepfather, yet ten times out of ten he would sneak out again to hack. Perhaps he felt he had nothing to lose.

Dutch smiled widely as he remembered the time they sent ten refrigerators COD to a bullying classmate's home for revenge. When caught, they were grounded for weeks and confined to their bedrooms. Fortunately, they thought, their bedrooms had computers.

This long friendship ended abruptly that July night when Ryan was arrested. Since then, Dutch had not hacked.

One year passed before the trial took place. Even though Ryan was a juvenile, the prosecutors were harsh. Ultimately, he was sentenced to six months in a juvenile correction facility. Hacking was seen as a crime no different than any other, for the weapons were their minds, and the bullets their keystrokes. Dutch felt responsible, and after the trial, the two never spoke again. Through it all, Ryan never squealed.

* * *

The sunlight peeked through the gray shades like a child demanding attention. The light blazed on the partially opened manila folders that lay next to Dutch. Upon awakening, Dutch looked briefly at the side-table clock flashing 12:00 from the temporary power outage, then quickly glanced at his wristwatch, which showed almost 7 a.m. Slowly lifting himself out of bed, he pushed the papers aside and headed to the kitchen for his morning dose of caffeine.

For a moment, no memory of last night's fight came to mind as he plodded through his tiny two-bedroom duplex apartment. Since the split, the apartment seemed empty. His ex-fiancé Jessica's parting gift was his name on the lease and three months' delinquency on the rent. No matter how much harder he worked, the mounting debt was overwhelming.

It was only seconds before the pulsating headache emerged as a reminder of the scuffle last night. He briefly massaged his temple. Entering the tiny kitchen, he slowly placed a mug of instant coffee into the microwave, pressed start, and stared aimlessly at the spinning mug.

Three head-splitting knocks sounded from his front door. "Police Department," the voice announced—in a deep and practiced tone—from the opposite side of the door.

Startled, Dutch's heart raced, as thoughts of the mysterious call he had received last night flashed through his mind. He then recalled the altercation that had taken place last night. Had the attackers talked to the police? But he had done nothing wrong.

As he reluctantly walked toward the door, the phone rang. Hastily, he picked it up. Again, he remained silent.

"John, ya there?"

"Steve?"

"Are ya ready to go?" Steve said.

"What?"

"Diving," Steve replied. "Open the damn door. I'm standing outside."

As the shuddering Dutch came to a calming realization that it was Saturday morning, he let out a long sigh. "Jackass," he muttered as he put down the phone. For years, the two had gone scuba diving on the weekends. A friendship of eight years traced back to *Marks' Towing*, Dutch's employer. Steve was the son of the owner. Dutch opened the door as Steve was about to pound on it again.

"Damn, what happened to you?" Steve asked, glancing at Dutch's blackened eye.

"Believe me, they got it worse," Dutch replied.

"Still up for diving?" Steve asked.

"Yep. I need to get the hell outside," Dutch said. "Let me get my coffee."

"I can't let you drink that instant shit. I grabbed an extra one for ya. Just get your stuff."

Dutch grabbed his pack of gear and threw it in the back of the Jeep, taking a moment to admire the outdoors. The radiant sun reflected from the many puddles on the ground. It was a beautiful and refreshing day after the torrential downpour of last night.

CHAPTER 4 THE EXERCISE

NEW BERN, NORTH CAROLINA
MAY 22

A GLIMMER OF DAYLIGHT remained as Dutch headed home along U.S. Highway 70. Dutch was exhausted. His black hair was still damp and smelled of salt water as the wind blew it freely. He settled low into the passenger seat, staring into the distance.

"The *Indra*," Steve broke the silence. "Always a good dive."

"Yeah," Dutch mumbled.

"U-352 is still on our dive hit list," Steve continued.

Harboring the sunken vessels, this stretch of the North Carolina coast was commonly called the Graveyard of the Atlantic. The *Indra* was a transport ship that had been purposely sunk, forming an artificial reef five miles offshore. The German U-boat 352 lay as a reminder of the naval battles fought off the Tar Heel coast in World War II.

"Don't you think?" Steve asked.

Dutch was silent.

"Y' okay?"

"Yeah, I'm fine," Dutch sighed.

"When we get back, we're gonna file a police report," Steve said.

"No! We don't need to," Dutch replied curtly. "Believe me, I'm fine."

"Just looks like you're thinking about something."

"Nothing. Really." Dutch paused. "Do ya ever get tired of the same old shit, just workin' your ass off just to get by? Same old stuff day-to-day?"

"Of course, but diving helps. Beer works better. Wanna grab one tonight?"

"I'm serious," Dutch said, his eyes pensive.

"So am I," Steve grinned.

"You ever want to get outta here?"

"What do you mean?"

"Leave New Bern."

"Not really," Steve said. "We have the ocean. It's only a half-day drive to the mountains. I love it here."

"I just feel so damn trapped."

"You've had a rough couple of months. You know, with Jess and all. Give it time."

"It's not that. I've always wanted more. Travel to new places. Hell, some adventure." He remembered the times when he had spent all night hacking. He could travel the world then with a touch of a button.

"I've always told you that you should be doing something with computers," Steve said. "I've never seen anybody better. Go back to school or something. Hell, you've kept my dad's ancient system alive for years."

Dutch nodded.

Steve wheeled his Jeep into the apartment parking lot. Before the vehicle came to a complete stop, Dutch jumped out. "How 'bout that beer?" Steve said, coming to a stop. "No excuses this time. It's Saturday night and you don't have to work."

"That's what I need, to run into Jess again. That'll cheer me up," Dutch replied. "Anyway, I need sleep."

"You'll get plenty of sleep when you die," Steve replied as Dutch mouthed the words at the same time. "Call me later if you change your mind."

Dutch reached in, shook hands, and grabbed his gear. Steve drove off.

As Dutch opened the storm door to his apartment, a brown package dropped onto the front step. He picked up the five-pound parcel and immediately noted the absence of a return address. Once inside, he grabbed a knife from the kitchen and made his way to the couch. He delicately laid the box on the coffee table. Paranoid, he entertained the thought that it might be a letter bomb or anthrax. Unable to resist, he ripped into the package.

He slid out the Styrofoam casing, exposing a small laptop computer similar to a Panasonic Toughbook. The black computer was sturdy and surprisingly heavy. There were no labels, no registered trademarks, no brand names. It was not a commercial laptop; it was an eerie-looking black computer that had obviously been independently assembled. Dutch pulled his hands away from the computer. He stood up and marched to his front window, briefly glancing outside before closing the blinds. Then he settled back onto the couch in front of the laptop and studied the casing of the computer. There were no external connection ports.

Dutch was the fish and the computer the bait. He slowly flipped open the laptop, found the start-up button, and switched on the computer. It went through a usual boot-up screen, then loaded the Windows operating system in seconds. Whatever CPU the laptop housed, it was the fastest Dutch had ever seen. After boot-up, the monitor revealed the skeleton Windows operating system. There was no software, nor an icon to click. He searched for software on the hard drive, but there was nothing.

Suddenly, the screen went black.

Look inside the box. Put on the earpiece, slowly ticked onto the screen, as though being typed. The connection was wireless. It had to be.

Frantically searching, Dutch again looked inside the package, discovering a tiny earpiece taped inside. He connected the earpiece wire into the computer, placing the tiny speaker end into his ear.

"Dutch, it's Skreemer."

"Why are you fucking with me?" Dutch demanded.

"What's with all the animosity?" Skreemer replied calmly.

"How can I be sure this line isn't tapped?"

"Relax. This computer provides a secure line," Skreemer said. "Our interaction is entirely encrypted. Only my computer has the decoding key. These days, it's the only way we can safely communicate."

"Convince me that you're really Skreemer."

"Ask me something."

"Name the password for the NASA hack?"

"Gazette."

"How about international calls? What was old reliable?"

"Hell, I don't remember the number."

"Then you're not Skreemer," Dutch said loudly, reaching up to pull out his earpiece.

"MCI radius. We always used the one you found with the 202 area code," Skreemer said. "Shit, you're still proud of that one, aren't you? What are you so paranoid about anyway?"

"How'd you find me?" Dutch asked.

"Wasn't easy. I must have searched a few hundred newspapers lookin' for a teenager who got arrested that night you left me the e-mail," Skreemer said. "The nasty storm that night of the hack narrowed the search down to the southeast. Articles said a New Bern teen. A little footwork and I uncovered a juvenile court case: Ryan Caldwell versus the State in violation of the North Carolina Computer Crimes Act. From there, didn't take much to track down his best friend."

"How could you tell I knew him outside of hacking?"

"You didn't give it away with words. It was just the way you two interacted."

"And STORM? Still together?"

"Alive and kicking."

"What about Ray and Skye?"

"STORM couldn't exist without them."

"Why are you contacting me? Why now?"

Suddenly, a flashing cursor appeared against the black computer screen. The cursor jumped down a few spaces, pausing periodically for several seconds, then continued until it stopped at the bottom of the monitor. The word *login*: suddenly appeared.

"I want to show you something. But first, I need to verify that you're really Dutch."

"A test," Dutch scoffed.

"Just being cautious."

Dutch focused intently on the word *login*. If he proceeded, it would be based upon an utter trust in Skreemer, a man he had never seen, and until last night, had not spoken to in almost twenty years.

"The old backdoor can't possibly still work," Dutch said skeptically.

"Well, you programmed it so that the code couldn't be found, right?" Skreemer replied.

Dutch took a deep breath, exhaling slowly, as though attempting to get rid of his doubt. "Here goes," he sighed.

He proceeded to type the old backdoor: *FIVE. Password*: then appeared on the screen.

This time, without a pause, he typed in the same four letters, all caps.

FIVE.

Instantly, *Access to Compound Five Database Granted* flashed onto the screen, then disappeared. The screen turned black for several seconds.

At the top of the monitor appeared the words: *THIS IS CLASSIFIED TOP SECRET. Examination by unauthorized persons is a criminal offense punishable by fines up to $100,000 and imprisonment up to twenty years.* A menu followed:

1. *Compound Five (C5) Physical Construct*
2. *Construct Control Center (C3)*
3. *Power Grid / Power Back-up*
4. *Tracking System: Plexus*

5. Security System: Perimeter / Core

A flashing cursor awaited a selection.

"I knew you couldn't forget," Skreemer said. "Nor resist."

"Oh shit," Dutch stammered, as he read the screen, acknowledging the fines and prison time.

"Don't worry. This connection is untraceable," Skreemer said. "Just watch. I'll take you through it."

Skreemer proceeded to press the first menu option: Compound Five (C5) Physical Construct. The hard drive light flickered.

Compound Five Physical Construct selected ran across the top of the screen.

> *Project: COMPOUND FIVE*
> *Authority: DARPA, U.S. Navy, Pentagon*
> *Classification: TOP SECRET*
> *Priority: National*
> *Subject: C5 high security facility structural design and tracking*
> *engineering*
> *Crossfile: Project WHITEWASH, Project OBJECTIVE FORCE*
> *WARRIOR, Project ELITE FIRE*
> *Delta designation confirmed.*

Topographical maps and structural diagrams of C5 populated the left half of the screen. To the right, GPS coordinates pinpointed C5 on a roughly pentagon-shaped island in the South Pacific.

"This is amazing. It's an island," Dutch acknowledged.

"Smack dab in the South Pacific," Skreemer said. "Closest neighbor: 250 miles northwest. There are five coastal access points, hence the name. The rest of the island is inaccessible due to massive volcanic cliffs."

"Why would the U.S. own a South Pacific island?" Dutch asked.

"It's a remnant of World War II," Skreemer replied. "Like Guam. Bikini. The Marshall Islands—you know, where all the nuke testing was done in the 1950s. But this island was uninhabited, secretly used for staging during the war. The U.S. retained possession."

"What's it used for?"

"DARPA combat research and testing facility now," Skreemer replied. "Top Secret for more than twenty years. They're finally opening it up to a small circle of nations, apparently for a counterterrorism initiative."

Skreemer moved the cursor to a blue circle icon at the center of the topographical diagram of the ten-mile-wide island. A tiny text box elucidated the icon: *Construct Control Center (C3)*.

The screen changed. Architectural and structural layouts of the C3 appeared.

Dutch took over the touchpad and began scanning the document.

Five miles inland from the surf line in every direction, at the island's center, the C3 was an underground steel-and-concrete-reinforced web-communications complex serving as the heart and brain of C5. The C3 housed the comm center and computer networks that controlled the exercises.

DARPA's High Productivity Computer Systems program pursued a new generation of computing systems for national security and industry. The initiative envisioned peta-FLOPS speed. The most powerful personal computers were rated at around 80 giga-FLOPS, or 80 billion floating-point operations per second; thus the supercomputer peta-FLOPS speed was tens of thousands times faster than any desktop PC.

Inside the mainframe chamber of the C3 was a classified network of ten modified Cray XT5h mainframe systems with a peak speed of over five peta-FLOPS. The fastest unclassified supercomputer was the Oak Ridge National Laboratory's Cray XT5 "Jaguar" supercomputer. The mainframe network at C3 dwarfed the Jaguar.

Dutch scrolled through the information briefly, reading bits here and there. The document was massive. Dutch did not understand why they would need such a powerful network. But he knew C3 could not be hacked from a remote location. Although it would feed information outside the compound, no information could come in remotely. There would be no hacking this one.

The screen went blank.

"What happened?" Dutch asked.

"Best not to overextend our stay," Skreemer said. "So, you've waited twenty years to see what you hacked. What do you think?"

"Why do they need that much computing power?" Dutch asked.

"A little suspicious, isn't it?" Skreemer replied. "This place defines top secret."

"I don't even know why I'm looking at this stuff," Dutch interrupted. "It's best I don't. How do I know you're not working for the NSA or DoD?"

"Trust goes both ways," Skreemer replied. "Why not report me to the authorities?"

"You know my name. Anonymity still applies to you."

"You have a point."

"Why do you want me to see all this? Why now?" Dutch asked.

"Consider yourself a consultant," Skreemer replied. "We're in need of your expertise."

"My expertise?" Dutch laughed.

"Since you left STORM," Skreemer began.

"I didn't leave STORM," Dutch broke in. "I didn't have a choice."

"Okay. Since you last hacked, we've infiltrated systems across the world—*Fortune 500* companies, banks, government systems—U.S. and foreign. For the last twenty years of my life, hacking is all I've done, and I can say without a doubt, I have yet to run across a hacker with better natural talent than you."

"That was twenty years ago," Dutch objected.

"There's a training exercise at C5 in two weeks," Skreemer said. "I guarantee I can have you back up to speed by then."

"Back up to speed for what?"

"To hack into the Construct Control Center."

"Can't be done."

"Nothing's impossible, Dutch. Of all people, you know that," Skreemer said. "As I recall, twenty years ago a group of five kids was able to hack into one of the most highly confidential, top-secret developments of this century."

"You read the same shit I did. Can't be hacked remotely."

"We have to go to the island."

"Go to the island!" cried Dutch. "You're shittin' me. I'm not going to some South Pacific island to hack into a system that is not only unhackable, but also unapproachable. Not even mentioning the fact that I haven't *hacked* in forever."

"We've got it all worked out," Skreemer insisted. "I can get us there. We already have codes for the perimeter security computers, thanks to your backdoor. Once inside, we'll hack the C3 computers and gain control of the exercise. Dutch, I can get us *to* Compound Five, but I need you to get us *in!*"

"I don't wanna hear anymore."

"How about one million dollars, Dutch?"

"One million?" There was a reluctant pause as Dutch digested the news. "I don't need the money," he replied.

"Get real! Your fiancée left you, you're three months behind in rent, and your fifteen-dollar-an-hour job towing trucks isn't gonna dig you out of debt anytime soon. Your hopes for fleeing New Bern…they're never going to happen and you know it. You need the money."

"How the fuck do you know…" Dutch began.

"That's my job," Skreemer interrupted. "Had to be sure you were really Dutch. Did line taps. Read your text messages and e-mails."

"You're fuckin' crazy!" Dutch fired back.

"Maybe so," Skreemer admitted. "Give it some thought. I'll be in touch with you tomorrow night at 11 p.m."

"Eastern, Pacific, or Mountain time?" Dutch asked.

"Don't try to peg me," Skreemer replied curtly.

The line went dead. Dutch sat staring into the void of the blank screen, his earpiece emitting static.

CHAPTER 5 TRAINING

NEW BERN, NORTH CAROLINA
MAY 23

DUTCH ENTERED the New Bern-Craven County Public Library and quickly moved past the front desk, avoiding eye contact with the librarians. His gray baseball cap was pulled low over his eyes, hiding most of his jet-black hair. A pair of old Levis, non-descript black tennis shoes, and a navy blue shirt finished out his non-specific ensemble. Paranoid, the generic outfit he donned was a vain attempt to hide his identity.

Usually, Dutch stationed himself in a corner on the far side of the quaint library where he could read in seclusion. He had read every book on computers, from cryptology to databases to hacking. Every title was stored in his cranial database. Every author was known. Yet, he never checked out any of the books. As for magazines, the first moment they hit the shelves, he consumed their contents. It was a hobby or perhaps an obsession—no matter; for the past twenty years, this is how many of his hours had been spent.

Dutch's reason for visiting the library this Sunday afternoon was quite different. Having already searched the Internet for newspaper articles on hacking, he positioned himself in front of the microfilm viewer and began scanning articles that spanned the past twenty years. They were not difficult to find. Stories were written almost daily on the subject now coined *cyberterrorism*.

For nearly four hours he stared into the lens of the viewer, reading feverishly on topics ranging from viruses to worms to Denial of Service to the latest bandwidth-consumption attacks. Dutch's eyes began to burn and water. He left with more questions than when he began. He still could not help but wonder whether STORM had had any role in these attacks. Moreover, nowhere was there any mention of STORM, nor of Skreemer, Skye, or Ray.

*　　*　　*

Sunday night came quickly. Dutch's apartment was silent. The commercial on the fifteen-inch TV was muted. Dutch sat alone on his couch, watching the blank, black screen of the laptop and tapping his fingertips against the coffee table. As 11 p.m. approached, he thought of a million reasons not to answer the call.

As the set time came and went, Dutch's hands began to sweat. His heart palpitated. The artery pulsed around his neck and head. He could feel his throat tightening.

At 11:04 p.m. the computer screen flashed. Dutch took a deep breath and exhaled. *Connected* appeared on the screen.

Frantically Dutch placed the tiny earpiece speaker into his right ear. "Where were you?" he asked in a whispered shout.

"Relax," Skreemer replied calmly.

"Why do you want to go there?" asked Dutch.

"We're not looking to do anything malicious if that's what you're asking."

"How are you getting paid?"

"Unfortunately, I can't give you specifics. It would compromise the operation."

"Then what are they paying for?"

"The Defense Department pays out billions annually to a slew of defense contractors. The money is there. All we have to do is take down the system, show it's vulnerable, and we get paid."

"They must want a malicious payload inserted. Virus. Worm. Something."

"No. Show the security system is compromised. Take the system down temporarily. Expose its vulnerabilities. That's it. Nobody gets hurt. No damage to the networks or system."

"It's too damn risky. Why do it at all?"

"We've been catching a lot of heat. It's all too risky now, Dutch. Ever since U.S. Cyber Command became the Defense Department's network-defense hub, they've gotten closer and closer to us. This is STORM's last hurrah. The final hack. We've hacked into some amazing networks over the years, but it's time for us to hang it up. This is our chance to get paid for our skills."

"So who's in this with you? Just the old STORM?" Dutch asked.

"Six of us: myself, Ray, Skye. The fourth is Lone Wolfe. He joined us four years ago. The fifth is Night Eagle. Eagle for short. He's a former Army Special Forces—you know—a Green Beret guy, hired by Lone Wolfe to get us into Compound Five. And the sixth is you."

"Ever try to get back in touch with Spyder?" Dutch questioned, as flashes of his old friend came to mind.

"No. The night he got busted was the last night we talked," Skreemer said.

"How do you know these other guys are okay?" Dutch asked.

"We don't. That's why we stay anonymous," Skreemer replied.

"Can't stay anonymous if you're gonna meet face-to-face."

"True. Lone Wolfe has been with us for some time. At least that's a little reassuring. Night Eagle's hired help, which makes me very uncomfortable. I've tracked him down and monitored him for months. Phone taps. Tracking e-mails. Kind of like you, going to the library every Sunday just to read about computers."

Dutch sat up a little straighter. "You've even followed me?"

"Nothing personal, man, but I had to make sure you were really Dutch," Skreemer replied.

"I think you're feeding me a line of shit," Dutch scoffed. "You guys are gonna hack Compound Five from the inside on an island in the South Pacific."

"You still picture us as kids, 'cause that's the last image you have of us," Skreemer said. "We're not kids anymore. STORM has spent endless hours hacking. We have so much delicate information and access codes to super-secret places that the U.S. government couldn't even friggin' imagine. But that information came at a cost. We're willing to leave it all now. Before we do, we want to get paid."

"You gotta understand where I'm coming from, Skreemer. I haven't talked to you in two decades. I thought STORM was history, until yesterday. Hell, for all I knew you were dead. It's just too damn much to take in." Dutch hesitated. "There's gotta be a better way than going to the South Pacific," he continued.

"Fuck, man! There isn't!" Skreemer shouted.

"How'd you plan to get into C5?"

"Are your eyes on the screen?"

"Yep."

Skreemer logged into the system and selected *Security Systems: Perimeter / Core* from the menu. A diagram of the island once again appeared, awaiting another keypunch to initiate the video.

"Dutch, recall this is a DARPA testing ground. All the latest technology and gadgets are here. Security is tight."

Dutch pressed the spacebar. The video began.

Recorded video from a helicopter showed treacherous volcanic cliffs lining the shoreline. Underwater trip wires and electrical fencing surrounded the entire island. It was an impenetrable fortress "to protect against any terrorist threat," the video proclaimed. It even detailed the next phase of security that included surface-to-air missiles.

Graphics then highlighted five beach access points, each laden with intelligent mines. A voice in the video discussed the novel anti-combat breach-response mechanism. Based on DARPA's anti-tank Self-Healing Minefield system, if mines were detonated, the other mines would move into position to cover the compromised region.

"This is where we go in," Skreemer said. "Mines are live. But don't worry, this is where Eagle comes into play."

The video continued. Hidden below the island's lush jungle was DARPA's plexus, an advanced tracking system, which along with the comm center included a subsurface metal alloy mesh—C5's nervous system—stretched across the entire surface of the island.

The plexus and comm center together served two purposes: to monitor and to protect. The system allowed for offshore tracking of all movement within C5. During a military exercise, any physical movement, intrusion, or landing from sea or air would be recorded, dissected, and scrutinized for error and development of future combat strategies. The plexus' second purpose was to protect against any unwanted visitors. With a 10-milliamperage electrical current, an intruder would not be able to move due to muscle tetany, while with 100 milliamps, the human heart enters into a lethal rhythm of ventricular fibrillation. The plexus could be controlled to stop intruders or kill them.

"The perimeter system and plexus are not active until the start of the exercise, so we have this worked out, too," Skreemer noted.

"What exercise?"

Skreemer returned to the main menu, selecting *Elite Fire Exercise Parameters*. A new menu appeared.

1. Participants
2. Command
3. Objective Force Warrior
4. Safety Requirements
5. Rules of Engagement
6. Main Menu

Skreemer pressed the number '1' on his keyboard.

A new video played. The Elite Fire Exercise was an international training exercise involving the elite counter-terrorist units from the U.S., Britain, New Zealand, Australia, and France. C5 was designated as the international base for the next combat exercise. Each CT unit participating consisted of five team members. Although still a training exercise, the combat, conditions, and weapons used made injury or even death a real possibility.

For the forthcoming C5 exercise, the M4 carbine, a collapsible-stock carbine version of the M16 assault rifle, had been further modified to integrate DARPA's High Impulse Technology. HIT was basically a stun gun with distance capability. Depending upon where one was hit, HIT created a range of responses from incapacitating severe pain to temporary unconsciousness. It was one of the first successful directed energy weapons, programmable such that if activated it could be lethal.

"This is unbelievable," Dutch whispered. He now knew why his old friend Spyder was delivered such a stiff penalty when it came to judgment day. STORM had uncovered a secret that defined top secret.

"There's more," Skreemer said, as he selected *Command* from the menu.

Dutch scrolled through the document quickly, his eyes darting across each page. Command was delivered from the offshore aircraft carrier USS *Ronald Reagan* and would serve as a control tower for each team. Each country's command center was located on an isolated area of the carrier. Pages were dedicated to meticulous rules and protocols. The more Dutch read, the more difficult it was to wrap his brain around the fact that this was real.

"This is some serious shit," Dutch said. "This all makes me very nervous. I still don't get why you need me."

"Up until a month ago, we had it all worked out. Then they changed the encryption-scheme of the perimeter security system. We can't break it. We're desperate and out of time. The exercise starts in two weeks."

"And you think I can break it?"

"You're the only one that has a chance. It's your hack to finish."

"This system is far different than the one twenty years ago."

"Dutch, we've run out of options."

"So I'm your last resort."

"Look, I'm taking one hell of a risk getting in touch with you. I wouldn't do this if I didn't believe you could do it. The others agreed that if I could get you up to speed in a week, we'd let you in on everything."

"When do I get to talk with the others?"

"In a week," Skreemer replied.

"Why wait?" Dutch asked.

"We have a lot of work to do," Skreemer said. "There's a lot to get through. Network protocols, security system manuals, operating systems."

"So, you have this all worked out—getting there and all?" Dutch asked, still doubtful.

"I've spent the past four years getting us there," Skreemer said adamantly. "In my mind, I've already been there a thousand times. I've got every square inch of the place memorized. Dutch, we'll be in and out of there before they knew what hit them."

"I'm committing to nothing," Dutch said. "But I'll take a look at the system."

"Fair enough," Skreemer replied.

"When do we begin?"

"Tonight."

CHAPTER 6 INFILTRATION

TALCAHUANO, CHILE
MAY 29

AN EARLY DAWN FOG settled onto the port city of Talcahuano, Chile. Dark clouds blanketed the sky.

Heavy-lift cranes lined the dockyard, each off-loading cargo containers from the ship *Cabo Tormentoso*. The vessel had arrived just after midnight, completing its three-day journey from the Easter Islands. Twelve of the ship's sailors were busy on the deck. The thirteenth seaman remained below.

Jose Montega stood alone in his cabin. He picked up an M4 carbine and gently placed it into the black duffel bag on top of the other dozen assault weapons. Slowly, he pulled the zipper closed. The veins in his forearms bulged like thick steel cables as he hoisted the eighty-pound pack onto his shoulder. The thin strap cut into his thick trapezius; his broad back muscles tightened.

He opened the cabin door, paused, and listened. The vessel's steel frame creaked. Ship horns bellowed in the distance. The crane engines hummed above.

Montega walked along the corridor and headed up a flight of stairs. The metal-grated steps banged loudly with each stride. When he reached the rear of the ship, he looked down. The stern ramp was vacant. He eased down the ramp, finally reaching the dockyard, and immediately tasted the salt lingering in the cool air.

He moved between the tall forty-foot-long cargo containers stacked two high. Within minutes, he reached a dirt road running parallel to the coast. He looked back. The fog had consumed the ship. He glanced at his Luminox wristwatch. His gait quickened.

Five minutes later, Montega saw the dim light outside his apartment piercing the slowly dissipating fog. The wooden sign above his door etched with the address 2363 was only visible when he arrived at his doorstep. He quickly unlocked the door and went inside, glancing again at his watch.

The one-room efficiency apartment was no more than 150 square feet. There was a tiny, rusted refrigerator in the corner next to a gas stove, an old ceiling fan that wobbled more than it cooled, and a metal-framed bed that took up most of the remaining space. A single bathroom was shared with the adjacent flat.

Montega moved into the apartment, grunting slightly as he hefted the heavy bag from his shoulder and carefully set it on the floor beside his bed. The weapons clanged inside.

He sat on the corner of the bed. The frame squeaked loudly. He glanced at his Luminox one last time, as his cell phone rang.

"Hola," Montega answered.

"Night Eagle, still on schedule?" the voice asked.

Since his arrival in Talcahuano six months ago, Jose Montega was the name he used to protect his true identity from his co-workers. However, Night Eagle was the name he used to protect his identity from his real employer—the man on the phone. Jose Montega was Night Eagle.

"Yep," Eagle replied.

"Okay. Did you get the package?" the voice asked.

"Yep."

"Good. You know what to do from here," the voice stated, then abruptly hung up.

Eagle moved to the floor, getting onto both hands and knees.

He dragged a cardboard box from beneath his bed. Lifting up his right pant leg, he pulled an eleven-inch black tactical knife from the sheath strapped to his calf. Deftly, he sliced through the taped cardboard box top. He reached in, pulled out an unmarked black laptop computer, and tossed it onto the bed. The bed again squeaked loudly. Kneeling on one knee, he flipped open the laptop and switched on the computer. It quickly booted.

Eagle stood up, nearly smacking his head on the ceiling fan, instinctively ducking away from the fan's rotating blades. He reached into his left front pants pocket and pulled out the tiny flash memory drive. He dropped back down onto one knee and inserted the drive into the port on the side of the laptop. He typed several commands, executing the desired computer program. A minute later, he placed the computer back into the box, re-taped it shut, and slid it back under the bed.

The changes were complete.

*   *   *

NEW BERN, NORTH CAROLINA
MAY 29

Dutch was fast asleep. In the past week, he had learned what he had missed over the last two decades. On most occasions, sleep was forfeited to endless hours of reading. He studied the operating-system manuals of the Construct Control Center and security systems of C5, searching for network vulnerabilities. Because he had never stopped reading about technology and computer hacking, his technical knowledge was strong, but he had lost much of his practical skills. This discrepancy did not last long.

Several rings from Dutch's home landline did not faze him. The answering machine picked up. No message was left. Shortly thereafter, the phone rang again; this time it woke him.

Another ring sounded before Dutch realized it was his home phone. He walked into the kitchen and grabbed his cordless receiver.

"Hello?" he answered.

"John, ya able to come in tomorrow?" It was his boss, Tony Marks.

"What?" Dutch said, walking back to the sofa. Dropping down hard, he put his feet up on the coffee table.

"You feelin' any better?" asked Marks.

"Yeah, ya just woke me up, that's all," Dutch said weakly, faking a cough. He stared at the black laptop sitting in front of him on the coffee table. The hard drive light flickered.

"What time is it?" he asked.

"9:30 or so."

"Oh, God," Dutch muttered softly.

"Is everything alright?" Marks asked.

"Yeah," Dutch replied.

"Steve tells me you got the damn flu. Ya sound awful. Why don't ya just take another day off?" Marks said.

"I think I'll take ya up on that," Dutch replied gratefully.

The computer monitor started flashing information—too fast to read.

"Alright, well, you get to a doctor, ya hear me? And get some rest," Marks continued.

"Yes sir," Dutch quietly replied as he hung up.

"Shit!" he exclaimed loudly. He quickly placed the tiny speaker into his right ear.

"Ray, it's not gonna work," Skye stated in her soft southern drawl.

"Well, do you have a better idea?" Ray replied.

Dutch listened closely, comparing the voices he remembered from twenty years earlier to the ones he was hearing today.

"No. But we just don't have the hardware," Skye replied.

"Hey guys," Dutch interrupted.

"Dutch. What the hell happened to you?" Skreemer questioned.

"I fell asleep," admitted Dutch.

"Okay, so you're the infamous Dutch that Skreemer's been talking about, to help us hack into this," Lone Wolfe replied. "So, how 'bout this. The network is running a modified EFS."

"Encrypting File System. Public key cryptography-based. It transparently encrypts on-disk data in real time. So you need the key?" Dutch elaborated.

"No shit, genius," Wolfe spat back.

"Hold up now, Wolfe," Skreemer said patiently. "This system has changed all the encryption for their remote access browsers from 128-bit to 256-bit cipher strength. All the keys we designed don't work anymore."

"In the past week, they've ramped up their security bigtime," Ray interjected. "They've changed all the access codes for entering the coliseum. We haven't been able to decrypt them."

"Damn, it's good to hear your voice, Ray. But why do you call it the coliseum?" Dutch asked.

"Well, you tell me what the difference is. Compound Five. It doesn't seem any different than the Romans and their gladiators."

"Don't get him started on that, Dutch," Skye chimed in.

"Skye, how're you doing?" Dutch exclaimed.

"Hey, we don't have time for a family reunion here. Any tricks, Dutch?" Wolfe jumped in.

"Would be doin' better if we could get this working, Dutch," Skye answered.

"So what's the real problem?" Dutch asked. "Do we need the recovery agent hardware or do we just lack computer power for decoding?"

"We have all the encrypted files right now," Skreemer said. "If we had the computer power, we could decrypt them—no problem."

"How 'bout university computers?" Dutch asked.

"We thought of that. University networks maybe have a couple hundred, at most a thousand computers," Skreemer said. "It would take weeks. We don't have that long."

"What about corporate systems?" Dutch continued.

"The corporate systems that have the power are heavily secured," Skye replied. "It would take weeks to months to hack them."

"We're hosed. Thanks for playing," Wolfe said loudly.

"Wolfe, do you believe in aliens?" Dutch asked matter-of-factly.

"Excuse me?!" Wolfe scoffed, astounded.

"Any of you heard of the SETI project?" Dutch asked.

"Yeah. The Search for Extra-Terrestrial Intelligence," Skreemer replied. "U.C. Berkeley started it, I think. Hunting for aliens."

"Am I the only one that hasn't lost their freakin' mind?!" Wolfe barked impatiently.

The group ignored Wolfe. Dutch went on. "In 1999, scientists at Berkeley wondered, 'Why not use personal computers around the world to process radio telescope transmissions during idle time on home computers?'"

"What's your point, Dutch?" Skye pressed.

"The SETI@home project has over a quarter million computers active," Dutch continued. "Last I read, it's like a 600 tera-FLOPS supercomputer. Hack that and you have access to the equivalent of one of the five fastest supercomputers in the world."

"If we could replace the radio-telescope data files with the encrypted files we have—then process the data and send it back—we could have it decoded in a couple days!" Skreemer burst out excitedly.

"We've got to hack into SETI first," reminded Ray.

"That's cake. Consider it done," Wolfe said.

*   *   *

NEW BERN, NORTH CAROLINA
MAY 30

Twenty-four hours later, Dutch sat on his couch, awaiting Skreemer's call. He sipped his lukewarm coffee, and then placed the mug on the coffee table beside his laptop. His gaze drifted back to the monitor positioned at eye-level. The earpiece connected to the computer was positioned loosely in his ear.

At 11 p.m., the blank screen on the laptop lit up. Skreemer was connected.

"We're heading out tomorrow," Skreemer started.

"What?" Dutch asked, shocked.

"Dutch, we need you there," Skreemer replied. "Have you thought about things anymore?"

"What's the status on the security codes?"

"Took a little longer than expected to get the data converted onto all the home computers, but decoding should be done tonight or early tomorrow," Skreemer replied.

"I still have no details on how you're getting there," Dutch continued, pausing momentarily. "I'm skeptical about the whole thing."

"I can't make any guarantees, if that's what you're looking for," Skreemer said. "Believe me, I know what's at risk. We've been careful, treaded lightly, maintained our anonymity, and prepared. I've spent many sleepless nights worrying, thinking, and re-thinking. It took four years of preparation to develop this plan and by no means is it foolproof. There's no way it could be. We've patched up every hole the best we can, but I can't guarantee success. What I *can* guarantee is that I've spent thousands of hours fine-tuning the plan. And I can promise you, this will be the ultimate hack."

"Certainly will be one hell of a hack," Dutch said.

"An airline ticket will come to your house tomorrow. You can either get on the plane or not. It's your choice."

"And if I get on the plane?"

"Pack lightly. Pack tonight. You'll need only one change of clothes. And make sure you bring the computer."

"Where are we headed?"

"You'll find out tomorrow."

"When I get to wherever I'm going, how will I find you?"

"You won't. I'll find you."

"Well, what do you want me to do when I get there?"

"Just hang out. Trust me, I'll find you. Oh, and by the way, *when* you get to your destination, you'll be Todd Mason."

"Todd Mason?"

Suddenly, there were several hard knocks at Dutch's front door.

"I gotta go," Dutch stated flatly. "Somebody's at my door."

"Dutch, I hope to see you tomorrow."

"Yeah," Dutch replied nervously.

The line went dead.

"Who is it?" Dutch yelled, jerking off the earpiece. He quickly slammed the laptop shut and shoved it under the sofa.

"It's me. Steve."

Dutch got up, walked to the door, and opened it.

"What's goin' on?" Steve asked, pushing past Dutch and walking into the room.

Steve wore khaki pants and a maroon Polo pullover shirt. His dark brown hair was neatly combed. "*Damn*, John, you look like shit!" he said, dropping down on the couch.

"Thanks," Dutch replied sarcastically, glancing beneath the couch to make sure the computer was hidden.

Steve reached over, picking up several letters lying on the coffee table. He propped his shoes on the coffee table and began flipping through them.

"I'm going out tonight. Wanna come?" Steve asked.

"Not really," Dutch replied.

"Have you even left the house?"

"Only to the cemetery to visit my folks."

Steve placed his feet on the floor and gently set the mail back on the table. "Man, I'm sorry." He paused. "What's it been? Five years since the crash?"

"Seems like yesterday," Dutch said. "Listen, I'm goin' camping this weekend. I need to get out of town for a little bit."

"Where?"

"I don't know. Maybe Uwharrie," Dutch replied, referring to the Uwharrie National Forest about 200 miles west of New Bern. "Can you cover for me at work?"

"Of course," Steve assured him. "Are you goin' by yourself?"

"Yeah...just need to clear my head."

"Y' okay?"

"Yeah, I'm fine. Listen—get outta here. Go have fun tonight."

Steve stood up, reached into his pocket and pulled out his cell phone as he headed for the door.

"Hey, Steve," Dutch started, pausing until Steve turned around. "Thanks."

"For what?"

"For being the brother I never had," Dutch said. "You know, always dropping by to see if I want to go out, even though I never go out anymore."

"Anytime," Steve smiled. "Just lemme know if you need anything."

Dutch watched as Steve got into his Jeep and drove off. For the next minute, he stood in his doorway, staring down the small street in front of his apartment, his thoughts drifting between STORM, Compound Five, his parents, and lonely New Bern.

CHAPTER 7 THE TRIP

NEW BERN, NORTH CAROLINA
MAY 31

"MOSTLY SUNNY TODAY with a ten percent chance of thunderstorms in the afternoon," the WCTI TV12 weatherman announced. Dutch was oblivious to the sound of the TV and the first three raps on his front door.

Bang. Bang. Bang. The knocks sounded again, louder this time. Dutch stirred, then awakened. He got up and walked to the window, pulling the dark-blue curtain-shade aside. The morning sun streamed in.

He squinted to see outside. A white FedEx delivery truck was parked in front of his place, the engine idling. The driver pulled the "Express Delivery" envelope from under his left arm and propped it against the door. The man dashed back to the truck, letting the storm door slam shut.

Dutch watched as the truck drove away. He glanced across the street at the two-story brick duplex. His eyes flashed nervously. A neighbor busily washed his white Ford pickup truck. Another walked his golden retriever along the shaded sidewalk where thick Spanish moss was draped over the broad, gnarling limbs of cypress trees hundreds of years old.

Moving to the front door, he opened it just long enough to

retrieve the package. He rushed back to the window, peeking briefly through the curtains before closing them.

Dutch walked back to his couch, sat down, and tore open the top of the envelope's paper flap. Inside was a printout of an Expedia.com electronic airline ticket.

Expedia.com itinerary number: 110597060403
Expedia.com booking ID: MO4JJO (1)
Main contact: John Newark
Home phone: (252)/555-2121
Work phone: (252)/555-7849

US AIRWAYS
One Ticket—One Way
May 31
New Bern (EWN-Craven County Regional Airport) Depart 11:55 a.
Charlotte (CLT-Douglas International) Arrive 1:20 p.
220 mi. (354 km)
Duration: 1 hr. 25 min.
US Air Flight 3239
Industry fare type—Economy/Coach Class—Unrestricted
Dehavilland Dash 8-300
Connection Flight at CLT
Charlotte (CLT-Douglas International) Depart 3:25 p.
Los Angeles (LAX-Los Angeles International) Arrive 5:31 p.
2121 mi. (3413 km)
Duration: 5 hr 6 min.
US Airways 193
Industry fare type– Economy/Coach Class, Airbus A3211 60%
    on time
Passenger: JOHN NEWARK
Must have valid form of identification with name exactly as it
    appears above in order to board flight
One Adult: $677.20

THE TRIP

Taxes: $59.80
Booking Fee: $2.50
Total Cost: $739.50

Dutch held the paper e-ticket in both hands. His breathing quickened; his eyes widened. "John Newark," he read aloud. He stood up and began pacing the floor. He read his name several more times.

Anonymity was no longer his ally. Friendship was questionable. If he was ever to get on that plane, he had no choice but to trust Skreemer. The more he paced, the more intrigued he became about the mysterious South Pacific island. Nervous excitement and a lucrative payout blinded him to doubt. Walking into the kitchen, he picked up the cordless phone and dialed the number to the Yellow Cab taxi service.

Ten minutes later, the cab horn honked in front of his apartment. The fifty-year-old cab driver stood beside the yellow taxi. The man had a round, red face and just a few strands of gray hair left on his head. A white T-shirt with a picture of the late NASCAR racing legend Dale Earnhardt fit snugly over his protuberant belly. The cab's trunk was already open.

Dutch carried two bags outside, handing the cab driver the black duffel bag containing the few clothes he had scrambled together. The driver placed it into the trunk, slamming the trunk shut. Dutch brought the computer bag with him into the back seat of the cab.

"To the airport, right?" the driver asked with a backwoods southern drawl.

"Yeah," Dutch answered briefly.

During the cab ride, Dutch gazed out at the sleepy little town where he had lived all his life. New Bern's Civil War heritage was embedded in the buildings on every street corner. The town had been spared the razings of General William Sherman as his army marched north of Savannah in 1865.

STORM

The cab continued south along the Freedom Bridge as they crossed over the Trent River. Colorful sailboats could be seen in the distance to the left of the cab in the east, sailing along the Neuse River as it intersected the Trent.

Captivated by the sun's reflection in the river, Dutch recalled the childhood story told to him many times by his father. The memory of one of the greatest sea raids in American Civil War history lurked beneath the blue-gray waters. Confederate Naval officer John Taylor Wood had led his handpicked crew in a seaborne assault and seizure of USS *Underwriter*, a 325-ton, steam-powered Union gunboat.

Early on the morning of February 2, 1864, Wood's team traveled the cypress-lined black waters of the Neuse. Dark storm clouds created a low overhead, while thick fog and sheets of rain blocked any light from *Underwriter*. Wood stood tall on the stern of his tiny boat, using the target's tolling bell as his guide.

Within 300 feet of the enemy, the Confederate raiders were spotted. Heavy gunfire rained down from USS *Underwiter's* crew of twelve officers and seventy-two men. Undeterred, the assault team tossed grappling hooks onto the enemy vessel, then battled their way aboard the bloody, rain-soaked deck. Within minutes, Wood and his team were victorious. Though they were ultimately forced to burn and abandon the ship, it was a pioneering raid, and in many ways, the birth cry of U.S. Naval Special Warfare. The tales of the famous raiding captain seemed to elicit more personal significance for Dutch now than they ever had before.

The Craven County Regional Airport was as quiet as New Bern. The cab pulled up at the departure area curb. Dutch handed the driver a ten-dollar bill, grabbed his luggage, and headed for the U.S. Airways ticket counter. He checked in his bags and entered the short line at the security screening area. Turning to glance back at the exit doors, he briefly considered the life to which he might never be able to return.

THE TRIP

*   *   *

LOS ANGELES, CALIFORNIA
MAY 31

The short connecting flight from New Bern to Charlotte was uneventful. Shortly thereafter, Dutch was aboard the flight to Los Angeles. On the ground, he retrieved his bag and waited.

He checked his cell phone repeatedly. No calls. He watched and listened to the voices and conversations of each passerby, but none were recognizable. Hours passed. Nobody approached him.

Perhaps STORM had bailed out. Maybe they had already gotten busted. Possibly this was some kind of sick joke. But who would have gone so far as to fly him out to California? Dutch stared at the one-way airline ticket receipt, shaking his head. He lifted both bags as he stood up, and began walking toward the automatic sliding doors exiting the airport.

"Passenger Todd Mason, please come to the Lan Chile check-in terminal. Passenger Todd Mason," the announcement blared over the airport intercom. At first it went unnoticed by Dutch. Then all at once he recognized the name. He turned, hurrying to the Lan Chile check-in counter. He stopped before entering the line.

Dutch scanned the area. A thin blonde desk attendant checked in an elderly couple. A security guard stood in the corridor. When Dutch glanced back at the Lan Chile check-in desk, the attendant stared back. The elderly couple walked away having completed checking in.

"Mr. Mason?" she said with a welcoming smile.

"Mr. Mason. We have your passport," she said again. "Aren't you Mr. Mason?"

Dutch eased his way to the counter without saying a word.

"Didn't you hear the announcements?" she asked. "A gentleman found your passport and ticket. Lucky I recognized you from your photo," she continued, handing over the passport.

Dutch flipped open the passport booklet and saw the picture of himself. But now he was Todd Mason.

"Thanks," he said nervously.

"You also lost your ticket," she added, handing it to him.

"Of course."

"Let's get you checked in," she said. "Your flight leaves soon. How many bags are you checking?"

"Just one."

"Hurry. Gate 32. Have a wonderful flight," she finished, handing Dutch the ticket.

He worked through airport security, then rushed along the nearly empty runway terminal toward Gate 32. "Final boarding call for Lan Chile, Flight 600 to Santiago, Chile. All rows—all passengers please report to Gate 32 for departure. Again, this is Lan Chile, Flight 600 to Santiago, Chile, final boarding call," crackled across the intercom.

Dutch raced down the corridor, waving his ticket above his head and yelling to the airline attendant. When he reached the gate, she quickly scanned the ticket, allowing him to board. He walked along the jet bridge leading to the plane. The faint smell of JP4 jet fuel filled the air. Dutch boarded the plane and made his way down the aisle of the 747. He glanced at his ticket—Seat 25F. The other passengers were already seated. His eyes moved from face to face, sporadically making eye contact.

Once he reached his row, two men were already seated. The man in the aisle seat grunted and rolled his eyes as he unbuckled his seatbelt and stood up, banging his head on the overhead compartment. The other, taller man, his long brown hair neatly combed, glared at Dutch over the top of his silver-wired Versace glasses while slowly getting up.

Dutch eased between the seats and took his spot at 25F, a window seat. The tall, thin man sat back down and began flipping through the airline magazine, glancing up every few seconds. Unconsciously, he repeatedly pulled his hair behind his ears. The man checked his Tag Heuer wristwatch, sliding his shirtsleeve back over the watch each time. He didn't utter a word. He watched Dutch's every move.

*   *   *

SANTIAGO, CHILE
JUNE 1

The wheels of the 747 touched the Chilean tarmac, awakening Dutch. Once the plane was parked at the gate, Dutch exited the aircraft, passing a large-print sign reading, "Aeropuerto de Santiago." The four-story-high ceiling stood above, while tall windows lined the terminal. Dutch moved with the crowd toward baggage-claim.

"Long flight, wasn't it?" the man with the Versace glasses stated, walking beside Dutch. Dutch glanced to his left; the thin, six-foot-three-inch man towered over him. Dutch nodded. With the back of his hand, he wiped the sweat off his forehead. He felt dizzy.

It was the man from the flight.

"Why didn't you carry on your luggage? I told you to pack lightly," the man with the Versace glasses said. Dutch stopped, turned, and glared at the man. He heard the voice of someone he considered to be a friend, but his eyes saw a stranger.

"Yep, it's me," Skreemer said.

"Fuck! You scared the shit out of me!" Dutch exclaimed.

"I know. Sorry I left you in the dark," Skreemer smiled. "I had to. C'mon. Let's walk. We don't have a lot of time. There's always a long wait at customs."

"Why didn't you say anything on the flight?"

"Just my usual paranoia," Skreemer replied. "Wanted to make sure you hadn't cut a deal with the FBI or something."

"You're nothing like I expected," Dutch admitted.

"Well, aren't we glad this isn't a blind date!" Skreemer replied, smiling and winking.

"Man, you scared the livin' shit out of me!" Dutch repeated. The two started walking again. Dutch hurried to keep up.

"What's next?" he asked.

"First customs. Then we have a three-hour drive ahead of us."

*   *   *

After passing customs, Dutch and Skreemer proceeded to the airport-parking garage. A blue Hyundai compact car waited. They loaded the car with their bags and were off, heading south on Highway 5.

"We're going to Talcahuano," Skreemer began. Dutch repeated the word several times in his head, unable to replicate its pronunciation.

"It's a small coastal town—300 miles away," Skreemer continued.

"Will the others be there?"

"Yeah, hopefully. Everybody flew out tonight."

"What's the plan?"

"There's a cargo ship leaving tonight from Talcahuano, headed for the Easter Islands," Skreemer explained. "Night Eagle's been working on the ship for the past six months and knows it like the back of his hand. The ship's path will put us within twenty-five miles of Compound Five. When we reach that point, we'll abandon ship."

"Hold on! Abandon ship?" Dutch interrupted. "How?"

"We'll jump."

"Off the ship? Into the ocean?"

"That's right. It's not as bad as it sounds. Just let me finish."

"Okay," Dutch replied, shaking his head.

"We'll have rafts to get us to Compound Five," Skreemer continued. "Ray and Night Eagle will circumvent the security systems. The key is that we'll enter C5 before the exercise begins. That's how we get around the plexus. Once we're on the island, we'll find the Construct Control Center. Then, you get your chance to hack."

"How the hell then are we gettin' *off* the island?!"

"We have a plan for that too," Skreemer said. "A submarine is gonna pick us up."

"A submarine? Won't the freakin' USS *Ronald Reagan* mind that a submarine is approaching the island?"

"Of course," Skreemer replied patiently. "But by that point, they'll be confused as to what the hell is goin' on. They won't know who to trust or what to believe anymore. They'll *assume* it's one of the other countries participating in the exercise. And because of this, they won't attack. They'll fear the repercussions."

"This is fucking insane," Dutch said incredulously.

"It's been in the works for four years now. Trust me. It's gonna work."

"It better work! What time is the ship leavin'?"

"At 1800...that's 6 p.m. for you non-military types," Skreemer said, smirking.

"That's only a couple of hours from now."

CHAPTER 8 STORM'S ARRIVAL

TALCAHUANO, CHILE
JUNE 1

EAGLE pushed the black drapes aside and peered outside, watching as a man and woman approached his doorstep. He gripped his 9mm Beretta pistol firmly in his right hand and moved away from the window.

Two raps sounded on the door. Eagle unlocked the deadbolt, opening the door slightly as the chain link tightened. "¿Quien es?" he asked cautiously.

"Just thought you should know that there's a bad storm coming," the man said.

Eagle nodded, undid the chain lock, and waved the two inside. He quickly closed the door behind them and tucked the gun beneath the waistband of his pants in the small of his back. "Skye," he acknowledged, greeting her with a handshake.

"The Night Eagle I've heard so much about," said Ray, extending his hand. "It'll be good to finally work with you."

"I take it Dutch and Skreemer haven't arrived yet," Skye said.

"Should be here anytime," Eagle replied.

* * *

Pulling off Highway 154, Skreemer turned onto the rutted oceanside street. Fishing boats lined the dock. The late-afternoon sun hung low on the horizon. Where the street dead-ended, Skreemer eased off the road onto the sandy, rocky shoulder. The two got out of the car.

Dutch stood with his door open, staring at the Pacific Ocean. The cool sea breeze blew through his hair. Seagulls perched on the dock squawked loudly. Further in the distance, cargo ship horns bellowed.

"It's beautiful here," Dutch said.

Skreemer walked to the back of the car, opening the trunk. He unzipped the black duffel bag and grabbed the 9mm Glock handgun. He popped the magazine into the chamber; a sharp click sounded. "What the hell is that for?" Dutch asked, catching a glimpse of the firearm as he moved to the rear of the vehicle. He stopped and took several steps back.

"Protection," Skreemer replied. "Don't worry; I'm not gonna off you," he said with a half smile.

"Protection from what?" Dutch asked nervously.

"Look, all you need to focus on is the hack. I'll worry about the rest," Skreemer said convincingly.

"A loaded weapon doesn't help me relax," Dutch replied.

"I don't know these people. Neither do you. It's just a precaution," Skreemer said as he tucked the firearm into his pants.

"It's all very *real* now," Dutch said. "Aren't you the least bit worried about..."

"Of course I am," Skreemer interrupted. "I know exactly how real this is and the ramifications if we get caught. At some point, you're just gonna have to trust me."

Dutch turned and faced the ocean. Part of him wanted to end the journey, but as he thought about his life back home, he convinced himself that he had no choice.

"Time to go, Dutch," Skreemer stated flatly as he closed the bag, slung it over his shoulder, and shut the trunk.

Dutch nodded.

"We're looking for 2363," Skreemer said, starting to walk down the road.

"Okay," Dutch said, following him.

"Listen, if things do get fucked up," Skreemer began, "remember this number: 1016555202."

"What's it for?"

"Repeat it back to me."

"1016555202."

"You have a mind like a computer, Dutch," Skreemer said admiringly.

"It's ten digits," Dutch replied. "But 101 isn't an area code. So if it's not a phone number, what is it?"

"Don't mention that number to anyone."

"Why?"

"We're here," Skreemer said, reading the address inscribed into a wooden sign fixed above the door.

"Trust nobody here, Dutch," Skreemer whispered as he knocked on the door.

Eagle cracked open the door without saying a word.

"Just thought you should know that there's a bad storm coming," Skreemer replied.

Eagle waved the two inside. Skreemer and Dutch quickly introduced themselves.

"Damn, we made it," Skreemer said, relief in his voice. For a few seconds, nobody spoke. Dutch silently stood with them, relinquishing his old imagined images of Ray and Skye with the ones now standing in front of him. Twenty years ago, Dutch never imagined such a moment. Even one month ago, it was not even a fleeting thought.

"Has Lone Wolfe contacted you with the codes?" Skreemer asked.

"Not yet," Eagle replied. "We don't have much time. The ship will be leavin' in a few hours. Let's go over things one last time and get Dutch up to speed." He pulled a black laptop from under his bed and booted it up.

"This is *Cabo Tormentoso*," Eagle explained, as the ship's layout appeared on the computer screen. "At 1830 we move out. We'll get on the ship at the stern and head straight to my cabin. These are tight quarters. You'll have to be quiet. Everything echoes loudly down there. The trip will take three days. On the third day, we jump ship."

"Skye," Eagle continued, "you'll be carrying the first boat. Skreemer and Dutch, you'll be riding with Skye. Ray will have the other. I'll be riding with him. Dutch, we'll go over the infrared strobe and UDT cast and recovery techniques when we're on the ship."

"UDT?" Dutch asked.

"Underwater Demolition Team," Eagle said. "Not important right now." He hit the spacebar, showing diagrams of the compound, panning through the security layout of the perimeter systems.

"We'll be arriving at the northwest shore of the island, at Gate Two," Eagle continued. "Ray and I will circumvent the underwater security systems. Skye will work on the perimeter gate. While you guys are doing that, I'll stow the gear. We'll be short on time, so we gotta move quickly."

Again hitting the spacebar, Eagle revealed the center of the compound and the helipad. "We'll then work our way to the center of the island, getting on the LZ," Eagle said, pausing to look over at Dutch. "LZ is the helicopter Landing Zone. Once there, Ray, you'll circumvent the security system. We'll gain access to the C3, but only to the area containing the mainframes. Keep in mind there are four personnel on the other side of the door at the terminal workstations." The video diagram panned into the C3, showing the ten mainframes and the target access panel.

"Skreemer will link up the mainframes to the laptop," Eagle continued. "Skye and Dutch, you'll hack the system. Once that's done, we'll upload our Inception Protocol."

"What's that?" Dutch asked.

"Gives us control of the compound," Skreemer explained. "It'll assign us non-combatant IDs, typically used for rescue personnel. If that doesn't work fast enough, we'll have to default to combatant IDs. Either way, this allows us to actually stand on the plexus without being detected. It'll take some time for the Inception Protocol to change the underlying system without it being detected, though."

"At this point, we'll have a short window to hack the—," Ray began.

"Then, we'll make our escape," Eagle interrupted. "We'll get out the same way we came in—through the LZ. But this time, the island will be covered with CT units. Their location will be transmitted to us so we can stay far away from battle. We'll move to Gate Two—the Inception Protocol will automatically open the gate. We'll make our exit. We'll retrieve our stowed gear, hit the surf, push out several thousand yards, tread water, and wait for the submarine."

"Dutch, we'll go over the details on the ship," Ray said. "We won't be getting much sleep. Keep sharp. No room for error."

*   *   *

Once their preparation was completed, Eagle led the five from the tiny apartment toward *Cabo Tormentoso*. They were outfitted in the standard issue navy-blue slacks and light-gray jumpers of the Compania Chile del Pacifico. Each donned a dark blue hat emblazoned with the flag of the Chilean shipping company—a blue moon centered on a white diamond with the letters CCP. With a black duffel bag slung across his chest, Eagle wove his way through the maze of crates on the loading dock.

Dutch pulled his hat lower; his eyes shifted nervously. His pulse quickened. Sweat beaded on his brow. He hurried to keep up with what seemed like a relaxed pace for Eagle. Skreemer followed behind Dutch, while the other three walked in a straight line in front of him.

"¿Qué pasa?" a worker asked, passing by Eagle.

"Keep moving," Eagle whispered to Ray.

Dutch slowed for a moment, as Skreemer nudged him to keep moving. Eagle walked over to the worker.

"Nada," Eagle replied loudly, staring down at the worker in an attempt to intimidate him into minding his own business.

"Ah, Montega," the worker acknowledged. "Muy bien." The man turned and walked away. Eagle worked his way back to the front of the line.

Arriving at the stern of the ship, Eagle took mental note of all workers. The rear ramp was still down. The ship was nearly loaded. The sun had already set; the deepening darkness would serve as cover.

Eagle led them up the stern ramp, onto the ship, and down a flight of stairs, until they reached his cabin. He opened the door, letting the others in. The windowless cabin was cramped—nothing more than a single bunk with a well-worn gray blanket—and it smelled musty.

Eagle quickly left the cabin room to perform his usual shipboard duties in order to eliminate any suspicion of wrongdoing. The four sat in silence.

An hour passed as they waited for Eagle's return. Several voices echoed outside the cabin door, none of which were Eagle's. Sounds of doors opening and closing were heard as Dutch glanced back and forth, catching the uneasy eyes of the others and finally settling on Skye's comforting eyes.

The voices grew louder. The rattling of keys sounded outside the cabin door, as the door's lock clicked. The door cracked open, and light beamed inside. Eagle quickly squeezed into the room, blocking the doorway with his massive frame. He shut the door behind him. "Everything's okay," he whispered. "They always search the ship for stowaways looking for a free ride. I'll check up in a bit."

The large cargo ship's engines began to moan as the ship eased its way out of port. It would take the bulk freighter three days to traverse 1,200 miles to the South Pacific island.

CHAPTER 9 PATIENCE

USS RONALD REAGAN
SOUTH PACIFIC
JUNE 4

FIFTEEN HUNDRED nautical miles from the Chilean coast, USS *Ronald Reagan*—nicknamed The Gipper—turned slow box patterns within site of Compound Five in waters too deep for anchoring. The 4.5-billion-dollar nuclear-powered carrier traveled at a meager two knots to maintain position three miles southeast of the island. Like a floating city, the massive carrier stretched more than three football fields long and housed over 5,000 sailors.

Five SH-60 Seahawk helicopters, the Navy's version of the Army's famous Blackhawk, lined the outer edge of the port-side deck, ready for the morning's counter-terrorism exercise. Amassed below the deck, F/A-18 Super Hornet and F-35C Joint Strike Fighter jets and dozens of support and surveillance aircraft—E-2C Hawkeye, C-2 Greyhound, and EA-6B Prowler—together composed an extremely formidable naval air combat unit.

Captain Walter McClure, commanding officer of the *Reagan*, sat in a high-mounted leather skipper's chair on the carrier's bridge and gazed across the flight deck beyond the glistening Pacific waters into the purple-orange sunset.

Preparing to assume his four-hour watch, Commander Joel Hutch, the ship's executive officer, stood to McClure's left and watched the radar screen, picking up a ship passing thirty miles off the port side. "Bulk freighter," McClure stated flatly.

"Yes, captain," Hutch replied. "*Cabo Tormentoso*: left port three days ago from Talcahuano. It stops at Hanga Roa, Easter Island. Final destination: Tuamoto Islands. Shouldn't be a concern, sir."

*   *   *

CABO TORMENTOSO
SOUTH PACIFIC

A booming sound, like that of sledgehammer, pounded against the bulkhead. Dutch scanned the ship's cabin. His eyes nervously met Skreemer's as he finished suiting up.

"Just the waves beating against the ship," Skreemer reassured him. Skreemer arched his back, stretching his long, thin arms to each side; his cramped muscles ached. He pulled off his shirt; his ribs were visible beneath his pale skin. He slid into the black wetsuit, strapped the seabag diagonally across his chest, and squatted to the deck.

With her back facing the others, Skye removed her shirt. Her sleek, muscular back glistened; her tanned skin was as smooth and flawless as a fashion model's. She put on a black sports bra and turned around, revealing her flat, ripped abdomen and rounded breasts. She pulled the wetsuit snug against her thighs, stretched it up onto her torso, and reached around behind her, pulling the long zipper up her back.

Ray glanced at his Omega Seamaster wristwatch, reading 1800. "It's time," he whispered. He cracked open the cabin door and glanced down the end of the short corridor. Eagle waited at its end.

Once they were together, suited up and each toting a seabag, Eagle led the way up to the ship's main weather deck. Huge cargo containers towered on either side, stacked four high. The southern hemisphere sun was now below the horizon. An orange glow was all that remained in the darkening sky. The ship's engines hummed. The smell of saltwater hung heavily in the air.

Eagle grabbed and tugged on two four-foot-long boat bags stowed amongst the cargo containers. He pulled one free and pushed it toward Skye, the other to Ray. Skye and Ray carried the thirty-pound boat bags to the ship's edge. They dropped each bag, unzipped them, and slid out the two three-person Zodiac inflatable rafts and battery-powered inflators.

Eagle followed behind, carrying in each hand a forty-pound outboard motor. His muscular arms were visible through the wetsuit. Minutes later, the fully inflated rafts, now outfitted with the motors, were ready to launch. Each raft was eight feet long and weighed nearly seventy pounds. Eagle and Ray hoisted the rafts, swinging and tossing them overboard one at a time. Next, the two men slung their seabags overboard.

"Why'd they do that?" Dutch said in disbelief.

"The seabags have beacons and they float," Skreemer replied.

"Your bag," Eagle demanded, reaching out and grasping Dutch's seabag. He proceeded until all seabags were overboard.

"Get far enough from the ship so you don't get sucked back towards it," Eagle advised. He moved twenty feet back, then sprinted across the deck and lunged overboard. A faint splash sounded over the roaring ship engines. "Oh, shit," Dutch muttered under his breath.

"It's a thirty-foot drop," Ray said. "Ship's goin' twenty-five knots. Be prepared for the impact. Hit feet first, or you're gonna get yourself killed." Ray ran full speed and leapt off the ship. Skye followed seconds later.

"There's no time to think about it," Skreemer said. He didn't wait another second as he dashed across the deck and hurled himself overboard.

Dutch stood at the ship's edge, glancing down at the dark water rippling away from the ship. Feeling dizzy, he stepped back slowly and grabbed the vertical beam on the cargo container to his right. His hands shook violently. His heart pounded fast and uncontrollably. An intense fear momentarily paralyzed him. Doubtful voices in his head questioned the reasoning that brought him to this point. He squeezed his eyes shut, opened them, and stared down the tunnel-like passageway created by the stacked cargo containers. Time was running out. The others were moving further away. Against all instinct, he took a few steps back, sprinted across the deck, and pushed off hard from the ship's edge. The vast ocean appeared like a black hole. He fell wildly, twisting in midair, his right side smacking into the water first. The hard impact stung his ribs and knocked his breath out.

Dutch plummeted ten feet beneath the waves. He kicked and pulled for the surface. He desperately needed air. As his head rose above the water, he gasped and coughed, inhaling a mix of seawater and much needed oxygen. The rumble of the ship's engine drowned out his coughing. His bruised ribs ached with each breath.

He watched as the *Cabo Tormentoso* moved away. The last glimmer of sunlight disappeared; a cool, night breeze blew across his face. The moonlight's reflection appeared like millions of mirrors. Nobody was in sight. Dutch hurried to switch on the infrared strobe.

Skye pulled herself aboard the raft, rolling onto her back. Bright stars illuminated the night sky. Her breathing slowed. She moved to the stern and tugged on the pull-starter cord; the engine sputtered, then hummed. She hurried to grab her NVGs, or night vision goggles, from her jacket pocket, placing them to her left.

As she looked up, a hand emerged from the water, firmly gripping the raft's tethered grab line. Skreemer's face appeared; he crawled and rolled onto the rubber boat. Skye grabbed his arm and assisted. "Did you find him?" Skreemer panted.

"Got here a minute ago. Haven't looked yet," she said. "You okay?"

Skreemer nodded. He pushed his wet brown hair away from his eyes and began searching across the black ocean.

Skye slid the NVGs over her head. Once powered on, the darkness turned into a field of gray-green. She toggled the goggles to IR mode and searched. "Where the hell are you?" she whispered.

"Do you see him?" Skreemer asked, a tinge of anxiety in his voice.

"I see him," Skye replied, finding the flashing IR strobe. "Starboard. 200 feet." She grabbed the steering control rod with her left arm, directing the raft toward the strobe.

Skreemer pulled the cast-and-recovery sling from his seabag. In theory, the cast-and-recovery technique was a simple water extraction tool for pulling somebody out of the water into a moving boat. In practice, it was not so simple.

Dutch drifted through the moonlit water, frantically searching for the others, as he heard the faint sound of the quiet motor. The approaching black raft appeared.

Relieved, he waved both hands side-to-side. Skye slowed the raft to ten miles-per-hour. Dutch kept his right arm bent at the elbow and high above water as Skye directed the vessel with Dutch located starboard.

Skreemer held the cast-and-recovery sling skipping in the water, as they approached Dutch. Skreemer hooked Dutch's raised arm, as Dutch quickly interlocked his hands. A forceful jerk pulled Dutch up, slapping him against the raft. As he skipped across the water beside the vessel, Skreemer grabbed his leg and yanked him aboard.

"Good show," Skye said.

"You okay?" Skreemer asked.

"Better now," Dutch replied, breathing heavily.

"Listen up," Skye said. "Once we retrieve the seabags, we'll be heading toward the northwest shore of the island, side opposite the carrier. The island is about thirty miles southwest. Little further than we wanted, but we take what we can get. Time wise, we're cuttin' it close. We must be inside by midnight."

* * *

EAST HOLLYWOOD
LOS ANGELES, CALIFORNIA

Above the mellow cafe *Sabor y Cultura* in East Hollywood, Lone Wolfe's second-floor apartment had served as command center for the past three months. Having rented the apartment with a fake ID, he blended unnoticed into the community.

For the third straight day, Lone Wolfe worked at assembling the security codes. Piece-by-piece, they were being decoded by millions of computers participating in the SETI project. The whites of his eyes reddened as he stared at the computer screen. He nervously stroked his graying light-brown goatee with his left hand. With his right, he reached into his pocket, pulling out a small white Ephedrine tablet. It was the fourth he had taken in less than 24 hours.

Lone Wolfe knew time was running out. STORM needed the codes.

* * *

OFFSHORE COMPOUND FIVE
SOUTH PACIFIC

Two hours turned the northward winds against STORM. Struggling toward the island, the two boat crews crouched down into the small rafts. "Any time now," Skreemer mumbled, as he raised his head up from his GPS unit.

Skreemer looked through his NVGs. A small speck of blackness appeared on the horizon, growing larger with each second. It was land: there, in the middle of the Pacific, was DARPA's Compound Five.

"We made it," Skye breathed.

Eighty-foot volcanic cliffs rose from the deep Pacific waters. The black cliffs were accentuated by streaks of pitchstone—glassy volcanic rock formed eons ago from rapidly cooling lava. Waves crashed against the jagged, rocky base; whitewater jetted into the air. The booming sound of the waves reverberated from the overhanging cliff face.

A thousand yards from the shoreline, Skye and Eagle cut the engines. Eagle, the self-designated scout swimmer, eased over the side of his raft and into the sea, and swam for the narrow beach carved beneath the cliff. The others waited.

Ray paddled and joined the other raft. "Get in," he told Skreemer. "We're gonna have to paddle hard once we get the signal." He firmly held the grab lines on both rafts, keeping them side-by-side. Skreemer boarded Ray's raft; Skye and Dutch remained in the other.

"Look at those waves," Dutch said.

"Eagle's a strong swimmer," Skye said. "He'll be okay."

"I'm not worried about him," Dutch replied.

"He'll find us a way," Skye said confidently.

"First he has to get by the trip wire," Ray said. "Sits ten feet underwater. Then the mines."

Eagle swam into the darkness, drifting out of sight behind the waves. The wind strengthened. The rafts bobbed and swayed. STORM paddled against the incoming tide to maintain position. Dutch glanced uneasily at the others, their eyes fixed on the shoreline. This was not the STORM he remembered. They were different. They were professionals. He sensed that he was surrounded by strangers. Dutch was an amateur and no longer fit in.

"Skye, where ya from?" Dutch whispered as a nervous diversion.

"Best we don't talk about this," Skye replied.

"I'm from North Carolina," Dutch said, annoyed. "I think if we're gonna do this, we should know a little bit about each other. That's all."

Silence.

Twenty minutes passed. A blue light flashed three times from shore. STORM paddled toward the beach, stopping fourty feet from the shoreline. "We swim from here," Skye said.

She popped the raft's inflation valve; escaping air hissed. Dutch and Skye drifted into the water as the raft deflated and submerged. Ray and Skreemer did the same. The two pairs tightly rolled their rafts, tucked them to their sides, and swam in to shore.

Eagle stood thirty feet inland on the sandy beach, completing his navigation of the corridor through the minefield. So far, the GPS coordinates had been flawless. But he did not trust GPS alone. He confirmed the locations of the mines using two additional techniques: ground penetrating radar and probing.

He finished the last several inches. Gently, he slid the non-metallic probe at a forty-degree angle into the sand. He probed every two inches, until the last mine-free step was outlined. Then he took the final step, his foot pressing into the soft sand. The minefield was breached. A successful corridor had been made.

Eagle stood inches from a galvanized-steel wire-mesh fence that stretched between the two cliffs, thirty-five feet inland from the water's edge. Razor wire spiraled along the top of the twelve-foot-tall fence. In the center, a sliding gate remained locked and closed. He flashed the blue light three more times.

The team proceeded onto the mine-littered beach and made a beeline for the marked corridor. Ray and Skreemer were first, carrying their raft and outboard engine.

Dutch hoisted the raft over his shoulder and started the traverse. Skye clutched the other outboard motor tightly to her chest and followed him. "Careful," she whispered.

Dutch took each step cautiously, the sand sinking under his feet. His thighs trembled; the raft's weight was feeling heavier with time. He quickened his pace. Skye followed, carefully brushing the footprints away with a branch wrapped with seaweed.

STORM completed the traverse. They gathered inches from the fence, which was buzzing with electrical current. "Let's de-rig," Eagle said. "I found a cave where I'll stow the gear."

"Huh?" Dutch questioned.

"We went over this," Ray said.

"Get out of your wetsuit," Skreemer interrupted. "Let's change into our dry stuff."

Dutch slid off his wetsuit and began putting on his land utility uniform. The others did the same, as Eagle packed the wetsuits together into one seabag.

Dutch pulled the C5 uniform from his seabag. It was a lightweight polyethylene black jumpsuit with the zipper along the front. He quickly stepped into it, pulled it over his shoulders, and zipped it up.

Already suited up, Skye probed the sand along the fence, finding a buried steel box; it was the gate's control panel. With both hands, she dug and pushed the sand aside until the panel door was exposed. She quickly unscrewed the panel door, opened the control box, isolated several multi-colored wires, and connected a laptop computer.

"Any word from Lone Wolfe?" Eagle asked.

"No," Skreemer reported, checking his satellite phone.

"We need those codes," Eagle said. He hoisted the seabag over his shoulder, across his chest, and headed for the cliff. He carefully walked along the fence line until he reached the cliff face. Then he climbed onto the rock, traversing five feet out over the ocean. The waves splashed onto his boots. The five-foot-deep cave was just inches away.

The faint thunder of helicopter rotor blades could be heard in the distance. With one hand gripping a large flake rock feature and the other holding the gear, Eagle slung the seabag into the cave. He climbed back toward the beach, traversing the volcanic cliff face, the black rock cutting into his hands. He leapt back onto the beach and sprinted along the fence line; the mines were inches from each step.

The helicopter drew close to the island; its spotlight glared onto the cliff face several hundred feet away; the pitchstone sparkled.

Skreemer stared at the sat phone. No codes.

"Shit. I see lights," Dutch muttered.

"Talk to me," Eagle said, rejoining the team.

Skye held her hands over the keyboard, anxiously waiting.

"We're fucked," Ray said.

"We've got codes," Skreemer shouted after finally receiving the transmission.

Skye pounded the numbers into the keyboard. The helo's spotlight moved onto the beach.

"Whadda I do with the motor?" Dutch asked.

"Once inside, hide it and run," Ray replied.

The gate inched open. One by one, STORM squeezed through the gateway and bolted onto the island.

Still outside the gate, Skye yanked the cords connected to the security panel. She slammed the panel door shut, kicking sand over it. The helo's spotlight approached.

"It's too late," Skye muttered.

CHAPTER 10 CODEZ

COMPOUND FIVE
JUNE 4

"GATE TWO is open. Please confirm," crackled over the pilot's headset from USS *Ronald Reagan*'s command tower.

"Roger that. Gate Two is open," the helicopter pilot replied.

"They're still running security checks out there. Check the area. Keep us updated. Over."

"Copy. Gate is closing now. We'll search the vicinity. Out," the pilot finished.

*　　*　　*

Following Skreemer, Dutch ran full bore, bobbing and weaving through the island's dense palm trees and thick underbrush. Lichen made the terrain slick as he struggled to keep his balance. The moon glowed dimly as Skreemer drifted in and out of sight.

Dutch looked back as the spotlight approached. The *thwop-thwop-thwop* from the helicopter blades intensified; a whirlwind of crackling leaves and sand formed behind him. He leapt behind the next palm tree he passed, then squatted and ducked. The deafening machine roared overhead. The spotlight bounced across the canopy of trees and drifted by and beyond him.

Dutch waited. He looked up; his eyes jerked, quickly searching the island.

There was no Skreemer. No Skye.

Gray clouds drifted past the moon several times, blocking what light remained. The roar of the helicopter began to diminish.

"Come on," Skye whispered, standing behind Dutch and sporting her NVGs. Startled, Dutch jumped back. "Don't do that!" he hissed.

"I don't think they saw us," Skye said. "Let's catch up with the others. We don't have much time."

"What's your status?" Eagle broke in via headset.

"We're clear. We'll meet up at C3," Skye replied.

"Copy that. It's 2320," Eagle said. "The plexus is gonna be activated at midnight."

Once active, the C3 and plexus—DARPA's advanced subsurface tracking system—would identify STORM as intruders. The only location undetected by the plexus was the original entranceway twenty years ago to the C3—what was now the helipad. Skye and the others knew if they didn't make it onto the helipad, they would be killed.

"Roger. Out," Skye replied. Turning to Dutch, she said, "Let's move. We have forty minutes to cover two miles in this pitch blackness."

*   *   *

Thirty minutes passed. Dutch and Skye listened to the sound of the helicopter's idling blades. They low-crawled to the outer edge of an open grass field, settling beside Skreemer, Eagle and Ray.

One hundred yards away, at the field's center, a Seahawk helicopter waited on the Landing Zone, or LZ—a ten-by-ten foot concrete helipad painted with a white "H." The rotator blades turned slowly; the pilot focused on his checklist, methodically inspecting his systems before lift-off. The other two crew members, the airborne tactical officer and sensor operator, prepared for flight.

One man dressed in a green Nomex flight suit sat in the helicopter bay. Five other men appeared from an in-ground doorway nearby the helipad, dropped to a crouch, and approached the helo. They wore standard issue U.S. Navy digital-camouflage utilities.

"Who are they?" Dutch whispered nervously.

"Not sure," Ray replied. "Representatives from the other countries, maybe."

"We're running outta time," Eagle mumbled, looking at his wristwatch, which now showed less than ten minutes until midnight.

"What's wrong?" Dutch asked.

"We have to be where that helicopter is by midnight," Ray said.

"Don't we have until 6 a.m.?"

"Dutch, the plexus is active at midnight," Skreemer answered.

The five uniformed men boarded the helicopter. The Seahawk blades quickened.

"Three minutes," Eagle said quietly.

The Seahawk lifted off, hovered for a moment, and turned ninety degrees. STORM anxiously watched and waited. The helo then nosed down slightly and thundered away from the helipad, ascending and moving out of sight.

"Move!" Eagle yelled. He and the others pushed themselves up to their feet and sprinted for the concrete slab.

At the pad, Dutch touched the cold concrete with his right hand. "We made it!" he breathed.

"Not yet," Skreemer said.

"Ten seconds," Eagle added.

"What the fuck?!" Dutch exclaimed.

Skye's body tensed as she closed her eyes and tilted her head down.

"What?" Dutch stammered.

"Five...four...three...two," Eagle counted.

Dutch trembled. His heart raced. His breathing stopped.

"One!" Eagle said, staring hard at Dutch.

Skye opened her eyes, took a deep breath and sighed.

"It's okay now, Dutch," Ray said. "You can relax."

"Tell me what just happened," Dutch demanded.

"We weren't sure if this glitch would work," Skye replied.

"Shit!" Dutch yelled. "Are you guys fucking insane?"

"Shut up," Eagle ordered abruptly.

The thundering of the helicopter blades lasted for several minutes. Skye sat with her seabag open, several items splayed around her: a laptop computer, a Glock 23 sidearm, a Taser, and her NVGs. She lifted the Glock, sliding the clip into place. She turned it side-to-side; the black sheen reflected the bluish moon.

Ray walked along the edge of the LZ, studying the structure. A thin layer of concrete blanketed the underlying steel door that had been used as the original entranceway to the C3. The main slab had a subtle yet noticeable defect along the edges where the steel door abutted the surrounding frame.

Ray shifted his seabag from his back to his side, unclasped it, and pulled out a pair of NVGs. He slid the goggles over his eyes and scanned the dark island that was now illuminated with a green tint. Gently lowering the seabag to his side, he dropped to both knees. He again reached into the bag and grabbed a small low-vibration drill, slotting a drill bit into place. He brushed off several pieces of dirt and some small debris from the LZ and pressed the trigger with his index finger. The quiet drill whistled as Ray exerted gentle pressure, pushing through the thin concrete and stopping just short of the steel door.

CHAPTER 11 CONTROL

CONSTRUCT CONTROL CENTER
COMPOUND FIVE
JUNE 5; 0202 (LOCAL TIME)

THE HUMMING of two geothermal-powered turbine generators sounded from within the lower level of the subterranean two-story Construct Control Center. The pipes rattled from the high-pressure 320-degree-Fahrenheit water being pumped from deep underground volcanic reservoirs and filling the heat exchangers. This hot water heated the recycling fluid to a high-pressure vaporous state, which drove the massive turbine wheels and supplied the C3 with a self-sufficient, perpetual source of electricity.

Kathryn "Kat" Lange, Edge Defense Industries' C5 project leader, rested within the dark sleeping quarters on C3's lower level, separated from the geothermal power plant by a few very thin walls. Lying on her back, Kat's blood-shot blue eyes were wide open, staring at the bottom of the top bunk. Because of the noise abatement system surrounding the geothermal plant, it was quiet in the sleeping quarters, but her concerns about the upcoming training exercise kept her awake.

She sighed anxiously, propped herself up on her elbows and pushed herself up out of bed. Her white T-shirt and full-length thermal underwear fit snugly against her petite body. She walked to the bathroom, flipped on the light, and stopped in front of the sink.

Pulling her sandy-blonde hair behind her ears, she splashed cold water onto her face—a few freckles scattered across her otherwise flawless skin lent something of a schoolgirl charm to her appearance. She headed back into the sleeping quarters and dressed. The standard issue U.S. Navy digital-camouflage utilities completed her outfit, hanging loosely on her five-foot-five-inch frame. Despite her status as a civilian contractor, her persistence for approval to wear the Navy's digi-cammies was successful, as she felt it necessary to fluidly integrate with the C3 military personnel.

Kat left the room, moved down a narrow corridor sandwiched between the living quarters and the power plant and walked up the steel-grated stairwell to the upper level. She slid a credit-card-sized Common Access Card into the CAC reader slot beside the door's handle, then tapped in her sixteen-digit PIN number. The panel's red light turned green as a beep sounded, followed by a click as the door unlocked. She pushed the door open and looked up, squinting into the brightly beaming overhead lights. Easing inside, she walked into the upper-level computer workstation area. The 5,000-square-feet upper level contained the web communications complex that served as C5's heart and brain. One-fifth of the upper level was reserved for the computer workstations, designated Northern and Southern Terminal Workstations. The rest of the upper level housed the Cray mainframes.

"I knew you wouldn't sleep," said Lieutenant Commander Justin Channing, similarly uniformed in Navy digi-cammies.

"Just don't understand why Gate Two opened," Kat replied. "It shouldn't have happened."

"An isolated problem: the plexus has been up and running smoothly since," replied the thirty-two-year-old Channing.

Kat briefly looked to her left toward the highly restricted

Southern Terminal Workstation, a network off-limits to her, searching for the three other officers housed inside the C3. Nobody else was there.

"The others sleeping?" Kat asked.

"Trying to," he replied.

Kat passed by a steel-alloy door to her right, beyond which were housed ten Cray mainframes that sat below the LZ. She settled in front of the center console of the Northern Terminal Workstation, beside the lieutenant commander; the other chairs remained empty. A large seventy-inch flat screen centered on the wall showed an aerial topographical map of the ten-mile-wide pentagon-shaped island. The five CT teams moving over the plexus and all real time combat operations would be monitored from this screen. Several smaller screens were illuminated with data feeds including Doppler weather, C3 and C5 security systems, and radar.

Kat glanced at the security monitors: no alerts. She took a mental note of the two-degree temperature drop in the mainframe chamber and turned her attention to the Doppler weather monitor.

"That's a hell of a thunderstorm," Kat said.

"The storms in this region can get bad," Channing said. "I estimate it'll hit us around 0630."

"Those SEALs had better find some shelter quick."

"They're DEVGRU," Channing responded. "They won't need shelter."

"DEVGRU?" Kat asked.

"They're actually a special mission unit of the SEALs," Channing replied quickly. "Very tough. Very well trained. For op sec reasons, that's all I can tell you."

*　　*　　*

NAVAL SPECIAL WARFARE COMMAND
CORONADO, CALIFORNIA
JUNE 5; 0346 (LOCAL TIME)

Rear Admiral Nicholas Briley entered the operations room at the NSW Command in Coronado, California. Briley nodded as he walked by the other SEAL Commanders and sat down at the head of the long, oval mahogany conference table.

The forty-nine-year-old Briley, a veteran of myriad special operations, glanced with piercing blue-green eyes around the table, then above at the dozens of monitors lining the surrounding walls, providing continuous updates on weather, radar, sonar, intelligence feeds, and naval fleet positions.

"Gentlemen. Welcome," Briley said. "As you already know, today is the landmark trial of the C5 counter-terrorist training site. Our finest CT team is there on *Reagan.*" Briley swiveled in his chair to the left and faced the wall-sized projected image of C5 before him.

"Mr. Edgewaters from Arlington is with us via teleconferencing," Briley said. "He'll give you the highlights."

Carl Edgewaters—a recently discharged submariner who had spent much time at sea on boomers, submarines armed with nuclear-tipped ballistic missiles—appeared on the bottom right corner of the monitor, telecast from DARPA, the central research and development organization of the U.S. Department of Defense.

The thirty-year-old Edgewaters adjusted his squared-lens eyeglasses higher on his nose and ran his hand through his short brown hair parted to the right, not realizing that he was already being telecast.

"Good morning, Mr. Edgewaters. Proceed," Briley began.

"Thank you, Admiral," Edgewaters said; his eyes widened as he straightened his back. "DARPA's mission has always been to take basic and applied research and development projects and bring their practical application to reality faster than ever for the battlefield of the 21st century. Compound Five is a result of that ideology and mission. C5 will provide the U.S. and our allies with the finest counter-terrorist research and development station."

"What protection does Compound Five have against a terrorist attack?" Briley interrupted.

"Protection against an outside threat is a top priority, Admiral," Edgewaters answered. "C5 is ready and capable of being entirely self-sufficient and can protect our assets against all sea, air, and land attacks. Beyond the plexus, minefields, and explosive tripwires surrounding C5, as an extra precaution, we have *Ronald Reagan* positioned offshore. After this initial test, there will be no need for such support."

Edgewaters tapped his keyboard; square red icons illuminated the shorelines of C5, indicating surface-to-air missile, or SAM, locations. "These SAM missiles were integrated to prevent an airstrike against C5, but they're disengaged for the exercise, sir," he said.

"Thank you. Proceed," Briley said.

"In less than one hour, we will kick off exercise *Elite Fire:* a force-on-force exercise between highly-classified CT units from the U.S., France, Britain, New Zealand, and Australia. We'll test the Objective Force Warrior in combat simulation today. The exercise will be complete when all opposition is destroyed or at the end of five days, whichever comes first. Once the exercise starts, we'll be able to see exactly what the operators on the ground see via their helmet-mounted cameras. In addition, via the plexus, we'll have 3-D reconstructions of each operator's movements."

"We all recall the deadly exercise two decades ago," Briley said. "Many in this room with more gray hair than not vividly remember our operators dying at C5. What have we done to prevent a similar disaster?"

"Admiral, safety is our number one priority," Edgewaters reassured him. "First, the technology today is far superior. Second, each of the operators has an emergency signal transponder. Any issues—they press the button—the exercise is stopped. We initiate our emergency rescue protocol."

"What if the exercise needs to be stopped for other reasons?" a commander asked.

"What other reasons, Commander?" Briley continued. "Unless all five countries agree to stop the exercise early, it runs the full five-day course. Everybody agreed to that. It was felt to be necessary in order to accurately test not only the Compound Five base, but also the OFW. For this exercise, I remind you, we've got an on-site crew at C5 at the Construct Control Center. We've even kept the supervising computer engineer, Katherine Lange, on-site. I've seen her work—she's incredible. Gentlemen, I can assure you this facility is safer than NORAD [North American Aerospace Defense Command]."

*   *   *

USS RONALD REAGAN
JUNE 5; 0524

Special Warfare Commander Mac Jacobs was standing inside the flag bridge, a confined windowless space below the carrier's bridge. The thirty-nine-year-old Desert Storm veteran stood with the admiral in charge of the carrier strike group beside him. Toward the rear of the flag bridge, five, twenty-seven-inch LCD monitors displayed the output of YUMA team's biomed sensors and GPS locations. Ten others congregated around the *Ouija Board*, a two-level transparent plastic table with etched outlines of the flight and hangar deck.

"YUMA. YUMA, this is Angel One Command. Do you copy?" Jacobs said.

"Copy you clear, Angel One Command," crackled the voice of Lieutenant Sean Graves, the SEAL officer-in-charge.

The DEVGRU SEAL element—consisting of Lieutenant Sean Graves and fellow SEALs Ron Spiers, Rico Cordova, Terrance Rock, and Matt Campbell—donned their C5 tactical suits three levels below. The basic Objective Force Warrior exoskeleton monitored vital signs and caloric consumption, and contained a microclimate-control system to modulate surface body temperature. DARPA's experimental biomed suit incorporated additional physiological sensors beyond the OFW exoskeleton to further understand the combatant's metabolism and sleep cycles during combat. DARPA's Peak Soldier Performance program focused on optimizing metabolic performance and identifying and eliminating areas of wasteful fatigue. The Preventing Sleep Deprivation program studied ways to alleviate the cognitive and psychomotor impairments of sleep deprivation.

One of DARPA's latest technologies, part of the Surviving Blood Loss program, was a method to measure plasma volume non-invasively. With a specialized device, blood loss could be monitored without actually drawing blood from the soldier, thus distinguishing which soldiers were salvageable during combat and enhancing rescue resource utilization and medical triage. If a soldier was dead, there was no need for a risky rescue mission. On the other hand, if a rescue was deemed feasible, injury severity and survival time could be estimated. The Surviving Blood Loss campaign's future vision was to induce a hibernation-like state, thus decreasing metabolic demands with the goal of delaying the onset of irreversible shock.

Matt Campbell, the YUMA medic, ran his hands across his chest, feeling for the paper-thin coin-sized plates used for electrocardiogram heart monitoring and plexus recognition. He could feel nothing because the small plates were so thin.

"Checking biomed-suit sensors," Jacobs said. He watched the monitor designated "Biomed: Campbell" as his temperature, pulse, respiratory rate, blood pressure, oxygen saturation, plasma volume, and heart rhythm were displayed. He glanced at the others' monitors. All were operational. "Looks good," he continued.

"Copy that. We're ready," Graves replied.

"Delta Zero is a go," Jacobs said. "I wish you all Godspeed." Delta Zero was the codename for the exercise in which Jacob's SEALs would be first targeting a unit from Britain's famed Special Air Service.

The five SEALs clambered up a series of stairwells to the flight deck. The cool sea winds flooded the deck as the emerging sun cast a golden glow across the morning sky. The dimming moon and stars hung low on the horizon. The massive blue ocean stretched out endlessly. Threatening storm clouds loomed far beyond the eastern horizon.

Two men in green jumpsuits led YUMA team toward a Seahawk helicopter. Others in a rainbow of jumpsuits—yellow, red, white, and purple—were moving busily about the deck. Each color designated the sailor's role with deck operations.

As YUMA approached the helicopter, the whirling blades filled the nearby air with jet fuel exhaust fumes. Cordova glanced to his right, down a line of five Seahawks, sizing up in his mind the four opposition teams climbing into the helos. A green-suited deck sailor gave the SEALs a thumbs-up as Cordova pulled himself up into the Seahawk, sat down, and buckled in. He briefly glanced across the faces of the team. His gaze settled outside the helo bay window, where he stared out at the massive ocean.

* * *

Captain Walter McClure sat in the leather skipper's chair, glancing across the deck at the five Seahawks. Ten miles to the northeast, fluffy gray-black cumulous rain clouds began darkening the sky. "Let pri fly know about the storm. Authorize lift off," he ordered, referring to primary flight control. He then turned to his lee helmsmen—the sailor responsible for steering the big carrier—and grinned widely.

One by one, the five Seahawk helicopters lifted off USS *Ronald Reagan*, each carrying their assault team destined for Compound Five. The staggered helos choppered across the twenty-mile stretch of awakening ocean to the island. The orange sun peeked above the horizon, beaming through the open helo door, outlining the five SEAL operators. Minutes later, YUMA team reached Drop Zone Two. The ocean water rippled in a circle below.

Lieutenant Graves gave a reassuring thumbs-up to his team. "Green light! You are clear to go. I repeat, clear to go!" pounded through the pilot's headset.

"Go, Go, Go," echoed from the cockpit into the bay as one by one the SEALs fast-roped to the beach below. Simultaneously, the five teams received the same message, as each CT unit landed on five different beaches and headed inland.

YUMA team quickly reached the sandy shoreline outside Gate Two, where the mines had been temporarily de-activated. The team trekked across the beach and proceeded through the open gate.

"Angel One, we're in," Graves whispered into his headset mike. "Proceeding."

"Copy that," Angel One replied.

"YUMA, three-pattern, double back, twenty-five feet. Keep your distance. Move out," Graves ordered. Spiers, their designated point man, pushed deeper into the island's forest.

CHAPTER 12 PROTOCOL

Exercise Day: One

COMPOUND FIVE
JUNE 5; 0602 (LOCAL TIME)

THE CACOPHONY OF INBOUND HELICOPTERS created a thunderous echo around STORM. Like a giant spotlight, the morning sunlight left them bare on the landing zone. A chiseled concrete-free line exposed the underlying doorframe and the dozen five-inch bolts fixing the door to its frame.

A subtle breeze blew the concrete dust into the air. Coughing from the dust cloud, Ray pulled his shirt over his nose and mouth. Dust stuck to the sweat on his brow. A chalky gray-white mixture of sea salt and concrete dust caked on his clothing and intermixed with his hair.

For the past six hours, he had worked meticulously to break into C3. Now he stood leaning over, straddling the break in the concrete. He applied firm pressure with a diamond-crusted tungsten-carbide bit-loaded drill and carved a tiny hole into the doorframe. Dropping to his knees, he tugged his already-open seabag next to him and grabbed a flexible fiber-optic camera, or flexcam. Lying flat on his belly and peering through the flexcam's viewer, he introduced the cam through the drilled hole and into the dimly lit mainframe chamber. In the distance, silhouettes and shadows of the tall Cray mainframe cabinets appeared.

Ray flipped the flexcam to infrared. Red lasers criss-crossed from wall to wall, inches from the chamber floor. He turned the camera back toward himself into a U-shape, scanning the immediate area around the door, and noted a fiber-optic sensor monitoring system. "Ah. Not so bad," he whispered.

"The CT units are in by now," Skreemer said, his eyes darting nervously between Ray and the nearby jungle. He glanced at Dutch.

"What's wrong?" asked Dutch, becoming increasingly anxious over their exposed location and slow progress.

"We're two hours behind schedule."

"What if I can't hack this thing?" Dutch said.

"That's not an option," Skreemer said emphatically, knowing the security systems would have to be disengaged before they could walk on the plexus and get through the perimeter gate.

"Dutch, you'll be in and outta there before ya know it," Skye interjected hopefully.

Skreemer turned to Skye. "Get the computer booted. Get everything ready," he ordered.

"Roger that," Skye replied.

Ten minutes later, Ray raised his head, making eye contact with Eagle. "We're good," Ray reported. Eagle nodded, then pulled a handheld drill to his side, positioned the drill on the first bolt, and pressed the trigger. Ray shifted anxiously on the ground with the metal-rumbling sound of each unscrewing bolt.

Minutes later, Eagle crowbarred a small opening between the 500-pound door and frame, hoisting the door inches away from the frame.

Ray wedged a hydraulic jack into the narrow space. Working it like a firefighter's "Jaws of Life," he created a man-sized opening.

"If the alarm goes off, it's over for us," Skye whispered nervously to Skreemer.

PROTOCOL

"Get your Taser ready," Ray instructed. "Remember, four others are down there." STORM was unaware that the civilian, Kat Lange, was a last-minute addition to the team within the C3.

Skreemer tightly strapped his seabag close to his right side. He pulled the infrared goggles over his eyes and belly-crawled feet first into the small opening, being careful not to bring any loose concrete with him. He slid into the chamber, pushing until the seabag popped beyond the narrow opening. He grabbed the sharp edge of the door's frame. His body dangled below the frame as he turned his head from side to side, sizing up a safe place to land.

Letting go, Skreemer dropped and landed on his feet facing the chamber's rear wall. Streaks of red lasered between his legs. He exhaled softly, shivering from the chamber's low-humidity air-conditioned space. A low buzzing emitted from the supercomputer behind him. He slow-stepped and turned to face the chamber's opposite end, then lifted his IR goggles and looked around.

The chamber was 4,000 square feet in size. Twenty black computer cabinets, each seven foot tall, lined the walls, leaving a narrow, dimly lit hallway in the room's center. At the end of the hallway was a steel-reinforced door.

Skreemer glanced across the room, reading the white lettering on each cabinet: "Cray XT5h" housed the main supercomputer processors, while "Cray I/O" housed the input/output hardware. The $50-million DARPA supercomputer project was right in front of him.

The cabinets hissed and droned as the cooling system constantly sprayed the chips with the nonconductive coolant Fluorinert. The liquid then evaporated and re-circulated after large amounts of water—thirty-three gallons per minute for each cabinet—chilled the coolant, maintaining a constant temperature for the high-powered processors. The sixteen-node configuration cabinets required liquid cooling, while the four-node cabinets required only air cooling. The air-cooled cabinets were much easier to get into undetected.

Skreemer pulled the IR goggles back over his eyes. He high-stepped over the lasers and headed to the third "Cray I/O" cabinet on his right. Settling into a laser-free area between the cabinets, he gently unshouldered his seabag, set it on the gray tile floor, and opened it. He pulled the IR goggles off his eyes, letting them hang loosely around his neck. Then he grabbed and positioned a small, halogen lamp onto his forehead and directed its white beam at the cabinet. With a flathead screwdriver in hand, he popped off the "Cray I/O" cabinet's side panel and propped it vertically against the cabinet. Horizontal stacks of thin circuit boards filled the inside.

From his right pants pocket, Skreemer pulled out and unfolded a paper schematic detailing the inside of the hardware cabinet. His eyes flashed quickly between the paper diagram and the hardware cabinet.

Bingo! A third of the way up, he located the Cray XT5h Computer Blade, a thin, tightly packed circuit board. He quickly popped it loose and slid it out, then pulled a new six-inch circuit board from his pocket and slotted it into the blue connection port.

Above ground, Skye waited anxiously for the wireless signal to be sent. The sky darkened. The wind began to pick up. Thunder crackled in the distance. A few raindrops landed on the LZ.

Ray pulled a black tarp over the chamber's opening. "Connection complete," Skreemer whispered into his microphone.

Skye pecked at several keys, then handed the computer to Dutch. "You're on," she winked.

Dutch wiped the sweat from his forehead, his heart racing. The time was here for him to prove his worth. Did they truly believe he could hack it? Why would they entrust him with the vital task? Failure meant not getting off the island.

He grabbed the black laptop and placed it in his lap. "Let's see what setup they're running," he said. He typed several commands. The screen filled with data.

****** Program Information ******
Real Time (sec): 6.091186
User Time (sec): 12.125577
Sys Time (sec): 0.028495
Vector Time (sec): 11.468935
Inst. Count: 937278529.
V. Inst. Count: 874561403.
V. Element Count: 104537182776.
FLOP Count: 82143574467.
MOPS: 8626.385359
MFLOPS: 6774.405413
MOPS (concurrent): 17179.574337
MFLOPS (concurrent): 13491.328818
VLEN: 119.530981
V. Op. Ratio (%): 99.940041
Memory Size (MB): 80.000000
Max Concurrent Proc.: 2.
Conc. Time (>= 1)(sec): 6.088620
Conc. Time (>= 2)(sec): 6.037041

"They're running one machine. Only two processors," Dutch stated, noting the third to the last line: *Max Concurrent Proc.: 2.* "Not even close to running at full capacity," he continued.

"What's that mean?" Skye asked.

"Means it'll be easier to hack," Dutch replied.

Skye smiled back. The C5 hack was underway.

CHAPTER 13 REQUEST

Exercise Day: One

CONSTRUCT CONTROL CENTER
COMPOUND FIVE
JUNE 5; 1126 (LOCAL TIME)

FIVE HOURS passed. A low incoming 1,500-foot cloud ceiling darkened the sky from gray to black. Flashes of lightning streaked above the island; the thunder blasted seconds later. The once drizzling rain devolved into a downpour, slapping the black tarp covering Dutch and Skye. Ray and Eagle scanned the surrounding jungle from opposite sides of the LZ. Skreemer remained inside the chamber.

Dutch continued to hack the Construct Control Center (C3) system. Already past innumerable firewalls, he planted dozens of "batch jobs"—little pre-defined programs executing a series of commands by the operating system—deep into the system. The "batch jobs" continuously launched covert attacks on the system, while Dutch attempted to find alternative entry points.

Elite Fire Exercise In Progress...Access Denied splayed across the screen again.

"How's it looking, Dutch?" Skreemer's voice crackled into Dutch's headset.

"Almost there," Dutch breathed.

"We're cutting this too damn close," Ray grumbled.

"Just get us access," Eagle demanded.

Positioned flat against the LZ's wet, concrete slab and propped on his elbows, Ray peered through his binoculars and scanned the distant jungle. "Eagle. I got movement. Three o'clock. 200 yards," Ray whispered into his headset mike.

"Fuck," Skye muttered.

"How many?" Eagle asked.

"One," Ray replied.

"We're in!" Dutch blurted excitedly.

"What?" Skreemer exclaimed.

"We're in," Dutch repeated, grinning.

Skye pulled the laptop from Dutch and rested it on her lap.

Access to DARPA C5 Network Granted, Skye read high on the screen.

"It's too late," Eagle barked. "Move inside."

"It's too fucking wet," Ray retorted. "It'll trigger the security system. The floor IR lasers are still active."

"Shut it down then," Eagle ordered Skye.

"Workin' on it," Skye quickly responded.

Eagle scanned the distant grasslands and palms through his M4 carbine NV scope. The stalks and brush vibrated with the wind. His right trigger finger readied. No people. No targets.

"Talk to me, Ray," Eagle demanded. Ray flipped his binoculars to NV. The jungle turned an odd luminous green.

"Security system's down," Skye reported. The lasers went dark below.

"Movin' inside," added Ray.

"Use your Tasers if you have to," directed Eagle.

Ray yanked a small Blackhawk tactical gear bag close, opened it, and grabbed the Taser X3, holstering it on his belt. When fired, the Taser X3 would deploy two four-inch-long dart-like probes capable of penetrating two inches of clothing, each attached to a thirty-five-foot-long conductive wire. After striking the target, the probe-wire system would carry bursts of electrical pulses, incapacitating the person's nervous system. The multi-shot X3 was able to incapacitate three targets simultanenously.

Ray crab-crawled beneath the tarp and wiggled feet-first into the hydraulically opened door. Wet gravel also streamed inside like a river. He grabbed the door's frame and pushed off, swinging his body into the chamber and letting go, landing feet-first next to the far wall. From his lower back, he pulled the Taser to a low-ready position. He sidestepped down the hall toward the far access door to the workstations. As he passed the third hardware cabinet, he nodded to Skreemer, who was on his right. Ray moved on and settled between two cabinets close to the access door.

Skye stuffed the laptop into her small Blackhawk bag, slipped it onto her back like a backpack, and cinched it tightly. She moved inside next and joined Skreemer. "Upload the Inception Protocol," Skreemer whispered. Skye pulled the laptop from the bag, flipped it open, and entered the command.

Eagle pulled the tarp away from the opening. Rain was blowing into the chamber; the wind whistled loudly. Eagle folded and dropped the tarp below and lowered himself inside.

Still above ground, Dutch hurried and squeezed between the door's small opening and the frame. The wet concrete slid beneath his fingers as he gripped the frame tighter. Suddenly his hands slipped and he lost his grip. Falling onto his left side, he crashed hard against the chamber floor below. Sharp pain pulsed through his left ankle and wrist. He pushed himself up onto his feet and limped toward the nearest cabinets.

Eagle hurried to release the jack, closing the chamber's ceiling door. The room fell silent. Eagle hurried opposite Ray, bringing his Taser up to the ready position.

*   *   *

"What was that?" Kat asked, seated at the Northern Terminal Workstation of the C3, as she heard a faint thud coming from the adjacent mainframe chamber.

"Gotta be the storm," the thirty-year-old red-haired lieutenant replied.

Kat glanced at the temperature and humidity readings of the mainframe chamber: sixty-eight degrees Fahrenheit and fifty-seven percent humidity. It was a three-degree temperature drop and a five percent increase in humidity over the past hour. The mainframe-chamber air-conditioning system kept the temperature between sixty-eight and seventy-two degrees, while humidity was maintained between forty-five and fifty-five percent.

Kat then noted the outside temperature and humidity readings: sixty-five degrees and eighty-seven percent. Thunder continued to crackle overhead. The chamber rattled as the monitors flickered. She tapped out several commands. Nothing showed up on the monitor of the chamber. "Shit," she muttered under her breath.

"What's wrong?" the lieutenant asked.

"The monitor keeps cuttin' in and out," Kat replied, concerned whether the malfunction could be more than just the storm.

"Try again," advised the lieutenant.

Kat pecked out several more commands.

The usual image on the monitor re-appeared.

"Of all the damn days to have such a storm," remarked Lieutenant Commander Justin Channing. "Are we still on-line with Angel One?" he asked, referring to USS *Ronald Reagan* Comm Center. He walked over to the Northern Terminal Workstation and stood behind Kat and the lieutenant.

Kat typed in several commands and initiated system-testing programs. "Angel One, construct control here. Do you copy?" the lieutenant queried.

"Copy you clear," affirmed Angel One.

"Are you still receiving all the feeds?" the officer continued.

"Affirmative," Angel One Command replied. "No problems here."

"Getting some power fluctuations from the storm, I think," the officer said. "But everything's working."

"Roger that. Let us know if anything changes," concluded Angel One.

"Roger. Out."

"There's an increase in humidity in the mainframe chamber," Kat reported. "I need to check it out."

"I'll check out the mainframe chamber," the chief petty officer volunteered, having heard the discussion from across the room.

"Okay, great," Kat said, standing up. "I'm gonna go check out the power plant below."

"You don't trust anything, do you?" Lieutenant Commander Channing replied, smiling at her.

"No," Kat retorted, calmly and curtly. "I don't." She stood up and walked to the door at the center of the workstation room that led to the lower level. She slid her CAC into the reader slot and entered her PIN; a quick, quiet *bleep* followed. She pushed the door open and headed down the stairwell.

In the top right corner of the C5 security system monitor, an icon started flashing, indicating deactivation of the chamber security system.

It went unnoticed.

*   *   *

Positioned between mainframe cabinets opposite each other, Eagle and Ray locked eyes.

"Can you lock the access door?" Eagle whispered into his mike.

"I'm workin' on it," Skye responded.

A fast, quiet *bleep* sounded from the access door. The door swung open. The overhead ceiling lights brightened.

The chief petty officer walked briskly inside the mainframe chamber, passing by the first several cabinets. He stopped suddenly, noticing wet boot prints, broken concrete, and puddles of rain on the chamber floor.

"What the hell?" he whispered, reaching for his Beretta 9mm.

A sharp pain instantly burst upon the middle of his back, quickly consuming his body. The sailor dropped, jerking violently from the Taser's electrical pulses.

Ray and Eagle sprinted through the access door and into the Terminal Workstation area. The lieutenant commander stood completely still ten feet away and stared back. Before the officer could react, Ray fired. Two probes punched through the lieutenant commander's uniform, one stabbing just left of his sternum, the other hitting his abdomen. He grunted as he fell to the ground and thrashed.

The lieutenant turned and bolted from his seat. A petty officer first-class followed behind. Eagle sprinted toward the lieutenant and fired. The conductive wires stretched the length of the room. One probe slammed into the lieutenant's right calf. The other probe missed, thus unable to incapacitate the target. Within seconds, Eagle fired again with the multi-shot X3 nailing both probes into the lieutenant's back. His body convulsed and flopped onto the floor.

Already inside, Skye fired at the sailor who fumbled with his holstered Beretta. The dropped Beretta slid across the floor as the twitching sailor fell. Ray and Skye immediately scoured the remaining Terminal Workstation area. There were no others. "All clear," Ray announced.

Eagle moved back inside the chamber. He zip-tied the plastic-wire handcuffs and blindfolded the officer. "Come on, let's move inside," he told Skreemer and Dutch.

Dutch peered from behind the mainframe cabinet into the hall. His hands trembled. His heart pounded. The pulsating sounds of the Tasers' shocks replayed in his mind.

"Dammit!" Ray exploded.

"So much for covert," grumbled Skye.

"Get 'em restrained and blindfolded," Eagle commanded, as he walked through the access door. "Remove their headsets. Let's get 'em downstairs."

Dutch followed Skreemer inside the workstation area. "You okay?" Skreemer asked.

"This is fucking crazy," Dutch replied, shaking his head.

"Nobody's hurt. Everything's okay," Skreemer assured him.

"I can't stop shaking," Dutch continued. He watched the others, competent and comfortable in their roles. While he felt increasingly guilty over his participation in the break-in, they seemed more assured and confident. No hesitation. Their teamwork was efficient, their senses heightened. It was clear that they'd done this before.

"We need to search the rest of the facility," Ray shouted.

"There're only supposed to be four people down here, right?" Dutch whispered to Skreemer.

"Can't be sure," Skye answered, overhearing Dutch.

"What about those?" Dutch asked, glancing at the security cameras located above the access door.

"They're only recording. They're not live feeds," Skreemer replied. "The Inception Protocol will delete the digital file."

"We didn't come all this way just for C5," Eagle whispered to Skreemer as he passed by. "Let's get workin' on the Intelink."

Skreemer led Dutch to the Southern Terminal Workstation, a mirror image of the Northern Terminal Workstation, with one glaring exception—it was connected to the Department of Defense's secure local area network.

Dutch sat down at the center terminal, one of five terminals positioned in a semi-circle. Seating himself at the terminal to Dutch's right, Skreemer pulled the sliding keyboard out and tapped the spacebar on the keyboard. The top of the monitor read:

Department of Defense
Defense Information Systems Agency
Secure LAN Connection
Authority: DoD, DARPA, U.S. Navy, Pentagon

Location: Compound Five
Intelink Status:
Intelink – SCI:	*off-line*
Intelink – P:	*off-line*
Intelink – N:	*off-line*
Intelink – S:	*off-line*
Intelink – C:	*ON-LINE*

Status: Secure
Encryption: enabled

Please enter user identity key:

"What's this?" Dutch asked.

"Have you heard of the Intelink?" Skreemer replied.

"The U.S. intelligence community's classified intranet," Dutch replied nervously.

"We have a unique opportunity here," Skreemer said. "A chance to hack the Intelink from a local workstation."

"You came here for the Intelink all along?" Dutch asked, shocked.

"Dutch. It's about control of information," Skreemer said patiently. "If you control the information, you can get anything you want."

"Yeah, but this is the U.S. government. Fuck, the military!"

"We're not gonna compromise top secret information," Skreemer reassured him. "Our goal is to have control of the information in order to have a bargaining chip, so we can get paid. This will make that cool million look like chump change. And of course, there is the challenge."

"Doesn't matter, it's impossible!" Dutch exclaimed.

"The Intelink is just like the regular Internet, just a little more secure," Skreemer continued.

"A little?" Dutch remarked with apprehensive sarcasm.

"The Intelink is only as good as the best civilian security

systems," Skreemer insisted. "The encryption platforms and intrusion-detection software are similar. Just a few more layers of protection. The real challenge is getting to a terminal that's hardwired to the network, so that we're not identified as hackers."

"You might need this," Skye declared loudly, walking over to Dutch and Skreemer with a Common Access Card in her right hand. She stopped and stood behind Dutch, reached over his right shoulder, and inserted the card into the thin CAC reader slot built into the keyboard. She then punched in a 16-digit PIN number. *Access Granted* flashed across the screen. The workstation was enabled.

"You knew about this, Skye?" Dutch asked.

She nodded. "We're close on time. Keep me updated," Skye said, as she turned and headed back to the Northern Terminal Workstation.

"I told you this would be the ultimate hack," Skreemer said with a sly half-smile.

"You lied to me," Dutch retorted angrily.

"I knew you wouldn't come otherwise," Skreemer shrugged.

"We're in over our heads," Dutch said.

"Is there are a problem here?" Eagle asked suddenly from behind Dutch and Skreemer.

"Not at all. Just figuring out our strategy," Skreemer reassured him.

"Good. Let's get movin'," Eagle said briefly as he walked away.

"Dutch, just hear me out," Skreemer urged. "There are several different Intelinks, based on the need-to-know and sensitivity of the information they house. The Intelink PolicyNet is run by the CIA; it links to the White House and other high-level intelligence users. The Intelink Commonwealth, or Intelink-C, links the U.S., the United Kingdom, Canada, and Australia. You probably recognize some of these countries as being part of the C5 Project."

"Uh-huh," Dutch agreed.

"There are three other services of the Intelink managed by the

Defense Information Systems Agency, or DISA, part of the Defense Department. First is the Intelink-N or NIPRNet. Stands for the Non-secure Internet Protocol Router Network. It's used for unclassified combat support applications. Second is the Intelink-S or SIPRNet. The Secret Internet Protocol Router Network. It's the Department of Defense's largest command and control data network. The main communications link for the military. It commands and interfaces land, sea, and air warfighting applications. Bottom line, the SIPRNet is the shit. The military is highly dependent on it. You still with me?"

"You want to hack the SIPRNet?" Dutch asked incredulously.

"Well, not exactly. A lot of classified information goes over the SIPRNet, but only up to information classified as SECRET// NOFORN," Skreemer replied.

"NOFORN?"

"Not Releasable to Foreign Nationals/Governments/Non-U.S. Citizens," Skreemer replied. "So, there's one more level. The Intelink-SCI. It operates at the Top Secret/Compartmented information level. The truly top secret intelligence is routed through this system. This *is* the top-secret Internet."

"Why do you want this so badly?"

"DARPA is highly involved in this so-called 'information superiority.' If we control the information, we have leverage."

"Leverage for what?"

"$10 million for each of us."

"This is absolutely insane," Dutch said.

Dutch tightened his hands into fists, attempting to stop the tremors. As though cold water had been unexpectedly splashed into his face, he awoke to the reality of this mission. Naïve excitement melted into the harsh reality that this was not a group of hackers, but a rogue paramilitary team. Dutch's juvenile vision of the operation was over.

"How would you hack this?" Skreemer insisted.

Dutch exhaled deeply, turned and watched the intimidating

Eagle as he secured the officers in the hall and moved them toward the stairwell. He felt he had no choice. He was one of them.

*   *   *

LOS ANGELES, CALIFORNIA
JUNE 5; 1145

Wolfe was fast asleep at his computer desk, his head lying on his folded arms. Suddenly, his computer alarm went off.

Seconds later, he lifted his head and rubbed his bloodshot eyes. A message had been received. A mouse click and decryption program later, Wolfe read the message: *Inception Protocol launched.*

A smile broke across Wolfe's face. He inserted the flash drive and proceeded to log onto the DARPA mainframe. Once inside, he sent an e-mail to the DARPA C5 project supervisor, a man by the name of Carl Edgewaters.

Lone Wolfe pulled a briefcase from under his desk and opened it. He grabbed a sat phone, dialed, and held it to his right ear. Several rings later, the line picked up.

"Yes," the man said curtly.

"Simple request has been sent," Lone Wolfe reported.

"But they're not even off the island yet," replied Joe Norman, vice president of Sentinel Software Incorporated.

In 1982, DARPA's Special Projects Office had been in charge of the secretive C5 Project, focusing on testing new combat technologies. At that time, aside from defense contractor SSI, which assisted with the security systems, the entire project was completed internally. This conventional way of developing newer technologies proved to be a disaster. DARPA and the Pentagon had cancelled the project and shut down C5 as a result of too many fatal training accidents.

When SSI lost the security bid for the re-development of

C5, Norman was furious—so much so that he hired Lone Wolfe, a former CIA operative who had worked with SSI on several government projects, to coordinate the takeover of C5. Norman's hopes were a future bid to regain the billion dollar security contract from DARPA.

"They will be soon," Wolfe replied.

"Won't that set off alarms, alert the *Reagan*?" Norman asked.

"Not important now that they're inside."

"Think they'll actually make it off the island alive?" Norman asked coldly.

"Don't care," Lone Wolfe replied. "I still get paid."

"You'll get paid only if the Inception Protocol works."

"It will," Wolfe asserted, abruptly hanging up the phone.

*   *   *

CONSTRUCT CONTROL CENTER
COMPOUND FIVE
JUNE 5; 1151

The usual knocks, squeaks, and whistles of the geothermal power plant emanated from the lower level. The 4,000-square-foot power room contained two 400-kilowatt turbines. A steel-grated walkway encircled each turbine, with a common walkway separating the two.

Kat completed her cursory overview; everything checked out. Convinced that a power surge had rattled the computer room's systems, she headed along the outer walkway back toward the entrance to the power room.

A human silhouette slipped along the northern turbine-generator assembly. Kat stopped—this time catching a glimpse of the unknown person outfitted in black, walking along the center walkway, outstretched hands holding a handgun.

Kat crouched and remained still for a moment, then moved

stealthily toward the already-open door exiting the power plant. She peered down the empty passageway and hurried down and across the hall until reaching a room at the far south end. She opened the unlocked door, entered, and quietly closed it behind her.

Her thoughts raced. How would she alarm *Reagan*? Were the officers dead? How many terrorists were there? Could this be part of a crazy exercise? Keeping the lights off, she reached and fumbled for the emergency flashlight affixed below the light switch. She grabbed it and switched it on.

The 150-square-foot storage space held the majority of the emergency equipment. Several non-tactical rescue suits hung from a hanger rod. Kat needed one to survive walking on the plexus.

Stripping down to her thermal underpants and bra, she stepped into the rescue suit and pulled it snugly over her body, then put her other clothes back on. Once suited up, she felt along her right pants leg until her fingers found the dime-sized tracking device. She popped the switch, turning on the device. The plexus would now recognize her non-combatant ID, intended for rescue purposes only. She firmly grabbed the emergency signal transponder, knowing it would only work outside the Construct Control Center.

Kat cracked open the storage door and peered down the passageway. One of the Naval officers staggered along in her direction. He was blindfolded and handcuffed. Another man followed. She quickly and quietly closed the door.

*   *   *

Eagle headed back upstairs to the Terminal Workstation area. "Lower level clear," he reported to Skye as he walked through the door into the upper level. "Ray and Skreemer are moving the last officer downstairs. We'll keep the crew restrained and locked in the sleeping quarters. How are you looking?"

"Upload complete," Skye responded. She quickly typed in the command: *run inception.exe*. The program began to launch.

"How long before the Inception Protocol re-configures the system?" Eagle asked.

"A couple of hours before it's integrated," Skye replied. "Before we have complete control of the compound."

"Let me know when we have control of the SAMs," Eagle instructed with regard to the surface-to-air missiles. Then he yelled, "Listen up! We're in a much different situation now. *Reagan* will realize something's wrong within the hour. Whether they will act or not, it's hard to tell. We have no idea what to expect. They might send in the helos to check things out. They may send in a shitload of Marines or SEALs. We have to be ready to move. Our sole mission now is to hack the Intelink, then get off this damn island."

*   *   *

Kat inched open the storage door again. The lower level passageway was empty. She sprinted into the power room and darted across the center steel-grated walkway.

At the far end, she unlocked and pulled on an extension ladder until it touched the floor. She climbed to the ceiling, briefly glancing back. Nobody was there. She continued higher as the exitway narrowed to a small tunnel-like protective railing and stopped at the emergency escape exit door.

She clung to the top rung of the tiny ladder. The cold aluminum chilled her hands. She pulled the emergency lever. The hydraulic-driven door inched open for the first time in months with a high-pitched steel-scraping creak. Rain and pooling surface water poured inside.

Kat crawled through the opening. Through the sheets of rain, she spied the broken concrete LZ. She hesitated for a moment, then turned and bolted toward the treeline, running 200 yards from the manhole across the tarmac toward the dark woods. She settled between a nest of three tall palm trees.

Exhausted and winded, she pulled the radio from her rain-soaked pants pocket and switched it on. She cupped her hand over her mouth, attempting to keep the rain off the receiver.

"Angel One," Kat shouted over the rain, gasping for breath. "This is Construct Control. We have a breach. Do you copy?" Static crackled over the line.

"Angel One, dammit!" she yelled frantically. "Can't you hear me? Intruders have entered the compound. Do you copy?"

No response.

"Angel One. Angel One. Do you copy?" Kat shouted over and over. Thunder, the pouring rain, radio static, and the pulse in her ears were all she heard.

*   *   *

The sharp shriek of the alarm sounded within the computer room. "What the hell?!" hollered Skye.

A red L.E.D. flashed on the monitor; an emergency exit door was open. "Where the hell's that?" Eagle demanded.

"Lower level. Power plant. Emergency exit!" Skye exclaimed.

Eagle rushed downstairs, joining Ray, who was finishing zip-tying the last officer on the lower level. With weapons drawn, the two scoured the lower level power room, moving along both outer walkways and meeting at the emergency exitway. The ladder was still fully extended. Light crept through the open exitway two flights above.

"Shit!" Eagle hissed.

Ray pulled his mike close to his lips. "Somebody else was here," he muttered.

"How many?" Skye asked.

"We have no idea," Ray replied.

"Skye, what's the status on the Inception Protocol?" Eagle

blurted into his mike.

"All radio comm was cut off between the C3 and *Reagan* minutes ago," Skye answered. "In five minutes, I'll have all CT operator monitoring feeds cut from *Reagan*. Also, the Inception Protocol is reconfiguring the combatant and non-combatant IDs. We won't have remote GPS locations of the CT units for another half hour. We don't have control of the SAMs yet either."

"Any chance of 'em getting a signal out now?" Eagle continued.

"Not a chance. I've jammed all comm," Skye replied. "Unless that person can get off the plexus and beyond the perimeter gates, there's no way. They'd have to do it from the beach."

"What about a radio signal while inside the Control Center?" Eagle asked.

"No way," Skye replied, aware of the two feet of signal-stopping steel surrounding the Control Center.

"As soon as it's available, I want to hear all CT units talking," Eagle ordered.

"You got it," Skye replied, glancing up at the large monitor at the Northern Terminal Workstation. YUMA and the French GIGN (*Groupe d'Intervention de la Gendarmerie Nationale*) CT team were nearing battle a half-mile east of the Construct Control Center. She mentally mapped out their escape route to the west.

Suddenly, a new icon appeared on the monitor. The plexus registered the icon as rescue personnel. The icon moved quickly east, headed directly toward the region of YUMA and the French GIGN engagement.

CHAPTER 14 ILLUSION

Exercise Day: One

COMPOUND FIVE
JUNE 5; 1401 (LOCAL TIME)

YUMA'S POINT MAN RON SPIERS knelt beside a sprawling patch of forty-foot-tall velvetleaf evergreens a half mile east of the island's center. Ahead, a hilltop clearing broke through the thick jungle canopy. Windswept eye-level grasses and dense shrubs were beaten by the thick, deafening rain that pooled into black puddles. The thundering gray-black sky loomed overhead.

Spiers, a fifteen-year Navy SEAL veteran, eyed the GPS coordinates of his team through the heads-up display of his helmet visor. The team moved in a diamond-shaped formation with Lieutenant Graves commanding from its center. Campbell, YUMA's medical corpsman, guarded the rear. On either flank, Cordova and Rock glassed the east and west perimeters with rifle scopes.

Spiers flipped up the eyepiece on the scope mounted atop his M4 carbine. He positioned his right eye behind the scope, switched it to NV, and searched the darkness.

Movement. Ten-o-clock.

Spiers dropped flat to the ground. The team simultaneously hit the deck. With his left hand, Spiers grabbed the Objective Force Warrior computer "mouse" strapped to his chest. Instantly, the digital message informing YUMA of the enemies' positions was sent. Spiers slowly proceeded forward, low-crawling through the wet, black mud.

"YUMA. Do you copy?" crackled into the team's headsets.

"Stand by, Angel One," Cordova whispered.

"YUMA. Thank God. This is Kat Lange from Construct Control. The compound has been compromised. Breached. Copy?"

Several bursts of lightning flashed, obscuring Spiers' view. He switched his scope to thermal sight. The cool rain blanketed the terrain with shades of aqua-blue. Twenty yards to the northwest, a red-yellow human-sized thermal silhouette approached.

Spiers switched on his scope-mounted digital camera: video feeds were instantly transmitted to YUMA. He watched the figure through his scope, took a deep breath, and exhaled a portion of it. Within seconds, the figure transformed itself into a woman, with shoulder-length hair blowing in the wind below the helmet. Completely unaware that she was being tracked through a rifle-scope, the woman walked quickly through the forest, crouching in a vain attempt to avoid detection.

"YUMA. The compound has been penetrated. We may have been taken over by terrorists. Do you copy?" Kat repeated.

The mud-covered Spiers inched forward for a closer look. Suddenly, lightning flashed and illuminated an M4 muzzle positioned in a divot atop a dead tree below the hilltop peak. The M4 was pointed in his direction. A figure crouched behind it.

Spiers mentally noted the time in milliseconds. He aimed his weapon at the hidden enemy. The adrenaline coursed through his veins, but his mind blocked it before his heart rate quickened. His breathing was unchanged as his index finger hungered for the trigger.

Too late.

A two-round burst of High Impulse Technology, or HIT, bullets struck Spiers inches behind his collarbone. A bluish flash followed. He jerked once, then lay motionless on the muddy ground.

At left flank, Cordova returned relentless fire toward the muzzle flash. *Crack-crack-crack* replaced the slapping rain. Tracers streaked across the small clearing. U.S. Navy SEALs were in a full-blown firefight with the French CT commandos.

"YUMA one is down," Graves yelled. "I have no pulse on the monitor! Verify status."

Campbell, the corpsman, low-crawled toward the right side of Spiers' lifeless body. He grasped Spiers' wrist, feeling for a radial pulse.

No pulse.

Campbell reached for Spiers' neck, searching for a carotid pulse.

Nothing.

"Angel One. Angel One. Man down!" Campbell shouted frantically into his headset. "Spiers is down!" he yelled again. He pulled the emergency signal initiator from his belt, flipped the top, and pressed the red button.

*   *   *

CONSTRUCT CONTROL CENTER
COMPOUND FIVE
JUNE 5

Skye sat at the center computer terminal of the Northern Workstation area. She slid the keyboard close to her, pecking several commands, until she heard YUMA's communications. Returning to the upper level, Eagle and Ray sealed the access door and joined her.

"They still tied up?" she asked.

"I checked 'em," Ray answered. "There're four. Only four. That's the intel we had."

"I'm tracking somebody new on the plexus," Skye reported. "Registers as a non-combatant ID."

"Get us linked up to all comm on the compound," ordered Eagle.

"Already done," Skye responded quickly. "But I'm catchin' some scary shit from YUMA."

"Put it through," Eagle requested.

Static crackled into Eagle's and Ray's headsets.

"Angel One! Angel One! Do you copy?" a female voice shouted frantically.

"Angel One. This is YUMA. Man down. I repeat. Man down!" Campbell yelled over the gunfire.

"Who's the woman?" questioned Ray.

"I believe it's the fifth person who was down here," Skye replied. "But what's going on?"

"It's a training exercise. Remember?" Eagle snapped.

"Doesn't sound like it to me," Skye retorted.

"At least we know they're not able to communicate with the *Reagan*," interjected Ray.

"Turn the radio off. The Inception Protocol is working," Eagle barked.

"We need to focus now on getting off the island," Ray continued. "Skye, how much longer?"

"Twenty more minutes and we'll able to walk on the plexus," Skye declared confidently.

"Dutch!" Eagle shouted across the workstation area, "We've only got twenty minutes!"

"Copy that," Dutch replied, the others unaware he had overheard the faint communication from the woman in distress.

* * *

DATA ACQUISITION CENTER
NAVAL SPECIAL WARFARE COMMAND
JUNE 5

"Black, this is Brown. I'm detecting a possible intrusion into the Intelink-U network," said Lieutenant JG Daniel Janssen, seated at the Naval Special Warfare Command's Data Acquisition Center. Appearing much like NASA's Mission Control Center in Houston, the expansive auditorium-style terminal workstations faced an amphitheater of large LCD monitors. The Data Acquisition Center housed top-computer security specialists who continuously searched for intrusions into U.S. military security networks.

"Roger that," Janssen continued. "Purple, this is Brown. I'm showing a stealth scan on IDS (Intruder Detection System) on Network STONEGHOST. Please confirm."

"Affirmative. An attack has been initiated," replied the officer designated as Purple.

"Green, this is Brown. Multiple Intelink networks are showing possible intrusions. Is this a drill?" Janssen asked.

"Brown, this is Green. This is not a drill. Multiple networks are being bombarded. The NIPRNet is now showing a possible intrusion."

"Standby. We also have some unusual activity on the SIPRNet," another specialist announced. The sound of flickering keys meshing in synchrony heightened.

"Brown, this is Black. I'm seeing what appears to be a lightning bolt inserted into the network." The lightning bolt was the hacker's symbol of gang graffiti.

Janssen, a twenty-nine-year-old self-described computer genius, stood up and walked to the center stairwell. He unconsciously pushed his oval-lensed eyeglasses back on his nose, and then looked up at the pixels of the lightning bolt illuminated on the theatre-sized LCD in the center of the room.

"Brown, this is Red. I have some information on that Network

STONEGHOST intrusion."

"Roger, go ahead," Janssen replied. "The lightning bolt appearing at that location is covering what the actual infiltration is. Request tracer assistance," he continued.

"Roger that. Initiating trace route program," Red said.

"Red, this is Brown. Can you give me some analysis on any of these network attacks? Where's the vulnerability?" Janssen queried.

"Brown, this is Red. Workin' on it. The lightning bolt is covering the ultimate target and origin of the attack."

"Any information from the trace?"

"Negative, Brown."

"Let's work this through, team. I need answers," Janssen directed loudly into his headset, staring at the networks under attack, a bit overwhelmed by the rapidly deteriorating situation and his immediate responsibilities.

The officers and specialists in the Data Acquisition Center had run the attack drill dozens of times, but this was a first. This was no drill.

The Intelink was under attack.

* * *

COMPOUND FIVE
JUNE 5; 1151

Matt Campbell, the SEAL corpsman, tugged at Ron Spiers' limp body, sliding the 280 pounds of dead weight (counting body weight, equipment, and the fact that he was soaking wet) through the rain and the mud. Dozens of HIT shells splattered the earth, spraying black droplets of mud across Spiers' face.

Campbell finished dragging Spiers into the treeline and behind a thick evergreen trunk. Automatic-rifle fire trailed them, smacking into the tree; shards of wood and splinters struck Campbell in the arm and face. He flipped his pack off his shoulders and dropped it at Spiers' side. From an outer pack sleeve, he pulled his trauma shears from their sheath and began slicing the front of Spiers' shirt in half, exposing his chest.

From the pack's top compartment, Campbell pulled two pads attached to a cardiac defibrillator. He stripped the bottom covering from the adhesive sticky pad and placed it onto Spiers' right upper chest. He positioned the second pad on his lower left chest. Then he switched the machine on.

Charging flashed across the screen.

Seconds later it read, *Charged... Stay back... Delivering shock.* Campbell inched away, aware of the water surrounding him.

Spiers' upper torso jerked fiercely several inches off the ground; his arms and legs flailed wildly. A second later, his body lay still. Two hundred joules of biphasic electricity had crossed his heart.

An electrical current conducted across the surface water, up Campbell's legs and into his torso. He gritted his teeth as his muscles tightened.

Spiers' eyes opened suddenly. His breathing started slowly, then quickened. Campbell felt Spiers' wrist. His radial pulse bounded.

Flat against the ground in the proverbial "no man's land" between the two opposing combat teams, Kat low-crawled backwards. Suddenly, a pair of large hands grabbed the back of her neck, tightening on it with a strangling grip and driving her face into the mud.

"Who the fuck are you?!" Rico Cordova shouted over the din of the firefight.

"Kat Lange," she sputtered from the side of her mouth.

Cordova yanked her shoulder, rolling her partially onto her right side. He firmly pressed the seven-inch tactical knife against her neck.

Kat's eyes stared back, blinking away both her fear and the raindrops. Her muddied blonde hair was matted against her face.

Her arms trembled and her chest heaved rapidly, her panting breaths silenced by the sounds of gunfire.

Cordova relaxed the pressure of the knife against her neck.

"Coronado. You were in the watch tower," Cordova stated abruptly.

"Yes."

"What's goin' on?" demanded Cordova.

"Intruders came in," Kat explained.

"What intruders?"

"I don't know who they are. They took over the Control Center," Kat continued breathlessly.

"Is this a test?" Cordova asked.

"Fuck no!" she replied vehemently.

"How'd these fake bullets take down our point man?" Cordova asked, dropping his head.

"They must have remotely changed the HIT bullets to lethal," Kat replied.

"Gimme your weapon," Cordova demanded.

"I'm unarmed."

Cordova patted her down. Found nothing.

"Try anything and I'll fuckin' kill you," Cordova stated flatly, lifting his M4-carbine scope above the grass and scanning the area. "If we shoot 'em, will these fucking stun-blanks kill them?" Cordova asked.

"I don't know," Kat replied.

*   *   *

"I did it," Dutch whispered to himself. He turned to look at Skreemer, who was seated in the swivel chair facing the opposite workstation down the hall. He knew his best option to get off this island would be to let them know he had finished the hack, yet he hesitated with the announcement.

"What?" Skreemer said, noticing Dutch staring at him. Glancing at the monitor, he patted him on the shoulder and shouted, "We're in!"

Skye swiveled in her chair, stood up, and dashed across the room. "No fuckin' way!" she breathed, staring at the screen.

Department of Defense
Defense Information Systems Agency
Secure LAN Connection
Authority: DoD, DARPA, U.S. Navy, Pentagon
Location: Compound Five
Intelink Status:
Intelink – SCI: *ON-LINE*
Intelink – P: *off-line*
Intelink – N: *ON-LINE*
Intelink – S: *ON-LINE*
Intelink – C: *ON-LINE*
Status: Secure
Encryption: Enabled
Full Access Granted

"You did it," Skye grinned, easing into the chair at Dutch's right. She slotted a small flash drive into the terminal workstation.

"What's that?" Dutch asked.

"A little program tellin' 'em STORM was here," she replied with a sly smile, keying in several commands.

The program upload finished in seconds. Skye pulled out the flash drive, slid it into her pocket, and headed back to the Northern Terminal Workstation. "It's done," she said, smiling as she passed Eagle.

"You sure the object was successfully uploaded?" Eagle asked, his mouth inches from her ear.

"Yep," she replied confidently. Eagle smiled broadly.

"How we lookin' with the Inception Protocol?" Ray asked.

"Couple more minutes," answered Skye.

"Let's get off this friggin' island," Ray declared.

"Listen up!" Eagle directed. "'Bout time to move out. We're leaving through the main exit. Remember, C5 is alive this time."

Minutes later, STORM grouped near the open steel access door between the Northern and Southern Terminal Workstations. A brightly lit stairwell extended up to the in-ground storm door. Skye entered and climbed the concrete steps until she reached the top. Mounted onto the stairwell wall adjacent to the storm door was a six-inch square black box. She popped open the access box and pressed a series of buttons on the numerical keypad.

The sound of screeching steel-against-steel echoed throughout the stairwell tunnel, followed by the clicking sound of the unlocking latch. The hydraulic-hinged in-ground door inched open. Humid, damp air wafted inside.

Eagle moved beyond Skye, lifting his head above ground and peering through the opening door. He brought his binoculars up to his eyes. The LZ and surrounding field were empty. The storm clouds gave the illusion of night. Distant trees swayed in the gusting wind.

Lowering his binoculars, Eagle grabbed his NephSystem PDA. With his large hand snug in the back strap, the anti-shock casing rested in his palm. Holding it below ground despite the already rain-streaked screen, he tapped several commands onto the touchscreen with his stylus. An image of the island appeared, along with icons indicating the location of each combatant in real time. It was a feature intended for rescue personnel only.

He turned to look down the stairwell at Skye and nodded. Only with his eyes did he ask the question: Would the plexus recognize him as an intruder? Or had the Inception Protocol changes worked? It would mean the difference between life and death.

Eagle raced into the clearing, then headed for the western tree line. Skye lifted her head above ground level, watching as he disappeared into the forest. Inhaling deeply, she too then rushed aboveground, across the LZ, and toward the tree line.

The others followed, as everyone quickly gathered together beneath the forest canopy. "We're headed to Gate Two," Eagle shouted. "It's a mile away. Let's move!"

*   *   *

Capitaine Paul-Henri Gastineau, the French GIGN commanding officer, reversed position, belly-crawling north away from the SEALs toward the hilltop. The four-foot-tall grass swayed and shifted under the barrage of HIT bullets cutting into the hillside. Sheets of rain blurred the muzzle flashes cracking along the southern tree line, while tracers arced and streamed into and over the muddy hill.

Gastineau, the team leader and a twelve-year-veteran expert rifleman, crawled next to one of his operators, tapped his shoulder, and moved down the backside of the low-lying hill. Further down the hill, he cautiously stood, crouching, then sprinted toward the tree line some twenty-five yards away. One by one, his fellow operators along the hilltop pulled back and raced toward the deep forest canopy.

*   *   *

The shooting ceased.

With Kat alongside, Cordova backtracked down the hillside and joined Campbell and Spiers, who were crouching behind the protective evergreen.

"Y'alright?" Cordova asked Spiers.

"I'm fine," Spiers quickly replied, looking up at Campbell; his brown eyes peered through his blackened, mud-covered face. He coughed to clear his throat several times. "Nearly had him in my sights."

"You just came back from the dead," Campbell reminded him.

"So don't sweat it."

"I should've shot you," Spiers said, shifting his gaze to Kat.

Their headsets crackled. "We need to clear this area," Lieutenant Graves' voice could be heard over the radio. "We know this is live fire; they don't. Cordova, I need you guarding the rear. And take your hostage with you."

Kat turned quickly to Cordova. "I'm not the enemy," she said.

"Copy that," Cordova whispered into his mike. Without looking at Kat, he said, "For our safety, we have to assume you are."

"What do we do with Spiers?" Rock asked.

"He can move on the plexus," Kat said into her mike. "It's just that all his equipment is deactivated since he got shot."

"Stay off the comm, miss," commanded Cordova.

"Can you walk?" Rock asked Spiers.

"I can fuckin' walk," Spiers snapped as he struggled to his knees, straightened his back, and managed to get to his feet.

"He's wobbly, but walking," Campbell reported into his mike.

"YUMA, we are tactical," Graves said. "Everything is live fire. Engage only if you come under fire. We are now at Two Whiskey [a previously determined codename for reconnaissance]."

CHAPTER 15 INTERVENTION

Exercise Day: One

DARPA
ARLINGTON, VIRGINIA
JUNE 5; 1825 (LOCAL TIME)

DARPA'S C5-PROJECT IT SUPERVISOR Carl Edgewaters leaned forward in his chair, propped his elbows on his desk, and rested his head against his open hands. Flecks of gray peppered his brown hair and tiny wrinkles around his closed eyes had emerged during his thus-far brief tenure at DARPA. The last six hours without any word from C5 seemed to deepen those creases.

Suddenly his computer began to emit a soft, musical beep: a new e-mail. He opened his eyes and glanced at the long list of unread e-mails, noting at the top of the list a sender labeled "unknown." How did an unknown sender make it through the spam filter and security network? He grasped the mouse, clicked and opened the e-mail message. "Shit!" he exclaimed seconds later. Immediately, he picked up the desk phone and dialed the secure, direct line of Naval Special Warfare Command.

*　　*　　*

NAVAL SPECIAL WARFARE COMMAND
CORONADO, CALIFORNIA
JUNE 5; 1831

Rear Admiral Nicholas Briley sat among the group of SEAL commanders, staring at the wall-sized projected image of C5. The plexus tracked YUMA. No problems identified. Briley turned toward the Doppler radar monitor showing the massive storm front dwarfing the island.

"Sir, I have Edgewaters on the line," reported a short, stout petty officer first class to his left. "He says it's urgent."

"Patch him through on speaker," Briley ordered.

"Aye aye, sir."

Edgewaters was connected. "Edgewaters, Briley here. I have you on speaker. You there?"

"Yes sir, I'm here," Edgewaters began nervously.

"What's going on?" Briley asked.

"Sir, minutes ago, I received an e-mail over one of our secure mainframe servers," Edgewaters explained.

"Well, what'd it say, son?" Briley asked.

Edgewaters cleared his throat, then read:

"Man accelerates toward war, as though horrified of peace. Unwillingness to act on our request will result in death at Compound Five. Electronically send US$250 million divided equally to the five locations listed below. Upon verification of receipt of these funds, we will allow you to regain access to Compound Five. The secrets you keep are now up to you. Trust nobody."

"Shit," one commander muttered.

"Any idea who sent the e-mail?" Briley asked.

"No, sir," Edgewaters replied. "The Admiral is the first person I notified about this e-mail."

"Do you think the threat is real?"

"Sir, I'm not sure," Edgewaters replied. "But it came across a highly secure internal e-mail server."

"Mr. Edgewaters, what else do you have?" Briley asked.

"That's all for the moment, sir."

"Please do what you do," Briley instructed. "Activate your intrusion protocols. Find this hacker and keep me updated on any leads or new communications."

"Aye aye, sir."

"You got a handle on this thing, son?" Briley asked.

"Absolutely, sir."

The line disconnected.

"Admiral, Compound Five is an anti-terrorist fortress by design," asserted Commander Christopher Toms, a forty-five-year-old special warfare veteran. "There's no way to get inside, sir. This threat isn't credible."

"Perhaps the intruders were already inside to begin with, Admiral," suggested one colonel.

"Are you insinuating that one of the exercise participants has taken over the compound?" Toms asked incredulously.

"We haven't had communication with Construct Control for six hours," the colonel reasoned. "None with YUMA for four hours, and now this e-mail."

"Look at the Doppler. It's the damn storm that's screwing up the comm," Toms said.

"What about the e-mail?" the colonel queried insistently.

"The threat has no merit. Our networks receive similar threats daily," Toms replied abruptly. "And I want to remind everyone that unless all five countries agree to stop the exercise early, it runs the full five-day course. We don't have a single emergency transponder activated. The other participants don't know anything about this e-mail."

"I need more intel," Briley insisted. "We need to verify the safety of our SEALs and personnel on C5, as well as ensure the security of one element we have yet to discuss—our Intelink."

"What are you proposing, sir?" inquired Toms.

"That we go in there and find out what the hell is goin' on," Briley declared.

"We'd have to go black."

"What other quick response assets do we have in that area?" Briley continued.

"We've got the Reagan Carrier Strike Group in the region and there's currently a FAST unit aboard," replied Toms, referring to the U.S. Marine Corps Fleet Anti-Terrorism Security Team. "They've been involved in a work-up with the SEALs who are on the compound, sir."

"Alright. Get McClure on the horn," Briley ordered.

*   *   *

USS RONALD REAGAN
SOUTH PACIFIC
JUNE 5; 1834

Walter McClure looked through the carrier's bridge window, across the rain-soaked deck, and into breaking storm clouds. The secure satellite phone to his right buzzed with a sharp tone. He picked up the phone. "McClure."

"Walter, any word from YUMA?" Briley asked tersely.

"None, Admiral."

"I need you to launch your FAST unit and figure this thing out," Briley ordered.

"Aye sir, consider it done, Admiral."

A call was immediately made to the FAST commander, Captain John Brice.

*   *   *

COMPOUND FIVE
JUNE 5, 1921

STORM quickly covered ground to Gate Two. Their entranceway now would be their exit. The evening sun had set unseen behind the storm clouds. The rain eased to a steady drizzle as the fresh-scented ocean breeze blew through the cliff break. The repetitive crashing of the heavy surf against the towering cliffs could be heard deep inland.

The exhausted group pulled themselves together at the gate. The twelve-foot-tall fence hummed from the electricity coursing through the galvanized steel. Eagle cautiously scanned the beach with his NVGs. "How much longer before the gates open?" he asked.

"Thirty minutes," Skye replied.

"Skreemer, Dutch, Skye, get the boats ready," Eagle ordered. "Ray, take guard high on the south side cliff."

Ray repositioned his seabag from his right side to his back, and then headed toward the south cliff. He climbed ten feet vertically and scrambled higher across the jagged cliff top to its ocean-side edge. Ray stood tall and stared into the vast dark ocean; the moon occasionally illuminated the rippling waves and swells through the breaking storm clouds. He glanced over the edge of the eighty-foot cliff; foamy whitewater from the crashing surf swirled and pounded at its base.

Dropping to one knee, Ray pulled his M4 carbine from his seabag, attached the NV telescopic gun sight, and slotted a loaded magazine into the carbine's magazine well. He positioned himself flat on the cliff top, the sharp volcanic rock stabbing into his torso, and began scanning the intended escape pathway.

Accompanied by Dutch, Skye located the Zodiacs and together they pulled one of the deflated rubber boats back toward the gate. Skreemer retrieved the other.

"We're almost home, Dutch," Skye said, inflating the boat with an automatic inflator.

"I don't know how we're gettin' outta here," Dutch muttered uneasily.

"We *are* gettin' out of here," Skye stated emphatically.

* * *

Offshore, a thousand or so yards beyond the island, Captain John Brice, a ten-year Marine Corps veteran, and his twelve-man FAST company waited in two Zodiacs for the scout swimmer's signal. Once the blue light flashed from the water's edge, indicating the zone was passable, the two boats' crews began paddling hard toward the beach and ultimately the corridor carved within the volcanic rock.

The high waves rhythmically crashed against the cliff base and violently tossed the two rafts. The crews fought the strong current, finally reached the beach, leapt from their boats, and quickly pulled them ashore.

The lone scout swimmer, already halfway up the beach, proceeded toward Gate Two. Behind him, a narrow, safe corridor was marked for his team.

* * *

"We got company," Ray announced briefly into his mike.

Eagle pulled his NVGs close to his eyes and located the Marine scout swimmer methodically moving up the beach. "Hide the rafts," he ordered quickly. "Take cover."

Skreemer and Dutch quietly dragged the partially inflated rafts into the tree line. Eagle grabbed his seabag and hoisted it onto his shoulder. "Skye, how much time?" he whispered into his mike.

"Any minute now," Skye replied.

"Shoot anything that comes through that gate," Ray demanded.

"Hold fire until I'm ready," Eagle barked.

Skye moved back, taking cover behind a tree twenty feet from the gate and bringing her weapon to a low-ready position. Her hands trembled. Her heartrate quickened.

Dutch lifted and aimed his Beretta toward the gate. *Fuck!* Dutch's mind screamed, as his fragmented thoughts and irrepressible emotions flashed from anger at Skreemer's deception to a looming fear of dying, and even worse, the impending possibility of killing. He tried to slow his breathing, so as not to be heard by the insurging Marines. His eyes darted around, searching for the others. Eagle and Ray were out of sight. Skye was hidden. Finally, he located nearby Skreemer, sensing a similar panic in him.

Eagle ran to the north-side cliff, climbed up the seven-foot face and scrambled up to the cliff top, positioning himself at the cliff's edge. "Gimme numbers, Ray," he said.

"Thirteen total," Ray said. "That's one-three. I got one halfway up the beach—two boats unloading right now."

Atop the northern cliff, Eagle dropped his seabag, unclasped it, and withdrew his M4 carbine. He slotted the magazine into place, tapped it gently, chambered a round, and took aim.

"Those gates are about to open," Ray said. "We've got only five minutes to get the hell outta here; otherwise, we're stuck on this island."

"Do not shoot to kill! Lay down a wall of fire to keep those jarheads outside," Eagle ordered.

"Then how the fuck are we getting' off this island?" Ray shot back.

"Too late for that now. We'll find another way," Eagle said.

"And if they make it through?" Ray insisted.

"If the enemy dares to come through those gates, take aim and unleash hell!" Eagle replied.

Sharp, shrieking beeps echoed within the canyon. The harsh grating sound of metal against metal commenced as the gate began sliding and squealing along its rail system. A dark figure charged through the partially open gate.

Ray opened fire.

* * *

The F/A-18E Super Hornet strike-fighter jet cruised through the night stratosphere above Compound Five at an altitude of 40,000 feet, having launched minutes before off USS *Ronald Reagan*'s deck. Dense storm clouds below temporarily blocked the thermal imaging transmissions from Raytheon's Advanced Targeting Forward-Looking Infrared pod attached to the jet's belly.

Awaiting the infrared display of the FAST company, Mac Jacobs, the SEAL team commander, watched the monitors in the crowded, windowless room of the carrier's flag bridge. The Doppler weather monitor showed an upcoming break in the storm front.

Static-filled communications from FAST broke through the overhead speakers intermittently. Finally, the thermal images flashed on screen.

Orange-red infrared heat signatures were illuminated around Gate Two. Three heat signatures were positioned inside the fence, while two were atop the cliffs. None of the five were part of the FAST company.

The heat signatures of four Marines charged up the beach, while a few others took false cover against the cliff's edge. Many did not move. They were already dead.

"Man down," blasted into the command tower speakers. "Man down... I'm hit."

"Rush the island," Captain Brice shouted over the gunfire.

Voice communication cut to static. The thermal images remained.

"It's a goddamn ambush," Jacobs mumbled. He stared at the thermal images as a phone receiver was placed next to his ear. "It's the captain," the sailor reported.

Jacobs pulled the phone closer to his ear, watching as more

heat signatures became motionless.

"Captain," Jacobs said.

"How soon can your SEALs be ready?" asked McClure.

*　　*　　*

Without a shot fired, Dutch hid behind the tree line. The *crack-crack-crack* of burst rounds splintered the nearby trees, sliced the brush, and ripped into ground with thin geysers of wet mud stretching into the air.

Five feet away to Dutch's right, Skye squeezed off several rounds with her Glock 23. The dark figure of a twenty-five-year-old Marine pushed quickly into the forest canopy as Dutch raised his 9mm Beretta pistol. The Marine got two bursts off, clipping Skye, then turned his weapon toward Dutch.

Three rounds clicked off as Skreemer fired at his target. The Marine dropped instantly. Momentarily stunned, Dutch crawled beyond the downed Marine and over to Skye. She was unconscious. Her blood-soaked shirt moved with her gurgling, shallow breaths. Her eyes slowly rolled into the back of her head. Dutch grabbed her shoulders and shook her forcefully.

"Stay with me, Skye," Dutch breathed, his voice cracking.

Skye's eyes shut. Her body went limp.

"Gates closing," Ray announced, climbing down the rock face.

"Move!" Eagle ordered, reaching the ground. "Move out."

"Skye's down!" Skreemer shouted.

"We're out of time!" Eagle yelled. "We gotta get out of here."

Ray reached Skye. He felt for her carotid artery. No pulse. Skye was dead.

CHAPTER 16 NSA

Exercise Day: One

NEAR GATE TWO
COMPOUND FIVE
JUNE 5; 1950 (LOCAL TIME)

DUTCH STOOD, trying to focus, searching for any sign of life. Bodies were everywhere. Fallen Marines were strewn along the electrical fence and across the beach. More Marines were slumped against the cliff base and bobbing in the distant surf. Frantically, Dutch paced along the fence as a fragmented blend of emotions coursed through him: fear, anger and bewilderment. Guilty voices argued in his head.

He was a tow truck driver thousands of miles from his small hometown. How could he have been so stupid? It was an innocent hack. He didn't belong here.

Dutch covered his eyes with his hands as if that might hide him from his own reprehensible deeds. Had he been so naïve as to think no one would get hurt? The bodies before him were United States Marines! Even though he hadn't fired a shot, his actions had contributed to the slaughtering of Marines. Even if they got off the island alive...how could he ever live with that?

The proverbial line had been crossed and STORM had pushed him over it—no choice offered. No amount of arguing that STORM had to do this to survive would matter. They were no longer hackers. They'd be branded as terrorists. *Murderers!* And there would be no turning back. Not now.

A raw anger permeated Dutch's entire being from deep within his body, running from his belly to his throat. He wanted to yell or punch something, furious that he had been put in this situation. Tears of rage stung his eyes as he looked over at Ray, who knelt over Skye's body several yards away.

"What the fuck have you done?" A silent voice screamed in Dutch's head, but no sound was emitted because he didn't dare. If he wanted to get off the island alive and not end up like the Marines, he had to control his anger. He pinched the bridge of his nose and closed his eyes.

"Dutch!" Skreemer shouted at him, as he felt the slap on his shoulder. "Are you okay? Were you hit?"

"They're all dead." Dutch's voice was flat.

"They would've killed us."

Dutch was silent.

"We had no choice," Skreemer continued, guiltily. "They would've killed us," he repeated.

"Get that gate open!" Eagle shouted.

"On it," Skreemer quickly replied. He whispered to Dutch, "We have to find the access node of the perimeter gate."

Dutch nodded.

Eagle walked up to Ray. Standing over him, he asked in a low voice, "What the fuck happened up there?"

"We had the advantage. I took the opportunity and waxed 'em. It had to be done. Hell, I wasn't the only one shooting," Ray replied.

Eagle gritted his teeth. "You just got us the death penalty," he said grimly. Turning to the others, he said loudly, "They'll be sending more."

*   *   *

NAVAL SPECIAL WARFARE COMMAND
CORONADO, CALIFORNIA
JUNE 5, 2002

Briley's war room was silent for what seemed like minutes. SEAL Team commander Mac Jacobs from USS *Ronald Reagan* had just reported the failed mission and presumed death-count of thirteen Marines to Rear Admiral Nicholas Briley at Naval Special Warfare Command in Coronado, California.

"What SEALs do we have in that sector?" Briley asked.

"None in the sector. Closest in the entire region are in South America. Colombia, I believe, sir," Toms replied.

"How fast can you have them on-line?" Briley continued.

"Half a day, maybe longer, sir."

"Okay. Let's send them," Briley directed. "And get me Edgewaters on the line."

A minute later, Edgewaters was connected. "Listen, son, we have a real situation here," Briley began. "C5 is no longer under our control. What else do we need to know about C5 before we send in a response team?"

"Sir, the Intelink may be a possible target," Edgewaters responded. "If so, a codebreaker would be useful on the mission, Admiral."

"Codebreaker?"

"Sir, regaining access to the Construct Control Center computer systems and confirmation of Intelink's integrity will require a highly-skilled technical professional," Edgewaters explained.

"Do you have somebody in mind?"

"We have some of the best codebreakers already on *Reagan*, sir," Toms answered.

"Edgewaters, what do you think?" Briley asked.

"Admiral, there's only one codebreaker that could get this job done," Edgewaters replied. "He works for NSA. There's no one better, sir."

*   *   *

NATIONAL SECURITY AGENCY HEADQUARTERS
FORT GEORGE G. MEADE, MARYLAND
JUNE 5; 2115

Fifteen miles southwest of Baltimore, Maryland, two high-rise NSA office buildings stood at the center of the Fort Meade compound. The bright moon reflected off the black windows of the secretive headquarters' building; within its walls were housed the U.S.'s premier codemakers and codebreakers.

Three stories below ground in an expansive ten-acre underground facility, Ryan Caldwell—operative for NSA's Vulnerability Analysis and Operations Group and PhD graduate in computer science from the Georgia Institute of Technology—hammered at the keyboard, attempting to hack through the latest CIA security firewall. That evening, he was the only person still on the floor.

Caldwell reached into the nearly empty bag of chips and tossed a few into his mouth, wiping the salty residue onto a crumbled napkin and flipping it back onto his desk. His fingers returned to the keys briefly, then he waited. "Impenetrable," he whispered sarcastically, as *Access Granted* flashed across the screen.

Noting the time, Caldwell stood and slung his red and black North Face backpack over his shoulder, then headed quickly toward the elevator. He scanned his ID badge and pressed the elevator button.

Minutes later, the familiar *ding* sounded as the elevator doors slid open. Caldwell's supervisor and two Navy officers dressed in starched khaki uniforms stood at the elevator entranceway.

"Ryan, there's a situation," Caldwell's supervisor began. "We need to talk."

"What situation?" Caldwell asked.

"Dr. Caldwell, I'm Lieutenant Commander Brad Lowry," said

the tall, broad-shouldered Naval Academy graduate, extending his large hand for a handshake. "This is Lieutenant Ron Kazel."

Nearly a foot shorter than Lowry, Lieutenant Kazel reached out and shook Caldwell's hand. "Sir, do you mind if we talk in the conference room?" Lowry inquired, motioning down the hall.

"Sounds important. Nothing I did, right?" Caldwell asked uneasily.

"We need your expertise, Dr. Caldwell," stated Lowry.

Caldwell nodded and followed the three down the hall toward the conference room. "Dr. Caldwell, we heard that you were the lead man on the Eligible Receiver exercise. Very impressive," Lowry noted as they walked down the hall.

One of Caldwell's many accomplishments involved an internal exercise known as Eligible Receiver, initiated by the Department of Defense. Caldwell was part of the adversarial "Red Team"—an NSA attack team comprised of hackers and often considered the Special Forces equivalent for military cyber-security. The team had been organized to infiltrate the Pentagon systems and the U.S. Pacific Command in Hawaii, which was responsible for all military contingencies and operations conducted in the Pacific theatre. On June 9, 1997, Red Team had accomplished this, as well as gaining access to power grids and 911 systems in nine major U.S. cities.

"That was a long time ago," Caldwell responded.

"And you were the Red Team hacker that uncovered and patched the network vulnerability in the Defense Department's GIG in '02," Lowry said, referring to the Global Information Grid.

"Uh-huh," confirmed Caldwell.

"And you helped shut down hackers during the '06 and '07 Pentagon attacks initiated from China," Lowry continued.

The four entered the last door on the left, a windowless, soundproof room with a square, black conference table surrounded by twelve empty office chairs. They sat down as Caldwell's supervisor shut the door.

"Before we begin, I must state that everything we discuss here today is top secret," Lowry stated.

"Understood," Caldwell replied.

"Compound Five. Have you heard of it?" Lowry asked.

Caldwell's eyes widened and shifted quickly back and forth from his supervisor to Lowry. He nervously tugged and loosened his light-blue tie. "Yeah, I've heard of it," he replied carefully.

"Perhaps you remember Sentinel Software Incorporated?" Lowry continued.

"What the hell's this all about?" Caldwell demanded.

"Listen, we're on the same team now, sir," Lowry reassured him. "The past that was buried has resurfaced. We need your help."

"Well, let me be very clear, gentlemen," Caldwell said bitterly. "I've been through this shit hundreds of times. I don't know what Compound Five is. I got caught before I could find out. The SSI mainframe was all I hacked."

"Indeed, you hacked into one of the top DoD security contractors," Lowry agreed. "The SSI mainframe held all the information regarding Compound Five."

"Dr. Caldwell, Compound Five is a top-secret military base in the South Pacific," Kazel spoke up. "It's a DARPA testing and training facility. Fully operational this summer. DARPA's using CT units from several countries to test the latest combat system of the Objective Force Warrior. The first exercise started this morning. However, the exercise appears to be compromised. We received a ransom demand at 1830 via DARPA's e-mail server. The notice requested $250 million in exchange for the lives of the men on C5. We lost contact with the team several hours ago."

"So what does any of this have to do with me?" Caldwell protested.

"We're told you're one hell of a codebreaker," Kazel replied. "The best Red Teamer there is."

"You've hacked into SSI in the past with little means," Lowry added. "We're not asking for you to tell us how. We're just asking you to do it again."

"Sure. Get me connected and I'll hack anything," Caldwell assented.

"Well, it's not that easy," admitted Lowry. "There's no remote access. You'll have to hack the security system from the island."

"We'll be sending you with the best team our military has to offer," Kazel assured him. "You'll be safe with them."

"I'm sure there're other hackers willing to go."

"We were instructed to get you," Lowry insisted.

"We'd give you time to think it over, but there's no time to spare," added Kazel. "We have an aircraft waiting."

"But I'm not a field agent and certainly not a technician," Caldwell protested.

"Twenty-five operators' lives depend on you assisting us. I hope you'll do the right thing," Kazel said.

"I guess I don't have much of a choice, do I?"

Lowry and Kazel turned and looked at each other for a second.

"Time is of the essence," Lowry said urgently.

"Then what are we waiting for?" Caldwell finished, standing up.

*　　*　　*

NEAR GATE TWO
COMPOUND FIVE
JUNE 6; 2203

Eagle glanced through the twelve-foot-high, electrically locked gate topped with razor wire, down the heavily mined beach, and into the crashing waves along the shoreline.

"What's the status, Skreemer?" asked Eagle.

"Still workin' on it," Skreemer replied.

"We lost our chance," Ray spoke into the mike as he dragged Skye's body behind a patch of dense shrubs and palm trees. "What the fuck are we gonna do now?"

No one answered.

With open laptop in hand, Dutch walked along the fence line with Skreemer. A sniffer program searched the wireless perimeter-security network for another access point. With the signal strength reading ninety-eight percent, Dutch sat down and placed the computer onto his lap. Through stinging, bloodshot eyes, he stared at the screen showing that a new wireless node address inside the network had been found.

Skreemer knelt beside him. "You realize it's encrypted, right?" Dutch asked.

"Of course."

"That's kind of a big issue," Dutch continued.

"Standard 40-bit WEP," Skreemer said, referencing the Wireless Equivalent Privacy encryption.

"I know that," Dutch said. "Uses Cisco's LEAP authentication protocol." He turned to face Skreemer. "Fuck, how could this happen?" he asked dejectedly.

"Get a grip," Skreemer snapped. "Focus. We gotta get off this island alive."

"I've tried for two hours," Dutch said as he shook his head. "There's no way past this encryption remotely. We'll need to head back to the C3."

"The C3 mainframe and peripheral security gate wireless system use two different protocols," Skreemer replied. "There's a window of time when the encrypted data is not encrypted. It's only milliseconds, but it's just enough time before it gets re-encrypted and transmitted to the mainframe."

"That's how bank ATMs work," Dutch thought, but DARPA's system was much more sophisticated. "Alright, here goes," he said, clicking several commands, then punching the *enter* key.

The two stared at the gate.

Nothing.

Moments later, Dutch reconnected to the access node and tried again.

Still nothing.

"Dammit, it's not gonna work," Dutch sighed. "We gotta go back."

"To C3? There's no time," Ray said. "This place is gonna be crawling with those fuckin' Navy snake eaters."

"We shouldn't have put a time limit on the system," Skreemer said.

"Pack it up," Eagle ordered. "We're goin' back."

CHAPTER 17 ECHO

Exercise Day: Two

NEAR SANTIAGO DE CALI
COLOMBIA, SOUTH AMERICA
JUNE 6; 0021 (LOCAL TIME)

MOONLIGHT FILTERED DIMLY through the forest canopy. The stench of the dank Colombian forest floor was heavy, the air thick, humid, and stagnant. The rhythmic humming and screeching of insects echoed throughout the valley in an expanse of rolling jungle-green hills.

Already on his third day of stalking and reconnaissance, Navy SEAL sniper Nat Mitchell took position 500 yards from the target—the main entrance to an underground lab of one of Colombia's largest cocaine-trafficking cartels, the Cali Cartel. Outfitted in a woodland ghillie suit, a sniper camouflage uniform, Mitchell tracked the two patrolling guards through the 16-power scope attached to his MK11 semi-automatic sniper rifle. "ECHO Two. ECHO Four. One guard, fifty yards, headed your way," he whispered into his mike.

Three hours ago, the seven-member DEVGRU Navy SEAL unit, ECHO team, had clandestinely descended upon the underground lab. Intelligence from the U.S. Drug Enforcement Agency indicated the lab was operated from prison cells, since most of Cali Cartel's leaders had been arrested in the 1990s. But ECHO wasn't there for a drug bust. Intel linked the cartel and the Revolutionary

Armed Forces of Colombia, a Marxist-inspired insurgent force, in the development of dirty bombs, a type of radiological dispersal device. This underground facility was believed to process more than coca.

Mitchell's reconnaissance detailed a shipment received twelve hours earlier via a nearby river. Based on traffic in and out of the facility, he counted eight men inside. Further up the valley, an aboveground building housed over a dozen heavily armed paramilitary guards.

Flat against the forest floor, Rick Chance, an eight-year DEVGRU SEAL positioned now as ECHO's point man, sliced the thin bundle of wires affixed to the enemy's underground bunker door explosives. "Bunker door disarmed," whispered Chance into his mike.

"ECHO Two?" said patrol leader Ben Rodgers. He was positioned low on the eastern hillside along with radioman Jack Tyler. M60 machine-gunner Samuel Brooks and corpsman Tyson Mann covered the western hillside.

"Status?" queried Rogers.

"ECHO leader, C4 in place," teammate Michael Drakowski whispered, moving twenty feet behind Chance.

"Copy that. ECHO Two and ECHO Four. Proceed," crackled into Chance and Drakowski's headsets. Chance gently lifted and opened the wooden door covered with dirt and grass. Peering through his NVGs and clutching his MK23 handgun with KAC sound suppressor close to his chest, he moved feet-first into the dark entranceway and eased downstairs. Drakowski followed and lowered the door behind him.

"ECHO Two and Four are inside," Mitchell reported.

Moments later, a second guard, armed with an M16 and unaware of the intrusion, approached the access door. A lit Marlboro cigarette hung loosely in his mouth.

"ECHO Two, you have one guard positioned at your exit,"

alerted ECHO sniper Mitchell. "Copy?"

"Roger that," Chance whispered back. He reached the bottom of the short stairwell and sidestepped along the low-ceilinged hallway.

No one was there.

Dim light emerged beneath two doors on opposite sides of and midway up the hall. To either side, wood planks supported the crumbling rock and dirt of the claustrophobic 2,000-square-foot structure.

Drakowski briefly glanced down at his handheld radiation detection device. It registered trace amounts of Cesium-137, a highly lethal radioactive powder. The most publicized exposure of Cesium-137 had occurred in September 1987 when a hospital in Goiânia, Brazil, moved to a new location, leaving its radiation-therapy unit behind. Scrap metal hunters dismantled the unit and sold the glowing cesium powder to curious buyers, leading to hundreds of exposures and four deaths.

With MK23 pistols in low-ready position, Chance and Drakowski reached the door on their right. Chance gently turned the doorknob. The door was locked. He turned to Drakowski and nodded.

Taking a step back, Drakowski lunged his right boot forward, kicking hard against the wood door near the knob. The deadbolt burst through the cracked frame. The lower hinge ripped loose, and the broken door dangled from a single upper hinge. Chance entered the room. Three men were inside, already facing him. The nearest one was only three feet away.

With his .45 caliber pistol, Chance moved swiftly, placing a single silenced bullet at the center of the closest enemy's forehead. The man's bloodied head flung back as the impact knocked his body several feet away.

The second, a short, stout Colombian man fifteen feet to their left, felt along his right side until he grasped a black automatic rifle strapped across his chest. The third man stood wide-eyed in the room's far right corner. His hands trembled as he struggled futilely to lay hold of his hip-holstered handgun.

Drakowski moved beside Chance and ripped two-round bursts into the chests of the second and third men. The two bodies jerked back, slamming into a long wooden table along the far wall. A small plume of white powder drifted into the air as the bodies hit the ground.

Chance scanned the small room. It was clear.

The commotion, however, did not go unnoticed. From across the hall, the door swung open and two more men emerged, weapons at the ready. Both Chance and Drakowski simultaneously popped bullets into the chest of a short, bearded Colombian, the leader of the two men. The impact of the big .45-caliber cartridge knocked the man back through the doorway.

"Ayuda! Ayuda!" a voice in the opposite room shouted into a radio. "Help!" Chance and Drakowski were quickly outnumbered, six to two.

From the enemy's M16, three-round bursts peppered the doorway and ripped through the room's thin wood and dirt walls. Chance and Drakowski hit the deck. Drakowski grasped the M4 carbine strapped across his chest, fingered the trigger, and returned fire into the dismantled doorway, suppressing the three left inside the opposite room.

Above ground, Mitchell saw four men running toward the underground facility. "We got company. I count four. Make that five, heading down the valley," he reported.

"We gotta get out of here," Rodgers ordered, "Abort, abort."

The patrol guard positioned near ECHO's exitway tossed his cigarette to the ground and knelt down. Running his hand along the bunker door's edge, he felt the cut ends of the explosive wires. Then he lifted the door and started to move inside. One silenced shot ripped into his back, splitting his spine in half and blasting through his torso, exiting his chest. His body rolled down into the stairwell.

"Tango One down," Mitchell reported.

"Copy that," Rodgers replied. Gunfire sparked from the surrounding jungle near Mitchell's position on the hillside.

Working their way back into the hallway, Chance and Drakowski fired occasional bursts to suppress the enemy inside the room, while backstepping toward the exit. At the stairwell, the two stepped over the guard's body, then hurried above ground.

"ECHO Two and Four are out," Mitchell announced.

"Copy that," acknowledged Rodgers.

Via a "center peel," basically a tactical "oh, shit" escape technique, ECHO withdrew. Chance, Drakowski, and Brooks formed the three-man front, while the others broke contact and hauled ass. Chance fired continuously, as Drakowski and Brooks "peeled" away on either side, moved to the rear, dropped to the prone position, and prepared to return fire. Before he could empty his clip, Chance peeled off, as Drakowski began firing.

"Everyone's clear," Mitchell reported, pumping rounds into the ever-increasing number of counter-attacking enemy soldiers.

Once Drakowski rolled back and hit the deck, he pulled out the small remote detonator, popped the safety switch, and pressed the wireless trigger. Some two hundred yards away, the earth erupted. Gray and black smoke billowed into the night sky. Drakowski pushed a second button. One hundred yards from the first explosion, the underground bunker roof ripped away and disintegrated as it somersaulted end-over-end into the air.

Sniper Mitchell clutched his weapon and eased away from his position almost invisibly, joining ECHO to the south, as they headed toward the extraction point on a remote cactus-strewn farmland.

*   *   *

COLUMBUS, OHIO
JUNE 5; 0112

Thirty-one-year-old Rashid Fahad sat upstairs at his desk in his quiet one-bedroom townhouse a mile from The Ohio State University campus. Nobody had visited since he moved in. The walls remained bare. There wasn't even a TV.

Having entered the U.S. six years ago under the auspices of a student visa, Fahad's façade as a student pursuing a PhD degree in Computer Science and Engineering was meticulous. With stellar grades and an outgoing personality, the highly educated computer engineer had quickly befriended many of his classmates. A natural leader, he was considered laid-back and well informed when it came to international affairs. But little did his "friends" know that Rashid held a core hatred for Western culture and society: American's infatuation with Hollywood stars, television, gossip, brand names, and expensive cars. These things sickened Fahad when he considered his family's plight of poverty back home in Afghanistan.

Although Fahad lived by himself, he did not operate alone. His team was one of several terrorist sleeper-cells of the Islamic Jihad Liberation Movement, a super-secret arm of the Jerusalem Force of Iran's Islamic Revolutionary Guard Corps. Fahad's five-man cell was composed of an expert in explosives, one in reconnaissance, one in surveillance, even a former CIA agent, all of whom were scattered across the Midwestern United States.

Communication between Rashid's teammates grew more difficult each year: telephone conversations, whether landline or cellular, were no longer possible. He remained in contact via brief conversations in encrypted e-mails and Internet bulletin boards on frequently rotating networks.

Fahad's relocation to Columbus was no coincidence. The DoD Network Information Center, one of the main military root name Internet servers, was only miles away. The Afghanistan-born extremist, who fancied himself a visionary, pecked away on his laptop and logged into the latest of his many e-mail accounts. A new message awaited in his inbox. He clicked and opened the new e-mail communication—a steagnography, a hidden message in an image file. Moments later, the decrypted image of Mickey Mouse translated into a four-word message: *Insertion successful. Lone Wolfe.*

* * *

BAHIA MALAGA
COLOMBIA, SOUTH AMERICA
JUNE 6; 0156

Arriving sixty miles northwest of Cali, Colombia, at the Base Naval de Bahía Málaga, ECHO offloaded the HH-60H Seahawk transport helicopter and moved inside a nearby two-story building. Once inside, Lieutenant Commander Miguel Mercado, a thirty-eight-year-old SEAL and expert on Colombian terrorist organizations and drug trafficking cartels, greeted ECHO as they entered.

"Glad to see you back, Lieutenant," Mercado said with a native Colombian accent.

"Glad to be back, sir," replied Rodgers, the ECHO team patrol leader.

Mercado guided the seven-member team into a windowless conference room. They filed in and sat down at a round aluminum table.

"Listen up," Mercado said abruptly. "We'll have a short debriefing tonight, but we have a situation in the South Pacific that requires your immediate assistance." Poring over maps, he drew on a Bolivar Cuban cigar. A smoky haze filled the room. "As you know, YUMA was slotted to participate in an international training exercise on Compound Five. Eight hours ago, we lost contact with the Control

Center and all combat teams. A FAST unit was deployed. All thirteen Marines were killed. We are actively gathering intel. We currently do not know who or what the threat is."

"Sir, any contact made by the hostiles?" inquired Rodgers.

"Received an e-mail yesterday saying hackers took over the compound's computer network," Mercado replied. "That's all we got."

"Sir, what's our op plan for delivery?" Drakowski asked.

"HAHO."

High Altitude/High Opening, or HAHO, parachute insertions consisted of a platoon jumping from an aircraft, typically with a commercial IFF (Identification Friend or Foe) signature flying in normal air traffic lanes, so as to not raise suspicion. Deploying at 30,000 feet with parachute opening altitudes of 27,000 feet would allow a team to traverse upwards of thirty miles. Using GPS for navigation, they could accurately reach the targeted landing zone.

"Sir, commercial or military aircraft?" Drakowski continued.

"Initially commercial," answered Mercado. "There's an Air Force Curtiss C-46 Commando prop plane that already has a commercial IFF signature and delivery route that runs approximately twenty-five miles from C5. They didn't wanna raise any international eyebrows before we figure out what the hell is goin' on down there."

Last used by the Air Force in 1969, only fifty of the original 3,000 Curtiss C-46s were still flying, mostly as freighters in Central and South America.

"Those things are ancient," Tyler said doubtfully.

"Fortunately, command's pullin' a C-130 off another run and gettin' it to Buenaventura for us," Mercado added.

"Sir, with the other CT units on the island, what are the rules of engagement?" Chance asked.

"It's gonna be tricky," Mercado said. "Trust nobody. We don't know if one of the other CT units is involved or whether a separate or a rogue group has entered. We know very little at this point."

"When's kick-off, sir?" Rodgers asked.

"A few hours," Mercado said. "We'll let you know. There'll be an NSA computer expert joining you on the mission. I'm told he's necessary and the best."

"Any combat experience, sir?" Chance asked.

Taking a deep draw on his cigar, Mercado faced Chance and shook his head. "None," he replied, blowing a thick plume of smoke across the table. "Even better, since you're the lightest, you'll tandem HAHO with him," Mercado finished grimly.

*   *   *

NEAR THE CONSTRUCT CONTROL CENTER COMPOUND FIVE
JUNE 6; 0201

A quarter-mile east of the island's center, Terrance Rock, YUMA's M60 gunner, glassed the area as far out as 200 yards for 360 degrees around him, as YUMA recon ordered its way toward C3.

"Angel One. Angel One. Do you copy?" crackled into Rock's headset as radioman Cordova attempted to contact USS *Ronald Reagan*.

In the distance, a low roar in the sky heightened into a deep scream as two F-18s streaked overhead. Rock instinctively ducked despite the fact that the jets were some 200 feet off the deck.

"They're gathering intel," Graves shouted over the roar of the engines.

"Movement, southeast!" Rock yelled, spotting two figures through his NVGs, 500 yards south of C3.

"Kill comm. Let's move back," Graves ordered.

"There are four men in danger down there," Kat whispered into Cordova's ear, pointing to the C3.

"Can't risk it right now. They may already be dead," Cordova replied.

*   *   *

On the eastbound path back to the Construct Control Center, Dutch purposely distanced himself from the others. Skreemer, Ray, and Eagle moved quickly out of sight as Dutch settled quietly into position behind a thick tree trunk. He put his back against the slick, moss-covered surface, slid to the ground, and sat down.

He lifted his PDA, rapidly switching modes to send text messages. His eyes darted across the forest ahead and to each side. No sign of STORM.

Intelink compromised. Must stop attack, he pecked rapidly on his handheld computer, sending the text, destined for Kathryn Lange, via the compound's emergency message system. He then lowered the PDA, clipping it to his belt.

"What are you doing?" Skreemer asked, shocked and breathless as he appeared around the other side of the tree.

"Tired," Dutch mumbled, feigning fatigue. His heart raced as panic overcame him. How long had Skreemer been there?

"No time to rest. Let's go," demanded Skreemer.

Dutch's unsteady legs trembled as he got to his feet. The two men hurried to catch up with the others.

Dutch covertly glanced down at the PDA. The text message had been successfully sent.

CHAPTER 18 INTEL

Exercise Day: Two

LOS ANGELES, CALIFORNIA
JUNE 5; 0231 (LOCAL TIME)

LONE WOLFE'S cell phone vibrated. The ringer was off. Wolfe, an ex-Case Officer in the CIA's former Directorate of Operations, now the National Clandestine Service, paused and stared at the caller ID number, then flipped open his phone. "You shouldn't be callin' right now," he said, irritation creeping into his voice.

"Any word from the team?" asked Joe Norman, anticipation in his voice. The Australian-born businessman and vice-president of Sentinel Software Industries, the former C5 computer-security contractor, felt the billion-dollar security contract from DARPA was within reach.

Wolfe, on the other hand, wanted revenge. Toward the end of his career, the covert and independent DO lost many turf battles with the FBI and the Departments of State and Defense. The DO was forced to become the NCS, and with the DO's end, Wolfe was pushed out.

"Are you on a secure line?" Wolfe asked.

"Of course."

"Got the first message. They're in. Still waiting on the second message. But we got a big problem," Wolfe began.

"What the fuck are you talkin' about?" demanded Norman.

"Thirteen Marines were just killed at C5."

"WHAT?!" Norman exclaimed. "How did you hear this?"

"Don't worry about it," Wolfe said. "I have my sources."

"Fuck!" Norman shouted. "What the hell happened?"

"Not sure," Wolfe answered.

"Can they get off the island?"

"Don't know and I don't care," Wolfe stated dryly.

"What about the Intelink? When can we verify it's been hacked?"

"It'll take the prion another twelve hours to work," Wolfe replied. "Then we'll know."

"What about the money?" Norman pressed.

"Patience," Wolfe replied. "The Iranians will pay the rest when we hand over access to the Intelink. They don't care about fucked-up operations."

"Well, I do," Norman spat angrily. "We're gonna fuckin' hang for this."

"We gotta get off this phone," Wolfe interrupted. "No more comm by phone. I'll be in touch by e-mail." Wolfe closed his phone. The line went dead.

*   *   *

AIRSPACE OVER COMPOUND FIVE
JUNE 6; 0235

The U.S. Navy P-3C Orion, a long-range maritime patrol and anti-submarine aircraft, cruised high above Compound Five, skimming the ceiling of the dark storm clouds. Carrying a crew of eleven, the aircraft's wings and fuselage extended roughly to the size of a baseball diamond in all directions. The drone of the four turbo-prop engines deepened from a high-pitched buzz to a low-pitched roar as the aircraft slowed, nearing the C5 airspace.

The non-acoustic operator stared intently at the monitor

receiving feeds from his three systems—the radar, infrared-detection-system optics turret, and the magnetic anomaly detection system—each housed in the long "stinger" in the P-3C Orion's tail.

"Pickin' up only a few heat sigs," the non-acoustic operator reported.

"Copy that," the tactical coordinator, or TACCO, answered.

"Circle back around," the patrol plane commander directed. "Launch the buoy."

"Roger that," the TACCO replied.

The P-3's left wing dipped as they banked, circled, and cruised south of C5. From inside the fuselage, a sonobuoy, a ten-foot orange cylindrical casing housing the sonar, was released. Within seconds a small, white parachute opened as the buoy drifted 35,000 feet to the ocean. Minutes later, the buoy transducer array deployed as the sonar signal began transmitting.

The acoustic sensor operator leaned closer as he monitored the transmitted signal on the screen. His eyes widened. He blinked several times, then refocused. He straightened up, turned, and glanced down the length of the cabin.

"Submarine!" he blurted. "One mile northwest of C5."

*   *   *

USS RONALD REAGAN
JUNE 6; 0239

Captain Walter McClure was briefly, unconsciously wringing his hands as reports of the offshore submarine emerged. He straightened his back in the leather skipper's chair. "XO, I want contact with that submarine, *yesterday!*" he demanded, turning to his left and facing the ship's executive officer, Commander Joel Hutch.

"Yes, sir," Commander Hutch replied.

"What's the status of the SEALs flying in from Colombia?" asked McClure.

"Still ten hours out, sir."

"Go ahead then," McClure ordered. "Authorize lift off."

Moments later, the two Seahawk helicopters thundered away from USS *Ronald Reagan*, each carrying a Marine assault team destined for Compound Five.

*   *   *

CONSTRUCT CONTROL CENTER
JUNE 6; 0315

Eagle and Ray sprinted hard from the treeline, across the rain-soaked grass field to the in-ground storm door of the Construct Control Center. Ray flipped open the access box and keyed the numerical access code, triggering the hydraulic door. The pistons hissed as the hydraulic engine emitted a low-humming drone. The door inched open.

Eagle hand-signaled to Dutch and Skreemer as the two also emerged from the treeline and ran toward the dim white glow created by the in-ground stairwell lighting.

With Beretta in hand, Eagle slid inside, established his footing, and then sidestepped down the stairs until reaching the already-open door to the Northern and Southern Workstation Areas. The air-conditioned breeze felt cold. The sound of screeching insects deadened as he entered the quiet workstation.

Eagle paused to let his eyes adjust to the bright overhead fluorescent lights. He raised his weapon, then burst through the doorway, turned the corner, and quickly glanced back and forth down the hall between the computer workstations.

Nobody.

Ray moved in behind Eagle. "Clear," Eagle said.

Above ground, Dutch and Skreemer quickly regrouped at the

now open in-ground storm door and clambered down the stairs.

With the four inside, Ray hurried to punch the key code. The storm door closed.

"Dutch and Skreemer. Hit the mines and gates," Eagle ordered.

"We gotta get a signal out," Ray said. "No comm with sub means sub leaves without us. Then we're really fucked."

Suddenly, a high-pitched beeping alarm sounded. On the large, flat screen monitor of the Northern Terminal Workstation, the green radar line sweeping over two moving circular icons indicated two fast-approaching aircraft.

"What is it?" Dutch asked.

Ray and Eagle moved closer to the monitor.

"Shit! Two bogies," Ray said.

"Helos," Eagle confirmed. "They're sendin' another team."

"What the fuck do we do now?" Skreemer said, uneasily.

"We wait," Eagle replied. "This won't be an issue in a few minutes."

At the screen's bottom, a seven-word message flashed: *STA Missile Silo One launch-ready.*

"The missiles are active?" Dutch gasped.

"Yes," Eagle replied grimly.

Dutch dropped in front of a network computer and began pecking frantically at the keyboard. "I can stop the launch."

"Get the fuck away from the computer, Dutch!" Ray shouted as his right hand moved toward his sidearm.

"If I don't, it'll kill 'em all," Dutch said, keeping his eyes fixed on the monitor.

Ray gripped his Glock, unholstered the weapon, and targeted Dutch's back.

"Cool it, Ray. Dutch, get up," Eagle ordered loudly. "We don't have a damn choice, gentlemen. If you want to get off this island alive, we have to work together."

Dutch turned and stood as Ray lowered his weapon. Eagle

moved closer to Ray, his mouth inches from Ray's ear. "Don't ever pull that shit again, understood?" he whispered sternly. Ray nodded reluctantly.

* * *

AIRSPACE NEAR COMPOUND FIVE
JUNE 6; 0319

A mile offshore, two staggered Seahawks, loaded with Marines, approached Compound Five.

Roger Winters, a rotary-wing pilot who had spent much of his time in special operations, tensed at the distinctive tone in the headset emitted from the missile warning system.

"SAM. Locked on. They've locked on to us," he announced to his co-pilot.

"Copy that. SAMs launched," the wide-eyed co-pilot announced.

"Initiating evasive maneuvers," Winters continued. "Brake right."

Firmly grasping the cyclic stick control, Winters banked hard right and rolled the machine, forcing it parallel to the ocean. The whirling rotor blades bit into the air as the engines screamed. The missile closed in. The Seahawk skimmed several feet above the ocean surface.

"Launching chaff and flares," the co-pilot said. The flares were a countermeasure for heat-seeking missiles, the chaff for infrared-seekers.

Two anti-missile flares launched from the sides of the helo, illuminating the sky with a brilliant burst of red-orange as they streaked away from the Seahawk. The chaff followed, as a cloud of tiny aluminum and metal composite sprayed to each side.

One hundred feet away, the missile did not deviate course. Winters pulled hard right, then upward. As the missile closed in, he yanked on the control stick, and the helo pulled away from the water.

The SAM clipped the tail rotor without detonation, then pounded into the ocean, detonating on impact. "I'm hit!" yelled Winters. The helo tremored violently and spun uncontrollably. Winters pulled up on the collective control stick, seeking altitude. The helo's tail hit first. Rubble scattered hundreds of yards away as the helicopter plummeted into the ocean.

CHAPTER 19 HOSTAGE

Exercise Day: Two

COMPOUND FIVE
JUNE 6; 0321 (LOCAL TIME)

THE CONSTRUCT CONTROL CENTER fell silent.

The four intruders—Skreemer, Dutch, Eagle, and Ray—faced the seventy-inch wall-mounted monitor at the Northern Terminal Workstation. The line of the radar-sweep circled in the lower left portion of the monitor; one helicopter disappeared, the other backtracked to the carrier.

"One down," Skreemer murmured.

"They'll keep comin'," Eagle said grimly. "Let's stay focused. We've got five hours to get a message to Wolfe or the sub's leaving."

"I can send a message from here," Dutch said nervously.

"Can't risk it," Ray replied, as he turned and began pacing up and down the hallway of the computer room. "Disengaging the radio-frequency jammers, even for a second, might be enough time for the CT units to communicate with *Reagan*. The last thing we need is five CT units on our ass. Right now, they don't know we exist."

"YUMA knows," stated Skreemer, pointing at the monitor. Six icons, representing YUMA's five CT members plus Kat, glowed on the screen, positioned in groups of two along the eastern treeline of C5's landing zone.

"We'll never get outta here alive," Dutch said despondently.

"They don't have real bullets," Skreemer reminded him.

"Those HIT bullets are the equivalent of Tasers, though," Ray interjected.

"Except they kill now," Eagle said coldly, turning away from the monitor and staring hard at Ray halfway down the hallway.

"What are you talkin' about?" blurted Skreemer.

"Wolfe re-programmed the Inception Protocol before insertion," Eagle said. "The HIT bullets are now set to lethal. This never was an exercise. It's no different than combat with real bullets."

"Why the hell wasn't I made aware of this?" Skreemer yelled.

"Enough!" Eagle shouted back, fixing his steely-eyed gaze on Skreemer. "We don't have time right now. If you wanna get off this island alive, then listen up. Dutch, get Gate Two open. Disarm the mines. Ray, come with me. We're gettin' the hostages."

*   *   *

From the eastern treeline, Cordova lay flat against the ground, firmly holding the night-vision goggles against his eyes. A misty rain dotted the lenses. He scanned across the empty grass field to the opposite side, where tree branches swayed, buffeted by intermittent gusts of wind. He then focused on the helipad, glancing back and forth at the hand-sized chunks of shattered concrete.

The blast and crackling sound of the missile-launch quieted. The faint, steady ratcheting of a distant helicopter disappeared. An occasional whistling of the wind remained.

"No movement," Cordova reported into his mike.

"Copy that," Graves replied. "We're in position."

Grouped into two-man assault teams, Graves-Spiers and Rock-Campbell staggered the treeline a hundred yards on either side of the Cordova-Kat team.

"Prepare to move," Graves directed.

"Copy," Cordova replied.

A faint vibration touched Kat's skin. Instinctively feeling along her leg, she discovered a handheld computer in her pants pocket.

"What is it?" Cordova asked, cautiously watching her movements.

She lifted the device and scanned the screen. "Intelink compromised. Must stop attack," she read aloud. "Somebody's trying to communicate with us."

"Who?"

"Probably Channing or one of others captured down there. I should respond."

"No. Could be staged, from one of the intruders," Cordova said. He keyed his mike, "YUMA Leader, we're getting a message via the emergency network reporting the Intelink is compromised. Unsure origin of transmission. No signature."

"Roger that. Do not make contact. Let's proceed as planned."

Kat leaned in next to Cordova. "If they're in there, the intruders can track us," she whispered. "They'll know we're here."

Flipping on NV mode and pulling his OFW visor down, Cordova turned to face Kat. "As soon as your finger touches the fingerprint reader and that door starts to open, run hard," Cordova replied. "Right back here. Understood?"

"Got it," Kat replied tersely.

"Ready to move," Cordova announced into his mike.

"Proceed," ordered Graves.

*   *   *

The blindfolded lieutenant hesitantly moved up the stairs from the lower level power room. His sweaty red hair was matted against his forehead. Unable to find a comfortable position, he nervously twisted his tremulous, clammy hands and wrists in the tight plastic zip-ties behind his back. For a moment, he stopped walking. The hard steel of Eagle's 9mm Beretta pistol firmly pressed into his lower back. He began walking again.

As he entered the computer room, the tense lieutenant sensed the brightness change through the white cloth blindfold creasing deeply into his temples. As he stepped onto the computer room floor, the toe of his black boot caught on the last stairwell step. A hard thud caused Dutch and Skreemer, both seated at the Northern Terminal Workstation, to turn around.

"What are they doin'?" Dutch whispered to Skreemer.

"Just focus on gettin' us outta here," Skreemer replied, turning away from the monitor.

"Get up," Eagle ordered loudly. He gripped the lieutenant beneath the armpits, hoisting him up. His giant hands appeared massive against the lieutenant's thin arms as he pulled him back up to his feet.

Shoved against the wall, the disoriented officer joined the line of C3 personnel—the lieutenant commander, chief petty officer, and petty officer-first class—with their backs facing the hallway between the terminal workstations. Standing guard, Ray aimed his M4 carbine at the four sailors. Eagle kneeled, slid his eleven-inch black tactical knife from the sheath strapped to his calf, stood again, and approached the five-foot-ten-inch lieutenant commander. "Listen up," Eagle said loudly, directly behind the lieutenant commander's left ear. He then paced back and forth a few feet behind the four men.

"We have no intention of killing you," Eagle continued. "If you do exactly as I say, you'll live. Try anything, and you will be shot." He moved behind the petty officer-first class—a twenty-two-year-old sailor roughly the same size as Dutch—slid his knife behind the plastic-tie around his wrists, and sliced it off. The petty officer slowly lowered his hands to his sides. "Keep your blindfold on," Eagle said. "Strip down to your skivvies."

"Why do..." the sailor started.

"Shirt. Pants. Now!" Eagle bellowed.

"Do as he says, sailor," the lieutenant commander spoke up. The young sailor unbuttoned his Navy digital-camouflage utility shirt, pulled it off, and dropped it to his side.

After deactivating the perimeter security system, Dutch glanced to his side, making certain that Skreemer was still looking away. He covertly opened the e-mail account and furiously typed a message: *Lone Wolfe is the man you're looking for.* He frantically hit *enter* and closed out the screen. The message was sent to Carl Edgewaters, IT supervisor for the DARPA C5 Project; Dutch recalled his name from the mounds of documents he had read in preparation for the trip.

"Security system's down," Dutch reported. "Mines deactivated."

"It's done," Skreemer confirmed, glancing at the screen, then turning and nodding at Eagle.

Eagle walked to the Northern Workstation and leaned in closely between Dutch and Skreemer, who were both still seated. "We're changing clothes with them," he whispered. "It'll confuse the SEAL team outside long enough to get us outta here. They're comin' after us for sure, so keep watching the monitor. When they move, let me know."

*　　　*　　　*

Cordova and Kat scrambled up to their feet and hurried across the open field, heading toward the in-ground emergency exit forty yards out. Cordova reached it first. Instinctively, he dropped to one knee and scanned across the grassy field ahead, then down at the dismantled concrete of the helipad. A short distance northwest, the standard entranceway remained untouched.

Out of breath, Kat dropped onto both knees next to Cordova. Her hands shaking, she fumbled with the access-panel door, opened it, keyed in the code, and firmly pressed her right index finger against the fingerprint reader. *Access granted* glowed in green on the LCD access-panel screen. The pressurized hydraulics of the in-ground door moaned and hissed. Above the sound of the sliding pistons, Kat could be heard hyperventilating.

"Door's openin'," Cordova reported into his mike. From the treeline, the two dark figures of Rock and Campbell emerged as they headed toward Cordova.

"Go! Get outta here," Cordova said, turning to Kat. Kat got to her feet and began backstepping. Cordova also inched back.

A deep, earth-rattling boom sounded as an earthquake-like tremor ripped across the field. The C4 charge, planted by Ray, warped the steel-alloy door and fired debris in all directions. Cordova was thrown nearly ten feet back. A large chunk of shrapnel ripped into the middle of his right thigh. Blood gushed from the wound. His cracked helmet lay several feet away. His bruised right eye swelled shut. Nearby, a dazed Kat drifted in and out of consciousness.

*   *   *

Positioned atop the stairwell extending to the main entranceway door, Ray felt the vibration of the C4 detonation course through the building. The screeching alarm of the compromised emergency exit sounded from the speakers in the computer room, echoing loudly inside the stairwell tunnel.

Ray glanced down the stairs. The four Navy men—blindfolded and outfitted in STORM's black uniforms—were tightly crammed together halfway up the concrete steps. The rest of STORM, grouped at the bottom, was now wearing the digi-utilities, as was Ray.

With his 9mm Beretta aimed up the stairwell, Eagle stepped back, turned it toward the monitor and fired, hoping to silence the alarm. The bullet pierced and shattered the screen's center. The high-pitched pulsing alarm continued.

"Lights off," Eagle ordered. "Let's go!" At the bottom of the stairwell, Skreemer hit the switch. The beaming fluorescent overhead lights went dark.

Ray punched the access code into the black box mounted on the stairwell wall. The door slowly opened with the now-familiar sound of hydraulic pistons hissing and the grating of steel-against-steel. Blackness was visible through the opening storm door. The rain dampened the top of the stairs.

Ray grabbed his NephSystem PDA clipped to his belt and tapped the touchscreen with his right index finger. The screen was instantly populated with an image of the island and icons indicating the location of YUMA. Ray looked up from the screen and nodded at Eagle at the bottom of the stairwell.

"Ready to move," Eagle shouted.

Four smoke grenades, the size and shape of a shaving-cream can, sat on the step at Ray's feet. He grabbed the closest grenade, pulled the metal pin and heaved the grenade out the now three-foot-wide door opening. One by one, he tossed the four grenades. Then he grasped his M4 carbine and pointed it at the darkness above.

"Blindfolds off," Eagle ordered. "Let's move!" The four captive men pulled the white cloth blindfolds up and off their heads. "Go! Go! Go!" barked Eagle. Ray followed.

The four Navy men clambered up the stairs, through the storm door, and into the darkness and the cool, drizzling rain. The wide-eyed petty officer was the last up the stairs; he slipped on the final step and landed face-first above ground. Disoriented, his face scraped and bloodied, he attempted to adjust his eyes to the darkness. He glanced to the east, where a hazy wall of smoke wafted. Moving in the wrong direction, he stumbled into the smoke, tripped on the broken concrete of the LZ, and crashed again to the ground a few feet away from Kat. The other three captives crouched and moved slowly toward the western treeline.

Skreemer climbed the stairs and moved above ground. Unexpectedly, moonlight broke through the storm clouds, dimly illuminating the field. "Move!" Skreemer shouted, as he positioned himself behind the three men.

From the opposite direction, the muzzle flashes began. Tracers streamed through the smoky haze. The popping and cracking of gunfire echoed across the compound's field. Ray returned fire.

Dutch reluctantly lifted his head above the ground door opening. Through a break in the wafting smoke, the first sight was that of a blonde-haired woman staring back, appearing frozen amongst the chaos of activity and gunfire. It had to be Kat.

Out of the corner of his eye, Dutch realized that Ray had seen the same thing at nearly the same time. Ray's gunsight honed in on Kat. The crosshairs locked on the target. Ray's trigger finger was squeezing.

Instinctively, Dutch punched at the weapon with his right hand, knocking the muzzle off its mark. The two-round burst fired into the darkness.

Knowing that this was no accident, the infuriated Ray glared at Dutch as he moved above ground and headed for the treeline.

Eagle climbed the stairs, tapping Ray on the shoulder as he passed by, and sprinted out of the kill zone. Ray turned to relocate his missed target; the cloud of smoke blocked all visibility. Dutch caught up with and ran a few feet behind the red-haired lieutenant. Half the distance to the treeline, Dutch lunged forward, tackling the officer and yanking him forcefully to the ground. "Stay down! The bullets are real!" he shouted above the din of gunfire.

The lieutenant briefly stared back at Dutch, not saying a word. Wanting to get back on his feet, the sailor attempted to push away. Dutch tightened his grip on the man's shirt.

"This is live fire. They think you're the enemy," Dutch shouted, tugging on the shirt as the confused officer continued to pull away. HIT bullets buffeted the short grass inches from the two men.

The sailor swung his fist wildly, knuckles connecting with Dutch's temple. The officer struggled to his feet as the stunned Dutch lost his grip.

One slug pounded into the lieutenant's mid-back. A bluish flash followed. He fell to the ground, jerked violently, then lay motionless.

Through the two-foot-high grass, Dutch crawled alongside the officer. The man was belly-down, his face tilted to the side, his eyes vacant.

"Let's go," commanded Eagle, grabbing the back of Dutch's shirt collar and lifting him to his feet. They ran toward the jungle. The moon disappeared and the compound darkened again.

As the HIT bullets ricocheted off the metal-alloy storm doorway, Ray dropped back below ground. The smoke drifted across the doorway. He shouted into his mike, "I need covering fire!"

*   *   *

Through the NV-scope, ECHO's Spiers scanned through the smoky haze for a clean shot. Nothing. He switched to the thermal-scope. "I got eyes on target," he said, watching the thermal image of a man crawling toward Kat.

"Take the shot," instructed Graves.

The HIT bullet ripped into the man's flank with a bluish flash. He dropped instantly. Kat crawled next to the downed man. He was unresponsive, his breathing shallow. "Jim!" Kat cried, instantly recognizing the man as Petty Officer-First Class Jim Reynolds. "Stop shooting!" she screamed frantically, seeing the black uniform. "They've changed uniforms!"

"Cease fire!" Graves shouted. "Cease fire!"

*   *   *

Before making his break, Ray glanced one last time at his PDA. One icon was missing. Cordova had disappeared from the plexus monitoring. Cautiously, Ray eased to the top step and lifted his weapon above ground, quickly scanning around the storm door. The spinning seven-inch tactical knife pounded into Ray's chest, just below his right collarbone. Cordova had hit his mark.

In the next second, Cordova appeared, lunging and colliding into Ray. The two fell back onto the stairwell and bounced violently down the flight of steps, their limbs flailing and striking each step and one another on the way down.

*   *   *

BUENAVENTURA
COLOMBIA, SOUTH AMERICA
JUNE 6; 0430

Landing in a Cessna-550 twin-engine jet at the airport in Buenaventura, Colombia, the NSA's Red Team hacker Caldwell gazed through the side window and into the black jungle as the plane rolled to a stop. He unbuckled the seatbelt, eased out of his seat, and moved hesitatingly into the aisle and down toward the front of the plane. The cabin door swung open. A wall of hot, humid air slammed against his face. Stepping down the short metal stairwell and onto the cracked, concrete tarmac, he glanced up at the night sky. The stars reminded him of lying in a dark, grassy field in his hometown as a child. Two men approached from the distance.

"Dr. Caldwell, welcome," Mercado said warmly, extending his hand. "This is Lieutenant Rodgers, ECHO's team leader."

Standing eye-to-eye with Caldwell, Rodgers seemed much taller than his five feet eight inches. With broad shoulders and a vice-grip handshake, Rodgers' shaved, balding scalp accentuated his chiseled jawline, prominent cheeks, and steely blue-gray eyes.

"Dr. Caldwell, sorry to move so quickly, but there's no time to waste," Rodgers said briefly. "Let's get you onboard. We'll answer all your questions once we're airborne."

The two directed Caldwell across the tarmac to the C-130 Hercules, a four-engine turboprop transport aircraft already boarded with ECHO. Caldwell climbed the rear ramp and stepped aboard, nodding as he passed by each SEAL until he was seated near the front of the plane. Moments later, the plane rolled down the runway, picked up speed, lurched slightly and lifted off.

Lightheaded, Caldwell shifted nervously in his seat as sweat beaded on his forehead. His face became increasingly pale as his nausea and fear about the operation worsened with the sharp elevation gain.

Seated next to Caldwell was a towering black man with a pockmarked face. "Don't fly much non-commercial, do you?" yelled Samuel Brooks over the roar of the engines.

"I don't fly much, period!" Caldwell acknowledged.

"Motion sickness is always worst with takeoffs and landings. You'll feel better soon. And since we're HAHOing, don't have to worry about the landing," Brooks smiled and winked.

Not amused, Caldwell wiped the sweat from his brow and glared at Brooks. Brooks reached out, handing Caldwell the nasal cannula, a two-pronged plastic tubing that supplied oxygen into each nostril. "What's this?" Caldwell asked, puzzled.

"Oxygen on demand," Brooks replied. "This bird's only been shipping supplies for the last decade. You might need a little extra O2 while you get used to the change in cabin pressure."

Caldwell placed the cannula into his nose and fitted the tubing over his ears to keep it in place. He took a breath through his nose as he felt two bursts of oxygen. For the moment, he breathed easier.

CHAPTER 20 PARACHUTING

Exercise Day: Two

COMPOUND FIVE
JUNE 6; 0432 (LOCAL TIME)

CORDOVA AWOKE to a sharp pain in his right thigh. He sensed the cinching tourniquet, a thin rubber strap, high up on his leg. Dark red blood oozed from his blackened leg wound.

With his right eye swollen shut, Cordova squinted through his left eye. Corpsman Campbell, YUMA's medical specialist, kneeled beside him. With a pair of heavy trauma shears, Campbell sliced the pants leg apart, exposing the steel shank—a piece of the hinge from the exploded emergency-access door—embedded in Cordova's leg.

"You with us?" Campbell asked as he worked.

"Uh-huh," Cordova mumbled groggily.

"Do you want morphine?" Campbell asked.

"Is the Control Center secure?" Cordova groaned.

"Yes," Campbell replied, glancing up as Spiers and Rock approached the motionless intruder's body.

"Do it," Cordova sighed. Campbell carefully peeled away Cordova's singed and torn shirtsleeve and stabbed the pre-loaded morphine syringe into his right deltoid. Ten milligrams of morphine, en route to his bloodstream, filled the muscle.

With weapons drawn and targeted, Spiers and Rock moved

closer to the unknown intruder's body. Blood pooled around the knife still embedded in his chest. Quiet transmission crackled through the downed man's earpiece. Spiers kneeled and pulled the headset off, bringing it close to his left ear. "Ray? This is Eagle. Do you copy?" transmitted through the piece.

*   *   *

COMPOUND FIVE
JUNE 6; 0441

Eagle, Skreemer, and Dutch re-grouped a quarter-mile northwest of the C3. Two hostages made it to the treeline with them. Two did not. Through the darkness, Eagle forced the two uncertain captives away from the C3, ensuring they were again blindfolded and restrained after the trek.

"What happened back there?" Skreemer asked.

"That officer attacked me," Dutch said hesitantly, unsure whether the others had witnessed him taking the lieutenant to the ground.

"Y'okay?"

"I'm fine," Dutch said, massaging his right temple. The lieutenant's vacant eyes flashed through his mind.

"We gotta go back," Skreemer panted.

"Forget it," Eagle replied tersely. "We can't go back."

"What about Ray?" Skreemer asked.

"Ray's gone," Eagle retorted. "They either have him or he's dead. Either way—makes no difference. We're not goin' back."

Skreemer pulled his PDA strapped to his waist back into view. Still no sign of YUMA. Instead, the screen was illuminated with icons symbolizing the British CT unit positioned at their exit, Gate Two. "We've got another problem," he stated.

"I know," Eagle nodded. "They've been movin' along the beach for several hours. I was hopin' they'd break away. We've got no choice. We wait."

*   *   *

COMPOUND FIVE
JUNE 6; 0523

Staff Sergeant James Osborne, a fifteen-year veteran of the British 22 Regiment Special Air Service, brought his CT unit to the western coast of Compound Five, just outside of Gate Two. Ten hours had passed since Osborne's last communication with command on USS *Ronald Reagan*. The overhead screams of the F-18s were now silenced. The explosive boom and crackling of gunfire had quieted.

Down on one knee, Osborne reached out with his right hand, touching the neck of the downed American Marine. His pale skin was as cool as the night air. He turned, faced the fellow operator kneeling beside him, and shook his head.

"Sir, we found another body," a third operator informed him.

"American?"

"A woman."

Osborne keyed his mike, then announced, "Prepare to clear this area. Assume live fire. This is no longer an exercise."

*   *   *

COMPOUND FIVE
JUNE 6; 0610

"I'm okay," Kat stated firmly, as Campbell flashed a penlight in her eyes. She was seated at the Northern Terminal Workstation. Rock and Graves returned to the workstation, having cleared the lower level of the Construct Control Center and finding no one.

"Miss, an explosive charge knocked you unconscious," Campbell said patiently. "Let me check you out."

"I'm fine," she insisted.

After being rebuffed by Kat, Campbell turned his attention to the injured petty officer.

Kat swiveled around in her chair, turning to face the wall-sized LCD behind her. The glass spidered from the bullet hole a few inches off-center. Her disoriented mind tried to focus on the face of the man who had disrupted the gunfire intended for her.

Turning back, she glanced down the computer room. Her eyes followed a bloodstain streaking along the off-white tile floor until it ended at the injured Cordova, his leg tightly bound with a tourniquet. A few feet away, Ray's body was positioned against the wall.

The once dead, now shocked-back-to-life Spiers slouched in a computer workstation chair along the eastern wall. Jim Reynolds, the wounded petty officer, was laid out on the floor, still alive. Campbell, now kneeling beside Reynolds, began cleaning the dried blood caked across the sailor's face.

Rock and Graves gravitated to the monitor of the Southern Terminal Workstation. From that distance, Kat was not able to make out the text flashing on the screen. The men's voices were barely audible.

Kat stood, swaying slightly with dizziness, then began walking by Campbell and moving toward the other end of the workstation. For the first time, she felt the swollen knot on the back of her head and the stiffness in her whiplashed neck. As she reached Rock and Graves, she noticed the lines of text flashing on the monitor. It appeared as though a computer program was assembling. The screen read:

PM2103T92 module construction in progress...
Completed.... Subsection 8 now 95% complete.
XP3882F82 module construction in progress....
Completed.... Subsection 8 now 97% complete.
TQM282F9 module construction in progress...
Completed... Subsection 8 now 100% complete.
Subsection 8 integrated.

Lynx Prion 91% reconstructed.
Proceeding to Module 9 construction.
TS28FM8 module construction in progress...

"What is it?" Graves demanded. "What the hell is a Lynx Prion?"

"Not exactly sure," Kat replied. "But a prion, if it even exists, acts sort of like a computer virus."

"Is this system connected to all Intelink networks? SIPRNet too?" Graves asked.

"Yes."

"Can we cut the hard line? Turn the damn thing off?"

"That'll only make things worse," Kat said. "I still don't understand the source of that communication. Reynolds said nobody in his group sent a message. There was no opportunity to do so."

"Might be a trap. Hold off on making any contact," Graves replied.

"One of them saved my life. Kicked out the weapon aimed right at me," Kat said.

"It's hard to know what really happened. Things were moving fast. A lot was going on," he replied.

"I know what I saw," she said firmly.

"We need to focus on regaining control of this compound," Graves insisted. "Is it possible to track the men that were in here on the surface via the plexus?"

"I can try," Kat replied.

* * *

COMPOUND FIVE
JUNE 6; 0832

Dutch and Skreemer held position a mile northwest from the Construct Control Center. Positioned just out of earshot, Eagle held guard over the two blindfolded captives.

"Why the hell are they still there?" Skreemer glanced at his PDA in frustration, watching the SAS team still positioned close to the gate, unknowingly blocking their escape route.

"What went so wrong?" Dutch asked in disbelief.

"We should be off this island already," Skreemer whispered. "Why did they have to send in those damn Marines? That fucked up everything."

"Stop bullshitting me. What are you hiding from me? What are you really after?" Dutch asked harshly.

Skreemer locked eyes with Dutch. "Okay," he said, turning to locate Eagle before continuing. Skreemer looked back at Dutch, who was still staring at him, his eyes like daggers. "Four years ago, we started hacking into foreign computer systems. A few times, we ran across some scary shit, to the say the least—information describing attacks against the continental United States. And I'm talking computer and bioterror attacks. A few months later, we started anonymously feeding this intel to the Agency. We figured it was the right thing to do."

"The CIA?"

"For six months, we gave those guys intel," Skreemer nodded. "When all of it checked out, it made 'em nervous. We had intercepted e-mails between Middle-Eastern-based terror networks to their networks' access codes. It wasn't easy. In the end, we all decided we should get some *real* money for supplying this info. The agency agreed to pay us $200 grand. But when it came to payday, they tried to bait us instead. We came close to biting, but none of us did. Now, they don't know whether we're one or many. We used no codenames. That's the reason for the secure lines and the throw-away computers."

"You've been fucking around with the CIA like that?" Dutch exclaimed.

"Hey, they're fucking with us!" Skreemer responded bitterly.

"So this is all about revenge? You've lost your damn mind!"

"It's leverage, Dutch," Skreemer objected.

"Leverage for what?"

"Two hundred and fifty million bucks," Skreemer replied without hesitation.

"As I remember, the U.S. has a policy not to give in to terrorists' demands," Dutch said.

"We're not terrorists," Skreemer replied. "Listen. You have to understand; the NSA, CIA, DARPA, and Navy—they all have secrets they keep from the Pentagon, even the White House. They even have their own internal secrets. Hell, things are no different than Frank Church's rogue elephant on a rampage. So, a couple million dollars to them—and they have very deep pockets—to keep things quiet is nothing. It's a drop in the bucket."

"What do you mean, 'rogue elephant'?" Dutch asked.

"Ever hear of Frank Church?"

"No," Dutch replied, looking around nervously.

"Church was a senator in the '70s during the investigation of the Agency. He referred to the CIA, FBI, and all the intelligence community combined as a 'rogue elephant rampaging out of control.' This is not an isolated situation. We're dealing with secrets that are bigger than any of that," Skreemer stated emphatically.

"The next big terrorist attack won't be from bombs or planes, but from computers," Skreemer continued. "There are across-the-board vulnerabilities throughout the entire North American computer infrastructure: from multi-national corporations to financial institutions to the Internet. Electronic warfare is far more devastating than any warhead. I know for a fact that there are gaping holes in the U.S. security systems. They think their new Cyber Command center will help. They don't stand a chance without us. I don't have all the answers, Dutch, but if they hadn't tried to screw us over, we would've been able to fill some of those holes. Fuck them. This is a way for us to make a statement."

"All this to 'make a statement,'" Dutch repeated, shocked. "This is your country! People are dead, Skreemer."

"I never wanted any of that to happen," Skreemer apologized. "I certainly never intended for anybody to die. Hell, the Marines took us by surprise. I didn't know Ray was such a loose cannon. And according to Eagle, he had no idea Wolfe activated the HIT bullets to be lethal."

"You've made me an accomplice to *murder*," Dutch said angrily.

"They'll never know we were here," Skreemer said.

"I'll know," Dutch replied.

*   *   *

AIRSPACE NEAR COMPOUND FIVE
JUNE 6; 1228

Over sixty years ago on this day, Allied Forces had invaded Normandy during Operation Overlord in World War II. The coincidence did not go unnoticed by ECHO.

For nearly twelve hours, the near-deafening engines of the C-130 Hercules roared 20,000 feet above the storm-gray Pacific. The rugged aircraft thrashed about as it passed through a series of up-and-down drafts and darkening clouds. The pilot—an eighteen-year Navy veteran who had served in Iraq and Afghanistan—closely watched the radar on the center console. Moments later, he eased the black steel control stick left, then gently rolled the aircraft closer to C5 in preparation for the HAHO insertion, mindful of the risk posed by medium-range surface-to-air missiles.

"Twenty minutes," he said into the mike.

The crew chief pulled down one side of his ear set and shouted over his right shoulder toward the cabin, "Twenty minutes!"

Seated in one of the forty-two fold-down wall seats lining the gray-colored bulkhead, NSA hacker Ryan Caldwell glanced across the cabin, out the tiny circular bay windows, and into the cloud-darkened sky. An occasional burst of sunlight flashed between the dark clouds and pierced the shadows inside the cabin. Ashen, Caldwell leaned forward, positioned his elbows on both knees, and lowered his head. He slowed his breathing, hoping to control the nausea, as saliva pooled under his tongue.

"Let's jock up!" Lieutenant Rodgers shouted above the roar of the engines.

Rick Chance, ECHO's lead jumper, lifted the helmet apparatus—goggles and oxygen mask affixed—and slid it snugly onto his head. The goggles rested atop the helmet above his eyes. With oxygen mask attached to one side, he pulled it up and over his nose and mouth, snapping and securing the other side to the helmet.

After first checking that the inhalation and exhalation valves functioned properly, Chance then turned the tiny circular knob of the oxygen tank. As bursts of oxygen filtered into the mask, he began to inhale deeply. Oxygen-rich air filled his lungs.

With both hands, he then positioned the tinted goggles over his eyes; his face was no longer visible. He stood up, moved next to Caldwell, and began securing their two harnesses together.

"Turn on your rescue transponder," Chance shouted to Caldwell. "Otherwise, the plexus will ID you as an intruder and you'll get us both killed when we land."

Chance reached down with a shaky hand, flipping the switch on the transponder strapped tightly around his ankle. A dim green LED light emitted from the device.

"Six minutes!" Rodgers alerted loudly.

"Six minutes!" each SEAL shouted back.

"When the ramp opens, we go," Chance bellowed at Caldwell through his oxygen mask. "Follow my lead."

The crew chief affixed and tightened his aircrew mask in anticipation of the drop in oxygen with ramp opening. He then exited the cockpit, moved past the SEALs, and reached the rear of the aircraft. As the ten-foot-long rear ramp opened, a blast of wind rushed into the plane's bay. Chance nudged Caldwell toward the ramp opening as Caldwell shuffled nervously toward the rear of the aircraft. Caldwell vainly attempted to control his shaking knees as he stared into the cloud-covered, darkening noon sky filling the void of the open ramp door.

The jump-signal monitor went from red to black. A second later, it flashed green.

"Go! Go! Go!" the crew chief commanded above the prop blast and the wind.

Caldwell hesitated momentarily. Chance slapped Caldwell's shoulder and the two men pushed ahead until they hurled off the ramp's edge into the whirling, roaring space 20,000 feet above the earth. Grasping the ripcord tightly in his right hand, Chance waited and stared at his wrist-mounted altimeter.

At 18,500 feet, he yanked the cord with a quick jerk.

The world was suddenly silent again. The aircraft droned in the distance. The two swung below a full canopy.

"You okay?" Chance shouted.

Caldwell, dizzy, shivering, with pulse racing, raised a shaky thumbs-up.

* * *

NSW COMMAND
JUNE 6; 1242

Lieutenant JG Daniel Janssen from the NavSpecWar Comm's Data Acquisition Center appeared on the teleconferencing flat-screen at Rear Admiral Nicholas Briley's right. The computer-security expert nervously adjusted his oval-lensed glasses and shifted in his seat as he prepared to deliver the message to Briley at the NSW command operations room.

"Lieutenant Janssen, I've already been briefed on the concerns regarding the integrity of the Intelink's security," Briley began. "Where do we stand?"

"The Intelink is currently secure, sir," Janssen replied hesitantly.

"Currently?"

"Sir, we've been tracking the source of several attacks," Janssen continued. "Most of which have led to zombie systems."

"Zombie systems?"

"Sorry, sir. Zombies are computers that are infected with code that can attack other computers on command at a later date. For the past few hours, we've tracked down systems in Russia, China, South Korea, Australia—all over the world. Hundreds of systems are attacking our Intelink. But one attack is unique. It's originating somewhere in the South Pacific. There's a top-level security DARPA system connected to the Intelink there. We're essentially being attacked by one of our own systems, sir."

"Can't you just cut off that connection?"

"Unfortunately, that's not possible."

"What happens if they gain access?"

"Sir, they could insert a virus, a worm, some other malicious program."

"What happens then?"

"Potentially, sir, they could take down the entire network," Janssen replied. "Meaning, we'd get knocked back to the 19th century militarily. Limited communication. Limited situational awareness. Extensive exposure."

"Lieutenant, we're working on eliminating the source of the attack," Briley assured him. "Please keep me advised of any changes."

"Aye aye, sir." The teleconferencing monitor went blank.

"What's the status of the SEAL insertion?" Briley looked around at the other officers in the room.

"The jump is ongoing as we speak, sir," said an officer seated at the table.

"Admiral, ECHO is aware of the time constraints," another officer added. "We're prepared for a strike at 1600 on the C5 Control Center."

*　　*　　*

COMPOUND FIVE
JUNE 6; 1247

The HAHO parachute pitched and yawed unsteadily in the turbulent wind as Chance directed himself and Caldwell toward C5. The hard rain drummed against the parachute's airfoil fabric. Through rain-beaded goggles, Chance glanced down at the island. The eighty-foot-tall cliffs, which in the distance appeared almost flat, were rapidly growing taller. A barely-visible haze of whitewater at the cliff's base marked the presence of the violent, unwelcoming ocean. He felt along his jumpsuit, then grasped his GPS, tilting it toward his eyes; they were only five hundred yards out.

Unsure if they could cover the distance and make it onto the island, Chance thought through the backup plan: using infrared strobes to locate the team in the ocean, then a short swim to the island.

"We're not gonna make it," Caldwell shouted.

"Hang on!" Chance shouted back, as his altimeter read 100 feet above the Compound, only twenty feet above the cliff top. Seconds later, the tandem parachutists headed directly toward the cliff peak, horrified to realize they were a few feet too low.

Chance frantically pulled down on the hand controls of the HAHO rigging. The men hovered momentarily.

Then an up-gust lifted them several feet, jerking the chute forward. Their boots grazed and skidded along the corrugated cliff top as they attempted to establish footing.

The chute lost lift. Wham!

The force of the ground sent the two tumbling, as they tucked their arms and legs in, sliding and rolling. Before they even stopped, a strong back-gust jerked the chute, pulling them back toward the cliff's edge. Chance punched the release mechanism in the center of his chest, instantly freeing the parachute canopy. It whipped over the edge of the cliff and away towards the crashing sea.

Just a few feet from the cliff's edge, Chance quickly unhooked the tandem link. "Let's go! Let's go!" he yelled, moving toward the distant tree line. Caldwell stood straight up and limped toward the tree canopy. "Dammit! Stay low," Chance shouted.

Having covered the distance quickly, the remaining ECHO parachutists cleared the treetops and landed at the island's center. The six SEALs—Brooks, Drakowski, Tyler, Mitchell, Mann, and Rodgers—re-grouped at the northern treeline outside the Construct Control Center.

ECHO leader Rodgers glanced across the grassy field. A wispy fog obscured the scant light that reached the ground. The partially open access door and the dismantled concrete helipad were clearly visible. He pulled down his helmet-mounted eyepiece, locating Chance and Caldwell on the GPS monitor.

"This is ECHO One," Rodgers spoke into his mike. "It'll take ECHO Two and ECHO Eight around thirty minutes to reach us. ECHO Five, work on contact with YUMA."

Using YUMA's communication decryption codes, radioman Tyler scanned through commonly-used frequencies. He keyed his mike and said insistently, "YUMA. YUMA. This is ECHO Five. Contact friendly on one-two-five-decimal-seven-five."

There was no response.

"YUMA. Do you copy?" Tyler said. "I repeat, YUMA, are you there?"

Nothing.

"ECHO, get ready to move. We're goin' in," Rodgers said.

CHAPTER 21 SPYDER

Exercise Day: Two

HALF-MILE NORTHWEST OF CONSTRUCT CONTROL CENTER
JUNE 6; 1325 (LOCAL TIME)

EAGLE, SKREEMER, AND DUTCH, along with the two blindfolded hostages, scrambled to reach a point one-half mile northwest of the Construct Control Center.

Perched behind a patch of dense trees, Dutch held watch over Lieutenant Commander Justin Channing, a dozen yards away from the other men. "Who are you? Why are you doing this?" Channing asked, his voice low and shaky. "Don't talk," Dutch said firmly. "I won't let them hurt you," he whispered.

Dutch's eyes flashed back and forth between Eagle and Skreemer and the other hostage. Eagle's face tightened as he stared at his PDA. "Are you seeing this?" he asked Skreemer, his voice tense.

Skreemer, positioned a few feet from Eagle, pulled his own PDA into view. Seven new ID signatures registered on the plexus grid. Two icons appeared at the northernmost tip of the island. The other five icons surrounded the C3.

"What is it?" Dutch fumbled to grab his PDA.

"More trouble," Eagle said grimly.

"How'd they get inside?" wondered Skreemer.

"Likely parachuted," Eagle replied. "There could be more."

"Who are they?"

"Not sure. Special Ops. Maybe Rangers," Eagle responded. "Listen up. We need to mobilize. The SAS has been slowly moving our way for over an hour."

"What about them?" Skreemer pointed at the two captive men.

"Two will slow us down," Eagle whispered to Skreemer, out of earshot of the other men. "But let's keep one for safe passage outta here," he continued, pointing at Channing in the distance.

"What about the other?" Skreemer asked quietly.

"I'll take care of him," Eagle whispered. "We're goin' north."

"But there're two men on the grid moving south, right at us," countered Skreemer.

"We can maneuver around them," Eagle asserted. "Remember, we know exactly where they are."

Skreemer nodded his assent.

"Move out!" Eagle commanded. "I'll catch up in a minute."

"Get up!" ordered Skreemer abruptly as he joined Dutch and Channing.

"Where we going?" Channing stammered.

"No talking," Skreemer cautioned, hoisting him up to his feet. Dutch, Skreemer, and their captive Channing headed north.

Eagle stayed behind. From his right pants pocket, he retrieved a small 100-milliliter vial labeled "Ketamine HCl Inj. HSP" along with a needle and syringe. He filled the syringe with the viscous liquid ketamine—a dissociative anesthetic with LSD-like properties. "Time for a nap," he muttered under his breath.

He moved next to the chief petty officer. Beading sweat covered the man's forehead, and his hands trembled at his side.

Eagle jabbed the needle deep into the man's thigh. The CPO jerked his leg in reaction to the sharp pain as Eagle forced him to the ground. The ketamine pooled within his muscle, then filtered into his bloodstream as he thrashed his arms and legs in vain.

Easily overpowering his captive, Eagle finished administering the entire syringe. It was ten times the amount used for general anesthesia, ensuring the sailor would not wake up for hours. It would take several minutes for the ketamine to take full effect. The CPO, feeling Eagle's weight lift off of him, yanked off the blindfold.

Eagle was already gone.

*　　*　　*

CONSTRUCT CONTROL CENTER
COMPOUND FIVE
JUNE 6; 1345

Victor Drakowski, a seven-year DEVGRU veteran and demolition specialist, molded the C4 plastic explosive into thick strips and pressed the modeling-clay-like putty into the crease of the in-ground doorframe. Every few seconds, he glanced up and panned across the Construct Control Center's immediate area. The warped steel of the exploded, partially open C3 emergency exit door was off to his left. The closed main entrance in-ground door remained shut to his right. The silence was unnerving.

As Drakowski moved around the in-ground chamber door, the crumbled chunks of concrete and dust slid beneath his boots. He continued working until nearly two pounds of explosives were packed along every inch of the doorframe.

Finished at last, he firmly pushed the detonating-cord clips— roughly the size of small pencils—into the off-white C4, then moved back fifty feet. He flipped up the remote detonator and positioned himself flat against the ground. "ECHO One, this is ECHO Four. The plastic's ready," he announced into the mike.

"ECHO Four, copy, fire 'em up," team leader Rodgers replied.

"Fire in the hole," Drakowski whispered as he flipped the detonator toggle switch up.

A red-orange blast flashed. A deep boom sounded. The earth rumbled. Concrete and dust were thrown into the air. The seven-inch-thick door was ripped loose from the frame; it cartwheeled ten feet down into the mainframe chamber. "ECHO. Move!" Rodgers shouted.

*   *   *

NORTHERN REGION OF COMPOUND FIVE
JUNE 6; 1349

The faint boom of the C4 explosive caught Chance's ears as he and Caldwell began the trek toward the island's center. Red, brown, and black rock formations—created by the settling ash from volcanic eruptions millions of years ago—glistened in the rain. The salty air whistled across the wind-beaten rocks.

Scattered trees and rare patches of tall grass offered little cover. The dense treeline was far in the distance. Instead, the man-sized gaps and spaces between the slabs and boulders created numerous hiding places.

"Hmmm, don't like this at all," Chance whispered, scanning across the rock field with his helmet-mounted monocle eyepiece—first with night vision, then infrared. "Too many places to hide."

He switched his head-up display to track his team members. Black icons representing ECHO illuminated the thumb-sized screen, showing ECHO infiltrating the Construct Control Center.

"What should I do?" Caldwell asked nervously.

"Stay here," Chance instructed. "Scan the airwaves and get us some intel. Let me check out what's ahead."

"Okay," Caldwell nodded. He nestled deeper into a two-foot rock divot covered by a three-ton rock slab. He pulled his pack close, extracted his handheld PDA, and began pecking away with his stylus. Looking up, he noticed that Chance had disappeared.

Caldwell tapped on an NSA scanner program and searched

the communication networks. Two comm frequencies were active. One comm was securely encrypted. The other had antiquated technology.

He tapped on the decryption program. Seconds later, he listened in on the comm.

"Let's keep movin'," crackled into Caldwell's headset. "They're trackin' us."

"Du—," he heard. "—movin'" came through brokenly. "Dutch! Come on."

In disbelief, Caldwell jerked his head up abruptly, pounding it into the slab. Trying to listen again, he lowered his head back down, rubbing the painful knot forming on his scalp. "Skreemer, shouldn't we wait for Eagle?" he heard.

The comm was from a voice he had not heard in twenty years. A voice he could never forget.

*   *   *

CONSTRUCT CONTROL CENTER
COMPOUND FIVE
JUNE 6; 1350

One by one, ECHO jumped into the twelve-foot-high chamber and moved through the haze of thick debris and dust, taking cover behind the closest standing mainframe column. Several of the nearest columns were no longer upright. The smell of fresh C4 and charred steel wafted through the air. The emergency fire-sprinkler system triggered, and water sprayed like a torrential rain from the ceiling.

Drakowski dashed down the hallway to the access door of the computer room and stood at the door's right side. All weapons were aimed at the door.

"This is Lieutenant Drakowski. U.S. Navy! Identify yourself!"

No response.

Drakowski signaled to Mann, waving him over.

Mann paced down the hall, popped the black side-panel open, inserted a CAC keycard, and entered the access code.

"This is Lieutenant Drakowski," he began again.

The hydraulic locks hissed, then clicked in three-burst pops.

"Stand down," a muffled voice sounded from the opposite side of the steel mainframe chamber door. "This is Lieutenant Graves of Team Six. Stand down."

"Put your weapons down; we are coming in!" Drakowski shouted.

"We cannot comply. Please verify your identity," Graves yelled back.

"This is a SEAL team. Put your weapons down. Hands in the air until we verify your identity," Drakowski repeated.

"Who's your team leader?" YUMA's Graves asked.

"Lieutenant John Rodgers," Drawkowski replied.

Five seconds of silence ticked slowly by. "Okay, we're opening the door," Graves complied. The door eased open. Rodgers was the first to enter, his weapon down.

"Damn, we're glad to see you!" Graves exclaimed as the two made eye contact.

*   *   *

NORTHERN REGION OF COMPOUND FIVE
JUNE 6; 1406

With his body pressed tightly against the sharp volcanic rock, Caldwell hunkered down in the two-foot crease. He nervously glanced back and forth across the rock field.

"ECHO Two, ECHO Leader. Copy?" transmitted into Caldwell's headset.

"Copy, ECHO Two. Be advised," Rodgers replied to Chance. "We've confirmed the presence of a rogue team with hostages.

I repeat. Unknown number of tangos—at least three—with two hostages. They may have switched uniforms with the hostages. Proceed with caution."

"ECHO Leader, I've visualized tangos. Need assistance," Chance said.

"I'm mobilizing help. We're three klicks away," Rodgers affirmed.

"Copy that. Out."

"ECHO Eight, ECHO Two. Do you copy?" Chance asked Caldwell.

"Copy that."

"ECHO Eight, four men are headed our way," Chance continued. "Stay put until I get back to you."

"Where the hell are you?" Caldwell demanded.

"Close by," Chance replied. "Stay off comm for now. Watch for hostiles. Out."

For ten minutes, Caldwell waited and listened. The sun filtered through the dark clouds, flashing shadows amidst the jagged rock formations. The wind whistled across the glistening wet rocks. Then, directly in front of him...movement.

One man drifted in and out of sight between rock formations, no more than thirty feet away. Caldwell pointed his 9mm Glock straight ahead.

Suddenly, the man appeared, his dark eyes directed at Caldwell's hiding place. The adversary lifted his weapon while retreating for cover. Caldwell apprehensively popped off two shots, then gasped in surprise as the second bullet hit its mark. The man dropped to the ground, now out of sight behind a small outcropping of boulders.

Caldwell drew himself further back into the already tight hiding place.

"ECHO Eight, ECHO Two here. You okay?" crackled into his headset.

"Fuck. I just shot somebody," Caldwell moaned.

"Stay where you are. I'm headed your way."

"Copy that."

"Dutch is down...Skreemer, get outta there," crackled into Caldwell's headset from the intercepted signal.

Caldwell eased out of the rock opening and scurried to the nearby boulder. A tiny streak of dark-red blood was spattered on the boulder. With weapon ready, he inched closer and moved around the boulder.

The man had pulled his injured left arm, bent at the elbow, tightly to his body. He held his gun loosely in his right hand.

"Drop the gun!" Caldwell shouted.

Dutch dropped the Beretta to the ground. With his right hand, he put pressure on the bleeding wound in his left shoulder.

"What's your name?" Caldwell demanded.

"John."

"John what?" Caldwell pressed.

"N-N-Newark. John Newark," Dutch replied.

Caldwell dropped to one knee.

Dutch looked up. His blood-shot eyes widened. He blinked several times.

"Spyder?"

CHAPTER 22 NEW STORM

Exercise Day: Two

CONSTRUCT CONTROL CENTER
JUNE 6; 1407 (LOCAL TIME)

"WHO'S THAT?" ECHO's Lieutenant Rodgers said, glancing at the only woman in the room.

"Kat Lange," replied Graves, YUMA's team leader. "Works for one of the defense contractors. She was stationed here for the exercise. The only one who escaped."

"Can we trust her?"

"Yeah. She was the first to inform of us of the intruders."

"Wait a second," Kat said. "You don't need to talk as if I'm not here. I can speak for myself."

"Good. We'll need your expertise," Rodgers said. "We've got a carrier off the coast, and I can tell you, at 1600 this Control Center is gonna get blasted unless we make contact with the CIC," he continued, referencing the Combat Information Center.

"Tyler!" Rodgers called ECHO's radioman over. "I need you workin' with Ms. Lange. Contact CIC yesterday!"

"Aye aye, sir," Tyler replied.

Rodgers turned to the others. "Brooks. Drakowski. Mann. Mitchell. Ready to move out. Let's get to Chance."

"Need anyone from my team?" Lieutenant Graves asked.

"Your guys look pretty banged up," Rodgers noted. "Best they stay here."

The five SEALS clambered up the stairs, waited for the in-ground door to open, then disappeared above ground.

Jack Tyler—a six-foot-four SEAL with his face painted black and green—moved next to Kat as she pounded away at the workstation keyboard.

"Kat, this is Lieutenant Tyler," Graves stated. Kat swiveled around and away from the computer and stood as the two shook hands.

"Can we use this system to contact CIC?" Tyler asked.

"No. Still can't get through," she answered. "I'm completely locked out."

"Any idea what they're after?" Tyler said.

"Let me show you something," she said, leading them to the Southern Terminal Workstation area. "This workstation is linked to the SIPRNet," she continued. "I don't know much about it, because I don't have security clearance for this system."

Multiple lines of undecipherable combinations of letters and numbers lit up the LCD monitor.

Tyler scanned the text and read the last line: *Lynx Prion 97% reconstructed.*

"What's a Lynx Prion?" Tyler asked.

"This is gonna sound crazy," Kat began.

"I'm all ears," Tyler assured her.

"When I started at Edge Defense Industries, I worked for our cyber-protection division," Kat said. "That's the first time I heard of it. A prion is part of hacker lore. Bloggers talk of this super-worm or super-virus developed by the government. From what I remember, hackers say it's a data-stealing program that covertly strips the contents of the computer network, then leaves it ineffective and useless."

"Is it real?"

"Not sure," Kat said. "I've only heard of it through

underground hacking websites and blogs. Never could really find much on it."

"We have less than two hours to figure this out," Tyler said grimly.

*   *   *

NORTHERN REGION OF COMPOUND FIVE
JUNE 6; 1408

As he inched toward Spyder to get a closer look, Dutch bit his lip in an attempt to keep from crying out in pain from the wound in his shoulder.

"ECHO Eight, ECHO Eight, get outta there," the order to Caldwell crackled in his headset.

"Dutch?" Caldwell asked haltingly, Glock in hand.

"Get down!" Dutch cautioned. "They can see you."

"Who?"

"STORM!"

"Wha..." Caldwell began, still on one knee.

"Get down!" Dutch shouted.

Caldwell crouched lower to the ground as a round from an M4 carbine struck the tree behind the two men.

Muzzle flashes seventy yards out sparked as Chance returned fire.

Caldwell moved deeper into the depressed rock and toward the patch of trees lining the northern side of the small three-foot deep crater.

"Dutch, you okay? Copy?" came through Dutch's earpiece. Dutch did not respond.

Round after round chipped away at the wall of boulders shielding Caldwell.

"What's goin' on?" Caldwell shouted at Dutch above the gunfire.

"Our PDAs are linked to the plexus," Dutch yelled back. "We know where everyone is!"

"ECHO Eight, talk to me!" Chance shouted into his mike.

"I can't get out!" Caldwell replied above the crackling gunfire.

"What's the status of the tango?"

"He's alive, but hurt."

"ECHO Leader, copy?" crackled in Caldwell's earpiece.

"Copy, ECHO Two," Caldwell heard from Chance.

"We're under heavy fire," Chance continued. "ECHO Eight is pinned. Need an ETA on backup?"

"Ten minutes, over."

"Copy that. Out." Chance said. "ECHO Eight, stay where you are."

"Roger that," Caldwell replied.

Caldwell low-crawled toward Dutch, grabbed Dutch's Beretta off the ground, and quickly retreated several feet. Bullets zinged and popped inches above his head as pieces of chipped boulder dinged his helmet. He lifted his weapon between a crease in the boulders and squeezed off several blind shots.

"Why are you here?" he questioned Dutch.

"To finish the hack," Dutch responded. "Our hack. I didn't know about the rest."

"What are you talking about?" shouted Caldwell.

"The Intelink," Dutch replied.

"But you stopped hacking?"

"I did."

"Then what are you doin' here?" persisted Spyder.

"I came here with STORM."

"STORM?"

"Our STORM," Dutch repeated over the intermittent gunfire.

Caldwell sank back down into the crater-like rock depression, staring at Dutch.

"Dutch, STORM got busted four years ago."

"Bullshit," Dutch said, shaking his head.

"I'm a cryptanalyst and a Red Teamer for the NSA, Dutch. It's true."

*   *   *

Eagle filed in next to Skreemer while he alternated firing on the two positions of Caldwell and Chance. "How'd he get so much distance from you?" he wondered.

"I was focused on the hostage," Skreemer replied.

"What's Dutch's status?"

"No word from him yet," Skreemer shrugged.

"Then he's dead," Eagle declared. "We have to go."

"I'm not leavin' Dutch," insisted Skreemer.

"We don't have a choice," Eagle retorted. "There are SEALs moving in from the south. We've got Brits to the west. If we don't leave now, we're never gettin' out of here."

"Skreemer, copy?" broke through Skreemer's headset.

"Copy that, Dutch. You okay?" Skreemer asked eagerly.

"I'm captured."

Skreemer looked at Eagle, "We'll need him if we have trouble at the gates again."

"We'll do an exchange," Eagle frowned.

Eagle keyed his mike, "Dutch, we're sendin' over a hostage as an exchange. As soon as you get outta there, run. We'll provide cover fire." He turned to the hostage. "Get up," he ordered.

Lieutenant Commander Justin Channing did not move. "Get the fuck up!" Eagle shouted. Channing got to his knees.

"As soon as I take this blindfold off, do not look back," Eagle commanded.

*   *   *

"They wanna do an exchange," Dutch told Caldwell.

"Exchange?"

"Me, for one of the Control Center hostages."

"I can't do that," Caldwell replied.

"ECHO Two, they wanna exchange hostages," Caldwell conveyed to Chance.

"Do not release your captive," Chance replied.

"The officer they're holding is in danger," Dutch said. "I have to go."

"But I have orders to keep you here," persisted Caldwell.

"I'm going," Dutch stated firmly.

"I will shoot," Caldwell threatened.

"If I don't go, they will kill us both," Dutch stated grimly. "Please."

Dutch crawled toward Caldwell till he was only inches away. Caldwell's 9mm Glock was aimed squarely at Dutch's forehead.

"FIVE," Dutch announced.

"What?" Caldwell asked, his finger on the trigger.

"The backdoor is FIVE," Dutch replied, referring to the Construct Control Center's system.

Dutch eased by Caldwell and crawled up the wall toward the outcropping of boulders. Caldwell briefly glanced into the distance, spotting the nervous Channing walking toward him with hands high in the air.

Caldwell keyed his mike, "Hold your fire. That's one of the Control Center hostages."

"I didn't know," Dutch said. He briefly turned around, then disappeared around the boulder.

Caldwell lowered his weapon, struggling with conflicted emotions. His thoughts raced from his childhood friendship to his teenage hacking days to the present moment. Their friendship had ended one night twenty years ago, and now he felt even less connected to Dutch. Caldwell felt frustrated and disappointed that he was unable to pull the trigger on a man that had now betrayed him and appeared to be a terrorist.

*   *   *

"Now!" Eagle ordered as soon as he saw Dutch. Depressing the M4's trigger, he peppered the region around Chance with gunfire.

Skreemer simultaneously opened fire on Caldwell, drumming the outcropping of boulders with bullets.

There was no return fire.

At the sound of the first shot, the captive Channing hugged the dirt. Holding his injured left arm to his side, Dutch sprinted past Channing toward his teammates. Upon reaching Eagle and Skreemer, he dropped behind the trees and fronds.

"Y'okay?" Skreemer asked.

"I've been shot," Dutch replied, wincing in pain. "My arm."

"You can still run. Let's move out," directed Eagle.

*   *   *

NSW COMMAND
JUNE 6; 1421

"Sir, Mr. Edgewaters is on the horn."

"Put him through," Rear Admiral Briley responded. "Edgewaters, go ahead."

"Sir, we received a message originating from a server on Compound Five," Edgewaters reported.

"I was under the impression that all comm to C5 was blocked."

"The individual who sent the e-mail must have taken down the comm jammer temporarily, sir," Edgewaters replied.

"What's the message?"

"Lone Wolfe is the man you're looking for," Edgewaters said.

"Who sent the message?"

"Don't know, sir. But somebody on the inside is helping us. We've cross-referenced with NSA's database and found digital traffic involving that handle."

"Could be a diversion tactic," Briley said.

"Yes, sir; however, we've traced the origin of the ransom e-mail to L.A. Encrypted phone logs also tie the codename Lone Wolfe to East Hollywood. We should have the exact address within the hour."

"Excellent work, son. Keep us advised," Briley finished.

CHAPTER 23 LYNX

Exercise Day: Two

NORTHERN REGION OF COMPOUND FIVE
JUNE 6; 1423 (LOCAL TIME)

AS THE GUNFIRE CEASED, Chance sprinted to the crater and dropped in hard. His body slammed against the opposite wall next to Caldwell. "Y'okay?" he panted.

Caldwell shook his head, staring at the ground.

Chance flipped down his helmet-mounted monocular and peered south between two boulders at a narrow vista of the jungle.

Thirty yards out, the hostage was facedown in the dirt, his hands clasped behind his head.

"Are you hurt?" Chance shouted to him.

"No," he answered.

"Can you make it over here?"

"I think so."

"I got ya covered," Chance reassured the frightened man. The captive looked up and caught a glimpse of a muzzle between the bullet-marked boulders. Hesitantly, he low-crawled until he reached the boulders, moving to the left of the rocks and into the crater.

"Who are you?" Chance asked, keeping his M4 aimed at the man's head.

"Lieutenant Commander Justin Channing, U.S. Navy," the man

replied shakily.

"Y' hurt?"

"No."

"ECHO Two. This is ECHO leader," transmitted into Chance's headset.

"ECHO leader, go ahead," Chance replied into his mike.

"ETA: One minute," Lieutenant Rodgers said. "Coming from your six o'clock."

"They're here," Chance announced with relief.

* * *

NEAR GATE TWO
COMPOUND FIVE
JUNE 6; 1445

A quarter mile out from Gate Two, Dutch stopped to rest. Winded and dizzy, he leaned against the nearest tree, a thin pine. Dried blood cemented the shirt against his wounded shoulder. Unsure if his arm was broken, he attempted to raise his hand above his shoulder. "Fu—ck," he cried out in a whispering shout at least ten decibels below the sound of the wind.

Stretching of the torn skin and muscle from the gunshot wound sent searing pain to his fingertips. He quickly dropped his arm back to his side. With his right hand, he flipped up his PDA screen and located the other teams on the island.

The Brits had retreated southeast. Caldwell, Channing, and Chance were moving toward the Construct Control Center. ECHO—the new team on the compound—approached from the west.

"Dutch, we gotta keep movin," Skreemer said, backtracking.

"They're trackin' us," Eagle acknowledged. "Get to Gate Two. Get the boats ready. I'm gonna slow 'em down."

"We're outta time," Skreemer stated. "The sub's gonna leave anytime."

"No choice," Eagle retorted. "I have to slow 'em down or we're all dead. If I'm not back by 1515, go without me."

*   *   *

CONSTRUCT CONTROL CENTER
COMPOUND FIVE
JUNE 6; 1451

"Anything yet?" ECHO's Tyler asked Kat, leaning over her right shoulder as she worked at the computer terminal.

"Nothing," Kat sighed. "The network's locked."

"ECHO Two. This is ECHO Five," Tyler spoke into his mike.

"ECHO Five, go ahead," Chance replied.

"ETA?"

"Five mikes."

"Copy that. Out."

"We'll have our NSA hacker here soon," Tyler said, turning back to Kat.

Still working on access, Kat inserted a back-up network CAC card into the keyboard reader slot, entered a PIN, then pecked out several commands to reboot the network. Seconds later, the monitor revealed the security system status:

Network: Construct Control Center
Location: Compound Five
Classification: Top Secret
Authority: DARPA, U.S. Navy, Pentagon, NSA, DoD

SECURITY STATUS

Plexus:	*ACTIVE*
Perimeter Ocean:	*inactive*
Perimeter Gates:	*inactive*

Perimeter Beach (Smart-Mines):   *ACTIVE*
Surface-to-Air Missiles: *ACTIVE*
Radar: *ACTIVE*
Wireless Network: *ACTIVE*
Communication jammer: *ACTIVE*

Enter command:

"Finally, something," Kat muttered.

"Work on getting those SAMs deactivated and the comm jammer off," encouraged Tyler.

"Won't be easy," Kat replied.

"At least the mines are active," Tyler added. "If they're still on the island, there's no way they're getting off now."

*   *   *   **

NEAR GATE TWO
COMPOUND FIVE
JUNE 6; 1455

Skreemer headed up the hill leading to Gate Two. He spotted Skye's body and stopped midway. Easing next to her, he kneeled down on both knees. Her half-open brown eyes were vacant. He reached out and gently closed her eyes.

Dutch continued past Skreemer and climbed to the top of the small hill. The twelve-foot-high security fence was wide open. Dutch rubbed his eyes as the salty air hit his face, then glanced across the sandy beach at the dozen dead Marines. He took a deep breath as the cool air chilled his lungs.

"Let's go, Dutch," Skreemer urged, tugging on the stowed Zodiac.

Dutch walked over to assist, grabbing the rope railing on the left side as the two moved through the open gate and onto the beach embankment. The black volcanic cliffs towered above them on either side. The sun hid behind the dark clouds, leaving the great cliffs shadowed.

"You sure about the mines?" Skreemer asked sharply.

Dutch nodded hesitantly. Uneasily, he moved down the beach toward the surf. The terrific pain from his shoulder forced him to walk slowly. He glanced down at his boots as the sand slid beneath each step.

Click.

The sand seemed to harden beneath his boot as he stepped dead center on a mine. He knew it would detonate if he lifted his foot. His heart raced. "I'm on one," he mumbled.

*　　　*　　　*

Eagle placed the last block of C4 into the small dirt hole, covering it with nearby fallen leaves. An entourage of tripwires and plastic explosive now separated STORM from the pursuing ECHO team. He backtracked slowly, waiting as the team moved toward him. "SEALs," he mumbled as he watched their tactical movements on his PDA.

*　　　*　　　*

CONSTRUCT CONTROL CENTER
JUNE 6; 1502

Chance, Caldwell, and Channing arrived at the treeline outside the open field of the Construct Control Center.

"ECHO Seven, we're at the perimeter," Chance reported to Tyler.

"Roger that, ECHO Two. Openin' the door now," Tyler replied.

The team of three men sprinted across the field to the opening in-ground door and down into the Construct Control Center.

"We don't have much time," ECHO's Tyler said, meeting them

midway up the stairwell. "Kat Lange is the project engineer. She'll be updating you on the system." He moved down the stairwell into the Northern Terminal Workstation.

"Ryan Caldwell. NSA," Caldwell stammered breathlessly. He glanced at the spider-cracked monitor on the wall, then turned to face Kat.

"Been trying for an hour and haven't gotten far," Kat said briefly. "Whoever hacked this system is really good."

"What's the infiltration?"

"Hackers got into both systems," Kat explained, walking him to the terminal workstation. "The C3 and Intelink networks."

"NSA needs to know ASAP about the Intelink," Caldwell said.

"One other thing," Kat added. "Have you heard of the Lynx Prion?"

Caldwell said nothing. His eyes widened and his jaw dropped as he stared back at Kat.

"So it is real," Kat murmured.

"Show me," Caldwell said.

The two hurried over to the Southern Terminal Workstation, moving around the makeshift infirmary for the injured SEALs. As Caldwell looked up, *Lynx Prion 99% reconstructed* flashed across the screen.

"This is an inside job," Caldwell stated emphatically.

"What?" Kat asked incredulously.

"The Lynx Prion was created by the NSA," Caldwell replied. "I helped create it. But the pieces were stored separately. Only the NSA knew the locations. Even if located, it takes days to assemble."

"Not if you have ten Cray mainframes," Kat stated drily.

"I need a workstation," Caldwell said anxiously.

"Wait a minute," Kat said, grabbing Caldwell's wrist before he could walk away. "Is it spyware?"

"It's the next generation of viruses and worms," Caldwell replied. "Except these aren't created by amateurs. Shit, I shouldn't be telling you any of this."

"If we have any chance of stopping this, I need to know," Kat said.

Caldwell sighed. "The prion hides in the network, moving within the software to elude detection. Once inserted, you can never find it. Once received, it'll execute an order, then kill the operating system."

"Execute what?"

"Depends on the prion," Caldwell replied. "Remember the F-35C design secrets stolen from the Pentagon? That was a prion."

"What's the Lynx do?"

"Data stealer. It'll grab anything you want. If it's ordered to attack the Intelink, it could expose all our undercover operatives."

"Can it be stopped?"

"We tried to create a patch. Never could get one to work," Caldwell said, tugging gently away. "Our first priority is saving the operators on this island," he continued. "I have an idea but I need a workstation."

"Some of the connections are down due to mainframe damage," Kat informed him as the two walked back to the Northern Terminal Workstation area. "I've been trying everything to get through," she continued. "I've gotten nowhere."

Kat inserted her CAC keycard and entered the PIN. The terminal activated. *Username:* flashed at the bottom of the flat-screen monitor. Caldwell entered *FIVE*.

Password: appeared on the next line. Again, Caldwell entered *FIVE*. Instantly, *Access Denied* flashed across the screen.

"Dutch, you son of a bitch," Caldwell muttered under his breath.

"There's somebody on the island trying to communicate with me," Kat whispered. "I haven't responded because the SEALs think it's one of the terrorists. I think it's from the man that saved my life."

"What?"

"Somebody's trying to help us," Kat said.

"Give me your rescue PDA," Caldwell demanded, as she handed

it to him.

Caldwell pinged and located the origin of the message. "They're just outside Gate Two," Caldwell acknowleged, turning to Tyler. "They're trying to get off the island."

"We have our team heading there now," Tyler acknowledged. "I'll let 'em know."

*   *   *

NEAR GATE TWO
COMPOUND FIVE
JUNE 6; 1510

The booming concussion of a distant, detonating C4 charge hit Dutch's ears. Seconds later, gunfire began popping in the distance.

"Shit!" Dutch blurted.

"The mines aren't active," Skreemer reminded him.

"I don't trust it."

Skreemer set the Zodiac down and unclasped his seabag, pulling out an ammunition box.

"We'll do it together," Skreemer said, moving behind Dutch with ammo box in hand. "When I transfer weight onto the mine, we'll go!"

"Wait!" Dutch insisted.

"We have to do this."

"Spyder was the one who shot me," revealed Dutch.

"What?!"

"He told me STORM got busted four years ago."

"Spyder is NSA. He doesn't operate in the field," Skreemer said in disbelief.

"It's Spyder."

"Why would he be here? Why would he shoot you?" Skreemer replied surprised.

"So it's true... about STORM."

"It's complicated, Dutch," Skreemer sighed.

"How else would you know he's NSA?"

"I'll explain later. Right now we have to go."

Dutch nodded reluctantly.

"On three," Skreemer said. "One. Two. Three!"

As Dutch jumped off the mine, Skreemer placed the ammo box where his foot had been. They sprinted several steps and hit the deck.

Lying on the sand, Dutch and Skreemer turned to look at each other. There was no mine blast.

"You were right," Dutch said, breathing a sigh of relief.

"You're sure it was Spyder?" Skreemer asked incredulously.

"Absolutely."

"We'll talk about this later. For now, let's get off this godforsaken island."

The two men got back to their feet and finished dragging the boat across the minefield to the water, sensing the clicking of the mines beneath their feet.

Skreemer hurried back up the beach to retrieve the motor. As Dutch sat on the side of the boat to rest, he watched one of the dead Marines bobbing with the incoming waves at the shoreline.

Returning, Skreemer hoisted the motor up and slotted it into place on the Zodiac.

"You're not really Skreemer, are you?" Dutch prodded.

"Of course I am."

"How did you always make phone calls back then?" Dutch probed further.

"Payphones, of course," Skreemer stated without hesitation.

"Who was our South African contact on the TRW hack?"

"Rabbit Ears," Skreemer instantly replied.

"How the *hell* do you know all this?" Dutch fired back irately.

"I told you. I'm Skreemer," he replied as he glanced down at his watch, which read 1515. "It's time," he concluded.

CHAPTER 24 TRANSMISSION

Exercise Day: Two

CONSTRUCT CONTROL CENTER
COMPOUND FIVE
JUNE 6; 1516 (LOCAL TIME)

KNEELING NEAR the top of the exiting stairwell of the Construct Control Center, radioman Jack Tyler scanned the radio frequencies in an attempt to contact the Combat Information Center.

"CIC, this is ECHO. Anybody there?"

Nothing.

He waited for a moment before heading downstairs into the Northern Terminal Workstation. "Somewhere around 1600, those F-35s are gonna light this place up," he said to Graves.

"We gotta be outta here," Graves replied. "It'll waste a quarter-mile."

"Caldwell, anything?" asked Tyler.

"Nope," Caldwell called loudly over his shoulder. He turned toward Kat, who was seated next to him at the computer workstations. "We're gettin' nowhere," he said. "Show me the mainframes."

"We don't have time," she replied, shaking her head. "We gotta go soon."

"We can't let them beat us," Caldwell said insistently. "Please, I can do this." He stood up and slung his equipment pack over his left shoulder. Reluctantly, Kat moved to the mainframe chamber door, opened it with her CAC keycard, and led the two inside.

The acrid smell of smoke from the C4 explosion lingered in the chamber. At the end of the main hall, cloud-obscured sunlight dimly outlined the square hole in the ceiling, a grim reminder of ECHO team's forced entrance. The three distant mainframe columns lay on their sides; the shattered casing and fragmented circuit boards were strewn across the floor. The nearest mainframe columns stood intact.

Caldwell stepped into the first row of mainframe columns and walked up and down between them, his right hand feeling across the smooth plastic paneling. Aisle by aisle, he searched until the uneven panel slid beneath his fingers. He stopped and dropped his bag to the floor.

"This is where they went in," he said excitedly.

*   *   *

NEAR GATE TWO
COMPOUND FIVE
JUNE 6; 1518

Skreemer stood in the surf, the waves rolling midway up his boots as he held the jostling Zodiac against the shoreline. Firmly grasping the rope railing, Dutch leaned against the raft, weighing down the bow against the sand. Both men stared anxiously up the beach at the perimeter gate, watching for Eagle.

Third Cray IO. Change the hardware, Dutch texted to Kat, unsure if she was still alive. He then lowered the PDA, monitoring Skreemer's gaze. His right hand gripped his Beretta while he hoped for a response. "Eagle, talk to me. Where are you?" Skreemer said into his mike.

Static crackled into his earpiece.

Who is this? glowed a text from Kat on Dutch's PDA. Dutch sighed with relief.

The man u saw, he replied, removing his hand from the Berretta to respond.

Why r u doing this? she texted back.

Dutch looked at the downed Marines, anger mounted.

Fix third Cray IO. Sorry. Must go, he responded.

"We're outside the perimeter gates; signals are jammed," Skreemer said loudly. He turned to Dutch. "We'll give him two more minutes." Then, noting that Dutch was using his PDA, he shouted, "What the fuck are you doing?"

Dutch grasped his Beretta and directed the barrel at Skreemer, his hand shaky. "What happened to STORM?" he demanded harshly.

"Lower the weapon, Dutch. We both know you..."

"No more lies!" Dutch yelled, firing a shot into the sand next to Skreemer's boots.

"You've heard of Moonlight Maze?" Skreemer asked quickly.

"Of course. Hackers hit the Pentagon, NASA, Energy Department, a bunch of systems," Dutch replied. "What's that gotta..."

"That was STORM," Skreemer interrupted. "Ray, Skye, and me. For two years, we hacked everything. We got our hands on some top-secret shit. I'm talkin' military installation maps, hardware designs. Made it look like the hacks originated from Russia."

"But Spyder said you got busted four years ago."

"That was the beginning of our end," Skreemer continued. "We got into everything. Pentagon systems. State Department computers. Took 'em over a decade to catch up with us. Four years ago, they got Ray and Skye. Not me."

"How'd you stay clean?" Dutch asked skeptically.

"Did everything underground," Skreemer said. "Stopped talking on the phone. Did all communication on-line. E-mails were encrypted. I alternated accounts every week. Changed laptops every month. No exceptions. They were on our tail."

A faint monotonous beeping, like the sound of a reversing dump truck, came from the gate as it began sliding on its railing system. Eagle was nowhere in sight.

"Dutch, none of us wanted this," Skreemer replied regretfully, glancing at the bodies. Skreemer looked back up the beach. Still no Eagle.

"Get in," Skreemer continued. "Time to go."

Dutch slowly lowered his weapon. He pushed the raft off the sand and climbed in, while Skreemer pulled it into the water.

"Who ended up busting Ray and Skye?"

"The NSA," Skreemer said. "A guy by the name of Ryan Caldwell."

"Spyder?"

*   *   *

CONSTRUCT CONTROL CENTER
JUNE 6; 1522

Kat peeked outside the mainframe chamber. The others had moved above ground, everybody but Caldwell.

"He's telling me 'third Cray I/O,'" Kat reported.

"This cabinet has clearly been tampered with; this is the one I'm going after," Caldwell replied. "We can't trust those messages. Hell, the third Cray I/O could be rigged up with explosives."

"There's no time left anyway," Kat said.

"Go ahead. Get outta here," Caldwell said. "I'll take it from here."

*   *   *

NEAR GATE TWO
COMPOUND FIVE
JUNE 6; 1525

Eagle emptied the clip from his M4 carbine into the jungle in front of him and dropped behind the nest of palm trees to reload.

Once he had slotted and popped the clip into place, he pulled the C4 detonator from his pants pocket and flipped the switch.

The earth quaked as Eagle grabbed hold of the thin jostling pine next to him for support. The boom rattled his teeth, and he instinctively covered his ears to protect them from the sharp, thunderous blast. Despite this, his inner ear rattled; a transient buzzing and throbbing ensued.

Before the trembling earth settled, Eagle began running again toward Gate Two. "Skreemer. Dammit! Can you hear me?" he shouted into his mike.

No response.

Bursts of gunfire cracked behind him, the rounds popping and whizzing nearby. Eagle dropped behind the next cluster of pines, quickly glancing at his PDA.

ECHO continued to close in.

Eagle turned and opened fire, unloading the entire magazine into the jungle. He kept moving. A minute later, he sprinted up the low-lying hill leading to the gate; the black cliffs towered to each side. "Fuck!" he shouted.

The galvanized-steel gate was closed. The electrical current buzzed, and the razor wire spiraled along the top.

Eagle glanced through the wire-mesh gate down the beach and watched as Skreemer yanked on the pull-starter cord. The engine sputtered, then cut off.

"Hey!" Eagle yelled, waving both hands high in the air.

Unable to get their attention, he pulled his M4 up to his side and popped off a round. Dutch and Skreemer jerked back and ducked into the raft.

Scrambling for his M4, Skreemer drew his weapon up; then he peered above the raft's side and realized it was Eagle.

Eagle pointed at the cliffs, then scrambled onto the volcanic rock and quickly ascended the rock face, reaching the eighty-foot cliff top in just a few minutes.

The wind hit his body, knocking him off balance as he moved to the edge of the cliff and looked straight down. The waves crashed against the cliff base as whitewater sprayed high into the air. A few feet from the cliff base, smooth boulders disappeared with each wave.

Timing the jump just right—before the water was at its highest—Eagle hurled himself over the edge. The massive free fall abruptly ended as his feet and legs hit the water like a sledgehammer and plunged deeply into the ocean. About fifteen feet below the surface of the water, his left leg smashed into an underwater boulder on the ocean floor.

Eagle thrashed his arms as he searched for the surface, gasping for air as he emerged. A few yards away, the raft drifted in and out of view as the whitewater splashed into his eyes. He gasped and moaned from the pain. Then he reached up for the rope cord along the raft's side, as he felt Skreemer's right hand grasp his shirt tightly.

"My leg's broken," he groaned.

The next wave slammed against the raft, nearly flipping it. The rolling water threw the raft against the cliff base. Skreemer lost his grip, and Eagle drifted underwater.

"Where is he?" Skreemer shouted.

Eagle popped back to the surface a foot away from the raft. He lunged and grabbed the rope cord with both hands. Dutch and Skreemer hauled him into the raft.

"Y'okay?" Skreemer panted.

"Go!" Eagle shouted, pointing toward the open water.

*   *   *

LOS ANGELES, CALIFORNIA
JUNE 6; 1530

Special Agent Alan Moran, an FBI veteran, stood to the side of the doorway, reached out with his right hand and quietly wiggled the landlord's key into the slot. He gently attempted to turn the key. It would not give.

The lock had been changed.

Moran nodded, signaling to another agent on the opposite side of the doorway. The other agent, a rookie, swung the four-foot hammer, ripping the deadbolt through the frame and tearing the upper door hinge off. Ten armed agents charged into the tiny second-floor L.A. apartment.

"FBI. Get down," the men shouted repeatedly, filing through the doorway and dispersing throughout the apartment. In less than a minute, the apartment was cleared.

There was no Lone Wolfe.

Moran stood in the center of the apartment and studied it suspiciously. The sunlight filtered through the shades, dimly lighting the 1,100-square-foot apartment. He glanced at the sparse living room furniture: a worn Lazy Boy recliner, a flimsy wooden desk, and a fold-up chair more appropriate for a porch. As he walked toward the back bedroom, Moran caught a glimpse of a tiny cable hanging loosely from the bottom of the desk. He dropped to one knee and peered beneath the desktop.

"Get out! Now!" Moran yelled. "Get out!"

The team pulled out.

Moran sprinted out the door, clambering down the back stairwell and out the building onto the street.

Sixty seconds later, the second-floor windows burst outward in an exploding, rapidly expanding ball of red-orange flame as shattered glass, masonry, and other debris flew into the street.

*　　*　　*

USS RONALD REAGAN
JUNE 6; 1556

Standing in the navigation bridge, Captain McClure lowered the white phone from his left ear and placed it back onto the receiver.

"It's a go," McClure confirmed to the ship's executive officer, Commander Joel Hutch.

"The F-35, sir?" Hutch said.

"Yes. With the SAMs still active, it's the safest way," McClure replied.

"These DARPA test missiles haven't been tested against the anti-missile system of the F-35 yet," Hutch said.

"I'm well aware of that, Commander," Hutch replied. "The specwar guys know as well."

Already loaded with two Paveway laser-guided bombs, each weighing 1,000 pounds, the F-35C Lightning-II Joint Strike Fighter moved onto catapult number one on the carrier's deck. The jet blast deflector, a protective piston-driven steel wall, swung into position behind the fighter's engine.

Outfitted in a green shirt and vest, the flight deck crewman confirmed that the catapult's equipment, a sling mechanism to compensate for the carrier's short runway, was in proper position. Steam wafted into the air as the catapult's cylinders charged.

The pilot gripped and pulled the throttle with his left hand, blasting the engine; the engine's thrust was resisted by the catapult's holdback system. Although motionless, the fighter jet was like a tiger tensed and ready for the kill.

The catapult officer released the holdback as the strike fighter catapulted forward. At 165 miles-per-hour and out of runway, the fighter shot into the air, ascended, and rolled to the left.

Its mission: to bomb the Construct Control Center at Compound Five.

CHAPTER 25 SUBMERGE

Exercise Day: Two

COMPOUND FIVE
JUNE 6; 1557 (LOCAL TIME)

DIZZY AND UNSTEADY on his feet, and weakened by the HIT-gun blast hours ago, YUMA's Ron Spiers struggled to walk with his arm slung across the upper back of ECHO's Jack Tyler. He and Tyler struggled and staggered side by side until they cleared the anticipated blast zone.

Arriving one mile north of the C3, the other evacuees—made up of members from YUMA, ECHO, and the Construct Control personnel—secured their position within a valley camouflaged by densely-packed pines, tall grass and brush, and moss-covered boulders.

Tyler gently lowered the winded Spiers to the ground, easing his head down against a smooth five-foot-wide boulder. Kneeling, he scanned the makeshift camp and did a quick head count.

One was missing.

"Where's Caldwell?" Tyler demanded.

"He wouldn't leave," Kat said with a shrug.

"Shit!" Tyler exploded. He turned toward C3.

YUMA's Graves grabbed him by the shoulder. "It's too late," he said, shaking his head.

"Caldwell, get the fuck outta there now!" Tyler yelled into his mike.

*　　*　　*

CONSTRUCT CONTROL CENTER
JUNE 6; 1558

Caldwell sat on the concrete floor of the mainframe chamber with his computer in his lap. Having relinquished all doubts, he had already opened the third Cray I/O cabinet that Dutch had led him to. There were no explosives. Dutch was telling the truth. It saved him precious minutes. Caldwell's nervous fingers pecked rapidly at the keyboard. He changed the remaining line of code, then hit the enter key.

The tiny laptop screen flickered on and off. The plexus monitoring system flashed on the laptop monitor, revealing the location of all exercise participants.

"Dammit, Caldwell, talk to me!" came through his earpiece.

Caldwell pounded out two more commands, and the system rebooted. "I'm in!" he blurted into his mike. "We'll have the default settings back in a couple of minutes."

"Three minutes. Leave now or you're dead," Tyler barked.

Caldwell pushed himself to his feet and hurried out the mainframe chamber and into the Northern Terminal Workstation. Before exiting the C3, he glanced back at the Southern Terminal Workstation, unable to get the Lynx Prion out of his mind.

He quickly ran over to the large LCD monitor to take a quick look. The screen read:

ZT39PM2 module construction in progress...
Subsection 10 integrated.
Lynx Prion 100% reconstructed.

The last line revealed:

Upload in progress...

*   *   *

AIRSPACE OVER COMPOUND FIVE
JUNE 6; 1600

Sunlight flickered through the canopy window of the F-35C Joint Strike Fighter as it cruised high above the storm clouds at 38,000 feet. The face of the pilot's helmet reflected a tinted golden sheen. The pilot, call sign "Whistler," eyed his light-green helmet-mounted display, taking note of distance to target: five miles.

The distinctive and repetitive short beeps of the F-35 missile warning system alarmed, as the infrared sensors of the distributed aperture system picked up the threat.

"I'm on radar lock," Whistler conveyed to USS *Ronald Reagan* with the calm, composed air of a man sitting on a lakefront porch, his pulse and blood pressure serene.

The DAS showed the missiles still grounded.

With the right side-stick in hand, the pilot rolled the F-35 hard to the right and reversed direction. His left hand cranked on the throttle as he was pushed deeper into the seat by the ensuing gravity forces.

"SAMs airborne," he reported as the DAS began tracking the incoming missile threat.

Two surface-to-air missiles approached, three miles out, west to east.

A giant booming explosion vibrated the jet as it went supersonic and simultaneously began a series of evasive maneuvers. As Whistler hit the chaff and flare buttons, the metallic spray and red-orange flames shot from the sides of the fighter. Seconds later, the SAMs missed, diverted by the jet's deliberate discharge.

"Shit!" he exclaimed under his breath.

At this altitude, surface objects and geographical features were unavailable to clutter the guidance system. "I'm gonna outrun 'em!" Whistler said into his mike.

The pilot knew the SAM had about a forty-second total burn time from light-off to flame-out if the missiles did not hit the target. He popped another round of chaff and flares, then pointed the aircraft straight down.

Wearing snug anti-gravity trousers tightly around his legs and abdomen, he grunted and tensed his torso and legs to combat the G-forces. Excess blood that pooled in his lower body from the high Gs would place him at risk for vision blackout and loss of consciousness.

One SAM hit the diversion, exploding upon impact of the chaff. Another continued its pursuit.

The pilot leveled the aircraft and maxed out the throttle. The SAMs had been in the air now for thirty-five seconds.

As the missile closed, Whistler banked hard right, rolling the F-35. The SAM began to lose speed and altitude. It flamed out.

"SAMs down," Whistler reported as he headed back toward the island and proceeded as planned.

*   *   *

USS RONALD REAGAN
JUNE 6; 1604

All eyes focused on the overhead loudspeaker within the flag bridge, as Mac Jacobs, the special warfare commanding officer, listened intently along with his commanding team aboard USS *Ronald Reagan*.

"Angel One, this is YUMA, copy?" the voice crackled across the speaker.

"This is Angel One," Jacobs replied. "Glad to hear your voice. What's your status?"

"Two men are critical," Graves said. "One of the station personnel is hurt bad. Another's dead."

"Is there still a threat?" Jacobs asked.

"Affirmative," Graves replied. "ECHO's pursuing at least three tangos. One confirmed dead."

"Have you secured the Control Center?" Jacobs continued.

"Roger, but evac'd, preparing for the airstrike," Graves replied. "We've got an NSA analyst still in the blast zone. He reports the system is back under our control."

The admiral in charge to his left nodded as he picked up the black phone on the wall.

"Call off the fighter," the admiral in charge ordered. "We've got friendlies in the red zone."

"We're callin' off the 35 now," Jacobs said. "Standby, YUMA. We're comin' for ya."

*   *   *

LOS ANGELES, CALIFORNIA
JUNE 6; 1615

Three blocks from the apartment explosion, Lone Wolfe walked briskly on the sidewalk, toting his black leather bag over his shoulder. An orchestra of musical car alarms sounded from the cars street-parked around the burning building. LAPD, fire, and paramedics whizzed toward the blast site; a fire-engine horn blared into Wolfe's ear as it passed by.

The name Joe Norman reverberated in Wolfe's mind as he tried to figure out how they had found him. Nobody else knew his location. His computer and phone trace technology were solid.

Minutes later, Wolfe reached his other apartment within a new twenty-five-unit upscale complex. He walked through the main entrance, climbing three flights of stairs to his front door. Nervously fumbling with the keys, he unlocked the deadbolt and paused before entering.

Wolfe unzipped an outer pocket of his leather bag and withdrew his 9mm Beretta, then opened the door. He flipped on the light switch as the lamp on the marble side table dimly lit the foyer. The walnut hardwood floors glistened. Silk curtains blocked out the sunlight. The space reeked of fresh paint.

Atop the kitchen table, he set his leather bag down, reached in and grabbed his laptop. Sitting down, he booted the computer, then proceeded to the university computer network at UCLA—the hiding place for the stolen Intelink data to be extracted by the Lynx Prion.

Paranoid, Wolfe checked over both shoulders, scanning the apartment. He then logged into the network account and began searching for uploads.

Nothing.

"Fuck!" Wolfe blurted. He pulled the sat phone from his leather bag and dialed.

"What's the status of the pick-up?" he asked.

"They've confirmed the prion insertion," the man on the other line said with a Middle Eastern accent. "Do you have the data?"

Beaded sweat dotted his brow; his breathing quickened. "Soon," Wolfe replied.

"Should we still proceed as planned?"

"Absolutely," Wolfe replied. "When they board the sub, kill them."

*   *   *

GATE TWO
COMPOUND FIVE
JUNE 6; 1618

Slowed by numerous explosives and tripwires, ECHO arrived at Gate Two and secured the immediate vicinity.

"Hear that?" point man Mitchell asked, listening intently.

The quiet, distant humming of a small boat's gasoline engine drifted in and out of earshot.

Chance shook his head, not hearing a thing.

"They're outside the compound," Mitchell stated. He wasted no time, and scrambled over to the cliffs and began to climb.

Once on top, he scurried to the cliff's edge. The sound of the boat's engine was gone. The high winds whistled in his ears. He pulled his binoculars to his eyes and scanned the massive blue-green ocean.

The distant speck of a raft came into view.

Mitchell pulled his pack off, retrieved his MK11 semi-automatic sniper rifle and slotted his 16-power scope in place. He laid flat against the jagged volcanic rock and glassed the wide-open ocean. Ten seconds lapsed before he relocated the vessel.

The strong ocean wind buffeted his body as he slowed his breathing and worked toward getting into rhythm as the boat bounced and bobbed through the open water.

"Shit!" he shouted angrily.

"No shot," he said into his mike. "They're over fifteen hundred yards out."

"I'll inform CIC," Chance reported. "They won't get far."

*　　　*　　　*

CONSTRUCT CONTROL CENTER
COMPOUND FIVE
JUNE 6; 1620

Caldwell remained at the Southern Terminal Workstation. Using an NSA-issued password, he continued to attempt the Intelink connection.

He was locked out.

"*Upload complete*," Caldwell read, as the Lynx Prion transmission finished.

"It's too late," he said in frustration.

"The F-35s were diverted," Tyler said. "You're safe."

"I know," Caldwell said. "But let the NSA, Pentagon—shit, let everybody know the Lynx Prion is out. The Intelink is goin' down."

"I'll let 'em know," Tyler reported.

"This will take months to clean up," Caldwell said bitterly.

"Hang tight; rescue and extraction will be in the airfield around the Control Center."

"Got it," Caldwell replied.

For ten minutes, Caldwell again tried and failed. Then he again recalled Dutch's mention of a backdoor.

ID: flashed on the screen.

He typed: *FIVE.*

Password: flashed on the screen. He again typed *FIVE.*

The text flashed onto the screen:

Department of Defense
Defense Information Systems Agency
Secure LAN Connection
Authority: DoD, DARPA, U.S. Navy, Pentagon
Location: Compound Five
Intelink Status:

Intelink – SCI:	*ON-LINE*
Intelink – P:	*off-line*
Intelink – N:	*ON-LINE*
Intelink – S:	*ON-LINE*
Intelink – C:	*ON-LINE*

Status: Secure
Encryption: Enabled
Full Access Granted

"Dutch, you son of a bitch," Caldwell mumbled to himself. He was in.

The Lynx Prion had already started and was actively ripping data and sending it to an off-site computer. Caldwell quickly located the destination of the transmission. It was at Internet Protocol address: 24.152.127.555.

Using an IP address locator, he searched the register. The IP address was assigned as owner UCLA. The data, however, was not headed to Los Angeles, California.

The IP address was attached to a computer calling itself "UCLA."

The location: Los Angeles, Chile, about 250 miles south of Santiago, Chile.

* * *

TWO MILES OFFSHORE COMPOUND FIVE
JUNE 6; 1622

Eagle pulled his pant leg up. His knife sheath was tightening around his swelling calf. He released the increasingly constricting holster. Then he felt along the outer leg; the swollen and torn flesh stung and burned from the salt water. Black, yellow, and purple bruises colored the skin surrounding the wound. Fortunately, no bone was protruding. The smaller lower leg bone, the fibula, was broken.

Skreemer cut the engine two miles offshore: the Zodiac bobbed and drifted. Seated at the bow, Dutch cocked his arm on his knee and stared out at the vastness of the ocean; the cool salty wind smacked his pale face and burned his bloodshot eyes.

"Where's the damn sub?" Eagle grumbled.

"I've sent the signal; they know we're here," Skreemer replied.

The distant rumble of the F-35C quieted as the faint sound of inbound helos heightened.

"Wolfe better not have left us here," Eagle said.

Twenty yards away, the water bubbled and rippled as the conning tower of the 250-foot-long Chinese Song-class diesel attack submarine emerged: the hull number was painted over black.

Skreemer and Eagle paddled hard to the submarine tower.

"Kuai (hurry)," the Chinese sailors yelled, as the three men were helped aboard. They climbed down into the submarine's hull. The team hurried to close and lock the hatch as the vessel began submersion.

"Dive, make your depth, fifteen hundred feet. Dive! Dive!" the captain ordered in Chinese. "Speed: twenty-two knots."

The captain eased up to Skreemer, staring directly into his eyes. "We were instructed to kill you," he said in surprisingly well-spoken English.

"I figured that," Skreemer replied calmly.

"Skreemer, you were very smart man to have worked with us separately," the captain said. "But we took a big risk."

"It will be worth it," Skreemer replied. "As we speak, the Lynx Prion is stealing top secret U.S. military data and sending it offshore. As soon as we reach land safely and confirm payment, you'll get what you paid for."

The captain remarked, "There's a sub and sonobuoy tracking us."

Anechoic tile coatings, super-quiet propulsion, and oxygen recycling muted the submarine's acoustic signature. This made it nearly undetectable to U.S. systems.

"Time to go silent," the captain finished.

*   *   *

USS *Springfield* (SSN-761), a Los Angeles-class nuclear submarine accompanying USS *Ronald Reagan* Carrier Strike Group, searched for the submarine detected by the sonobuoy of the P-3C Orion aircraft as it moved along the western shoreline of

Compound Five.

"The P-3 lost the signal," stated the acoustic sensor operator aboard USS *Springfield*.

"What about our sonar?" the captain inquired.

"We're seeing nothing, sir," the submariner reported.

"We've lost track of the enemy?"

"Affirmative, sir. The submarine's gone."

*   *   *

CONSTRUCT CONTROL CENTER
COMPOUND FIVE
JUNE 6; 1635

Kat stared blankly across the grass field at the commotion, as injured men were stretchered onto a Seahawk. Another helicopter descended, while foreign operators emerged from the treeline. Kat squinted to keep the circulating debris from hitting her eyes as dust from the dismantled and destroyed landing zone was lifted into the air by the helo's rotor wash. Her muddied blonde hair blew wildly in the turbulent wind.

Lieutenant Commander Justin Channing walked up and stood at her side, silent for a moment.

"Lange, y'okay?" he shouted as he moved closer.

"DARPA was concerned about an attack," Kat muttered. "There was an increase in e-mail chatter. That's why they wanted me out here. To make sure network security was tight in real time. I knew this system better than anyone. I failed."

"Well, if it weren't for you, YUMA might be dead. We might all be dead."

"Still a nightmare," Kat said. "Did you even see any of them?"

He nodded. "Just one. They called him Dutch."

EPILOGUE

PACIFIC OCEAN
JUNE 7

THE CHINESE SONG-CLASS SUBMARINE moved through the warm Pacific water fifteen hundred nautical miles off the Chilean coast.

Sitting alone in the submarine's spartan mess hall, Dutch hovered over a bowl of lentil congee, a rice porridge soup, dipping his Lotus-seed bun with his uninjured right hand; the other arm was snug against his body in a sling.

Moments later, Skreemer eased onto the metal bench; the two men stared at one another across the steel mess table.

"How's the arm?" Skreemer inquired.

"Don't act like you give a shit," Dutch spat. "Why'd you even bring me along?"

"You were the only one who could pull this off," Skreemer replied.

"That's bullshit!" Dutch shouted, knocking his metal bowl across the table and onto the floor as congee splattered everywhere. "People are dead. American soldiers—dead!" He reached across the table, grabbing and yanking Skreemer's T-shirt collar.

A jolt of pain radiated down to Dutch's fingertips as Skreemer grabbed and squeezed his injured shoulder. Dutch took a deep breath and released the shirt.

"Sit down," Skreemer ordered. "I'll explain everything."

Lightheaded, Dutch eased back onto the metal bench, grimacing in pain.

"You remember the name Joe Norman?"

"Of course," Dutch replied, recalling the user name of the attempted hack of the Sentinel Software Incorporated network the night Spyder got busted two decades ago.

"Norman is a vice president with SSI," Skreemer said. "I contacted him after SSI lost their C5 contract with DARPA. I made him an offer: $50 million payment for access. I'd deliver the access he couldn't get any other way. Lucky for me, he's one greedy bastard. Norman thought if he could disrupt C5's security system, he'd win back the DARPA contract."

Dutch interrupted, "Where does Lone Wolfe fit in?"

"He was the contact person," Skreemer replied. "Norman hired Wolfe to coordinate the operation to infiltrate C5. Ex-CIA. Of course, I'm not supposed to know that, but I profiled everyone. Wolfe selected the members of this new STORM. The others were mercs. Skye was our techie. When I asked whether or not she'd be able to handle the physical stress of the mission, turned out she was a competitive triathlete. She could've outdone both of us."

"Ray and Eagle?"

"Both Army," Skreemer said. "Ray, a former Ranger. Eagle, Special Forces. Versatile. Knows three languages. Perfect guy on the ground in Talcahuano."

"Why would Eagle and Ray be willing to become mercenaries against their own country?"

"Why were you willing to hack?" Skreemer asked.

"I'm not sure anymore," Dutch answered. "Everything got so fucked up."

"It was supposed to be an in-and-out job," Skreemer said. "Hack the system. Show the system was vulnerable. SSI would regain the security contact from DARPA. We'd get paid. When we learned about the Intelink, the potential payoff became much larger. There was a bidding war between China's People's Liberation Army, Iran's Islamic Revolutionary Guard Corps, Quds Force, Lebanese Hezbollah—those kinds of guys. Wolfe, it turns out, changed a lot of the software. I didn't know."

"How'd you get involved with extremists?"

"Call me paranoid, but I didn't trust Wolfe," Skreemer admitted. "My intuition was dead on. His plan was to never get us off the island alive. So I started looking into making my own deal. He made a deal with the Iranian Mullahs. I made a deal with the Chinese."

"Bidding for what?"

"The Intelink," Skreemer replied. "The reliance of U.S. security on the Intelink is excessive. The top-secret data stored in its networks are more profitable than any other commodity in the black market. Governments and terrorist groups around the world have been trying to hack it for years. Cyberspace is where the wars are fought now, because you're never sure who attacked you."

"But why help terrorists?"

"It's only letters and numbers, Dutch. Just data."

"Just data," Dutch said, his brown eyes glaring back at Skreemer.

"You wanna know what happened to the real STORM?" Skreemer asked.

"Not anymore," Dutch said tiredly. "I'm done with all this."

"There's $10 million in a bank account in Buenos Aires under your false name: Todd Mason," Skreemer offered with a glint in his eye.

"I don't want your damn blood money!" Dutch exploded. "I just wanna go home."

"You can't go back," Skreemer stated with a shake of his head.

"What do you mean?" Dutch gasped.

"Spyder saw you," Skreemer explained. "They'll be waiting at your apartment. I have a place for you in Argentina. Your new home."

"I don't want to live in South America."

"It's the only place you'll be safe."

"What about you? What are you gonna do?" Dutch asked.

"I'm going into hiding," Skreemer said. "There'll be a lot of people lookin' for me. But I'll do what I do best: go underground." He slid a tiny, folded piece of paper across the table, leaving it in front of Dutch.

"What's this?" Dutch asked.

"The bank and account number," Skreemer said.

"So that's it? I'm a lifelong fugitive?"

Skreemer nodded.

"How will I ever get in touch with you in the future?" Dutch asked.

"You already know," he replied.

*　　　*　　　*

NSW COMMAND'S DATA ACQUISITION CENTER CORONADO, CALIFORNIA JUNE 8

Lieutenant JG Daniel Janssen sat close to his network computer in the expansive stadium-seating auditorium filled with computer workstations. The officers and specialists clicked away on the keyboards days into their investigation of the possible Intelink intrusion.

"You're breaking up; say again," Janssen spoke into his mike, adjusting his earpiece.

"Your system's infected," NSA's Caldwell said. "This prion only makes its presence known after it's done stealing all the data. By then it'll be too late."

"We've tracked all intrusions non-stop for days," Janssen replied. "We're not seeing any compromised networks."

"We have to assume the worst before it's too late," Caldwell insisted.

"Any idea who's responsible for these attacks?" Janssen asked.

"No clue," Caldwell replied.

"What do you recommend?" Janssen asked.

"Power down all Intelink servers," Caldwell said. "System-wide, we need to go off-line."

"Shut down the Intelink?" Janssen said. "It's never been done before. That's just not possible."

"If you don't, this will prove to be the worst infiltration into a U.S. network to date," Caldwell replied.

"Brown, this is Black. We've got a problem," came across Janssen's headset.

"Dr. Caldwell, hang on a second," Janssen said, switching connections to Black.

"Go ahead, Black," Janssen replied.

"Remember that lightning bolt that was covering the infiltration?"

"Yeah."

"Well, it's back."

Janssen looked up at the central theatre-sized LCD, as the lightning bolt glowed in the center of the screen. He stood, moved into the walkway splitting the center of the auditorium, and faced the amphitheatre of LCD monitors.

One by one, the monitors went dark. Moments later, the officers' and specialists' individual network monitors also went black.

"Dr. Caldwell, you there?" Janssen asked.

"I'm here."

"All our systems just went down. Some sort of power outage. I'll need to get back to you."

"Are your lights still on?" Caldwell asked.

"Well, yeah, that's strange," Janssen replied.

"No power outage. We're too late."

*　　*　　*

LOS ANGELES, CALIFORNIA
JUNE 9

Lone Wolfe eased open the silk curtains; his eyes adjusted to the dawn sunlight warming his face. He gazed into his apartment complex's courtyard. The freshly cut lawn glistened with morning dew. At the center, water spouted from the top of the four-tier pedestal marble fountain. This was the first time in three days that Wolfe had looked outside.

The sat phone, already in his right hand, rang loudly. He lifted it to his ear.

"Yeah," Wolfe said.

"Updates?" Rashid Fahad, leader of a terrorist sleeper cell of the Islamic Jihad Liberation Movement, said with a Middle Eastern accent.

"My sources tell me two of our team were found dead on C5," Wolfe said. "From what I can determine, Ray and Skye were the two killed."

"And the others?" Fahad asked.

"They cut a deal with the Chinese," Wolfe said.

"We must find them."

"Already working on it."

"Do you even know who this Dutch and Skreemer are?"

"Not yet," Wolfe replied.

"Our mission is in jeopardy unless we find them," Fahad reminded him.

"I'm well aware," Wolfe said.

*   *   *

MARIA DOLORES AIRPORT
LOS ANGELES, CHILE
JUNE 14

Dutch waited in the lazy terminal of the Maria Dolores Airport, in Los Angeles, Chile, as he prepared for his flight to Buenos Aires. His arm—no longer in a sling for fear of recognition—throbbed. Sweat beaded on his forehead, streaking down along his temples and cheeks. Unshaven, with a baseball cap pulled low, he glanced up and down the short terminal, carefully watching each passerby.

Approaching with her father, a young girl who couldn't have been more than four or five years old skipped along happily, smiling widely at Dutch as she passed by.

Dutch pulled the tiny, folded paper from his right pants pocket. He unfolded the crimped paper and stared at the handwritten information, wondering if the money was even there.

He balled the paper into one hand. In the opposite hand, he gripped his black bag tightly, stood and moved across the walkway toward a trash can. He extended his hand over the trash receptacle for several seconds; then he placed the crumpled paper back into his pocket.

As Dutch looked down the terminal again, four obviously American men in black suits appeared in the distance. Dutch ducked into the nearby restroom and hurried into an empty stall, his body trembling. Dizzy from fear, exhaustion, and the pain in his throbbing arm, he focused on his breathing, slowing it to prevent passing out.

"If things don't go so well..." Dutch recalled. "Remember this number," Skreemer's words replayed in his mind.

1016555202.

Possibilities flashed through Dutch's mind. Finally, it came to him.

Reverse the numbers. That's what STORM did twenty years ago.

202-555-6101.

Area code 202. Washington, D.C.

Dutch dropped the bag to the floor. He plunged his hand inside it, grabbed the sat phone, and dialed the number.

"Hello?" a man's voice answered.

"Skreemer, is that you?" Dutch asked.

"This is not Skreemer, " the man replied with his thick New England accent.

"Who is this?"

"Is this line safe?" the man asked.

"Yes," Dutch replied.

"It's Ray," he said. "The real Ray."

Dutch's journey continues in the next STORM novel.

www.stormnovel.com

ABOUT THE AUTHOR

Dave Pearson was born and raised in Vero Beach, Florida. After graduating from the University of Florida, he attended medical school at Vanderbilt University and completed residency training in Denver, Colorado. He is currently a practicing emergency medicine physician and lives with his wife and son in Charlotte, North Carolina.

This is his first novel.

15740073R00166

Made in the USA
Lexington, KY
13 June 2012